I Gave You All I Had

also by zoë valdés

Yocandra In the Paradise of Nada

I Gave You All I Had

a novel

ZOÉ VALDÉS

TRANSLATED FROM THE SPANISH BY Nadia Benabid

Arcade Publishing | New

FIRST ENGLISH-LANGUAGE EDITION

This is a work of fiction. Names, places, characters, and incidents are either
products of the author's imagination or are used fictitiously.

Originally published in Spain under the title *Te di la vida entera* by Planeta, S.A.,
Barcelona

ISBN 1-55970-477-2
Library of Congress Catalog Number 99-73646
Library of Congress Cataloging-in-Publication Information is available.

Published in the United States by Arcade Publishing, Inc., New York
Distributed by Time Warner Trade Publishing

10 9 8 7 6 5 4 3 2

Designed by API
BP
PRINTED IN THE UNITED STATES OF AMERICA

To Mami

ACKNOWLEDGMENTS

I thank Attys Luna, Ricardo, my friends, Editions Actes Sud, the Ecole des Hautes Études en Sciences Sociales, and the Centre National du Livre for their trust and assistance.

If in the end, I have to write
the story of my world,
If in the end, I have to spell out
my most heartfelt days,
I would mostly speak of you
who've been my recompense,
my love, my joy, my dream,
sentiment and chimera.

By Juan Arrondo,
as sung by Clara and Mario

Prayer for My Head

Igba, baba, igba yeye, igba echu alagbana
(Give leave father, give leave mother, give leave echu Alagbana);
igba ile akuokoyeri, igba ita meta bidigaga
(Give leave house echu akuokoyeri, give leave corner 3 and ficus
      tree);
kinkamache oyubona, kinkamache apetevi
(Salutations godmother, you of the second chair, salutations to the
      one who watches over Orula);
kinkamache ori mi kinkamache gbogbo oricha
(Salutations to my head, salutations to all the orisha);
agbalagba kinkamache kinkamache komalebe
(Salutations to the ancestors, salutations to the privileged head);
agbaniche, oba ni omo
(Orisha of ocean depths, thy son be King);
ona kuni obani ye emi
(Be alert on the roadway, the deer belongs to Obatalá);
kachocho eni kachocho
(Give word Obatalá with the right).

1

Havanity, havanity, all is havanity . . .
I am twice bereaved, for night and
for the city. To remember is to open
a Pandora's box of pain and smells
and nocturnal music . . .

— GUILLERMO CABRERA INFANTE

1

Be Careful, It's My Heart

Be careful, it's my heart.
It's not my watch
you're holding,
it's my heart.

By Irving Berlin,
as sung by Bola de Nieve

I *AM NOT THE AUTHOR OF THIS NOVEL.* I am the corpse. But never mind that now. Telling, that's what matters now, with the yapper full of worms if need be, like the dead narrator making his way from *A* to *Z* in my favorite movie, *Sunset Boulevard* by Billy Wilder. In due time, I'll produce official evidence of my death, but not just yet. Just prick up your ears and listen up now, or better yet, plunge into these pages where my spirit has managed, with more than its fair share of love and pain, to survive:

It was in 1934 that Cuca Martinez was born in Santa Clara, a city in the province that used to be known as Las Villas and is now Villa Clara. Her father, a Chinese cook, had journeyed from Canton to Mexico. There he changed his name and traveled on to Cuba to strike it rich. Her mother was a Dubliner by birth but left that city behind when she was two. Cuca's grandparents on her mother's side had come to Cuba with three fledgling girls in tow and high hopes of making a killing in the horse meat trade. Cuca's grandfather was a butcher; they called him the King of Beef Jerky. In no time, the wee ones blossomed into blue-eyed redheads. The youngest, who had taken to reciting French poetry at the local playhouse and who went in more for exotica than for Eastern Asia, fell in love with the kitchen cook, the Chinaman adrift from kith and kin. Five children would spring from the union of mulberry and Irish rose: one died an infant, the other was stricken by polio at fifteen, the third laid low by asthma and chronic Catholicism, the fourth laid up with a nervous condition, and the fifth — Cuca Martinez — was the healthiest of the lot and wasn't always toothless and ugly and old. Believe me, Cuca Martinez was *once fifteen*, which is how you say it in Havana when you mean she sure was pretty, a real dish, stopped cars and buses everywhere on streets and avenues.

When Cuca Martinez, known simply as the Girl, turned ten, she was sent to live with Maria Andrea, her godmother, because her lady mother — she of the stormy red hair and the sea blue eyes — felt compelled to resume her forgettable career as an actress or a soliloquist. She ditched her Chinese husband, the Girl's father, took up with an eighteen-year-old, and bade them all a good out-of-sight, out-of-mind. Unable to take on all four children, the Chinaman kept two and loaned out the other two to Maria Andrea, the black woman who had taken a godmother's vow and was beset by unrelenting and tenacious toothache. From her, the Girl would learn to scrub and launder, to cook and iron, and all manner of chore befitting her sex (I could gag for sinking to such malarkey!). In her free time, which was negligible, Cuca got permission to play with a beer bottle fixed up in doll's clothing. Because to tell the truth, though the Girl never went hungry, toys were something else again — she couldn't have had too many, maybe none. But she didn't have time to get bored; she was either working like a mule, or whiling away an hour with her bottle-doll, or warming alcohol in her mouth to spurt it up later in tepid mouthfuls into Maria Andrea's decaying mouth so as to dull the pain of cavities. The Girl Cuca's brother, laid low by asthma and chronic Catholicism, also lived with them, as did the godmother's twenty-three-year-old son.

On a night of stifling backwater heat and boredom, the god-mother left the house to attend a spirit gathering, leaving the Girl forsaken and forlorn. Done with the pots and pans, the Girl sat down to sew a new dress for her bottle-doll. She was intent on threading a needle when the damn-near-white mulatto son of the godmother Maria Andrea appeared before her. His cock was stiff before he even entered the room, a cudgel going before him toward the Girl. With one smack he knocked her onto the divination board, where she lay dazed amidst the cowries. He hurriedly ripped off her panties and spread her skinny rash-covered thighs and was about to force his meaty rod into her dry little bald pussy, when the godmother Maria Andrea reeled in, still heaving with spirits and in full rapture, and picked up a plank with a nail poking out its end and slammed it on the back of her son, the rapist, who lit out of there, gashed and gush-ing blood like an open tap. Along the way and on the wing, he jammed his prick into a calf, came, and considered hanging himself. But as it was stolen rope that would have done the trick, and as the shopkeeper from whom he filched it had spotted him, he didn't get too far before the police picked him up right in front of the tree that could've been his gallows.

With a swirl of blood burbling about her tongue, the Girl Cuca came out of her swoon. Maria Andrea called in the midwife to ver-ify that her goddaughter was still a virgin and shed a very puny croc-odile tear or two on learning that her son was in custody. She'd never liked that boy, and he returned the feeling. She was vinegar to his oil. In fact, she even breathed a sigh of relief. Why, who's to say? Prison might rehabilitate him. She hastened to quash the thought, amend-ing it with that chestnut about once crooked never straight, and arm-ing herself with lighter fluid, she buckled down, like one without a care in the world, and polished the cement floors to a shine.

The damn-near-white mulatto spent the subsequent six years in and out of the slammer, no sooner out and in he'd go again for the usual infractions — violent assault, attempted rape, car theft . . . Even so, he regularly wangled day passes and eventually even man-aged to get out for good. He'd often stop by his mother's house, never staying beyond the fifteen to twenty minutes it takes to make coffee and drink it, without talk or anything, just there, just drinking, present and brooding and fuming up the place with his criminal sweat and his breath.

The Girl Cuca's brother, laid low by asthma and chronic Catholicism, was now settled in the damn-near-white mulatto's hole of a room, walled off by a wooden partition from the pigeonhole where his little sister slept. Not that she was so little anymore, now that she had reached adolescence. It was a morning of pouring rain when the Girl (she'd only shake the name as a full-grown woman) heard something like the parched panting of a horse, the rustling of bedsheets, and the rip of yielding cloth. Twas not curiosity, but fear, the kind that chills and convulses the belly with a simultaneous urge to shit and vomit, that sent her spying through a crack. The scream she stifled dangled in her open mouth. There was her brother, forcibly pinned down by his hair, all naked, all wet, slobbering, tied and scratched up, weeping and mumbling an "oh my God! oh my God!" beneath his breath. Buttocks glistened like tallow in the grid of moonlight sifting through the slats, the damn-near-white mulatto's peninsular penis pumped away, in and out, plunging with the ease of a Turkish saber into a heart. The Girl Cuca saw her brother's ass, chafed and raw, and that other one's cock smeared in shit and blood. She wanted to scream, call for help, rescue her brother, the Catholic laid low by chronic asthma. But the damn-near-white mulatto chose that very minute to come, to pull off the finale of the century, sealing his moans with a bite to the other one's back. Laughing and crying in one breath, the other one whimpered away — "oh, my sugar angel, my mulattokin, my honey cock." And then, he too was coming in some intergalactic orbit, and his lungs opened up and he breathed deep like a frogman, like an amphibian creature. The Girl Cuca looked on in pain and terror and saw only too well what pleasure her brother, the Catholic laid low by chronic asthma, had felt. From that moment on she began to learn about silent suffering; she'd never play again. That rank spectacle with its asshole vapors would traumatize the Girl Cuca, and from then on and for the rest of her life, sex would fascinate and disgust her.

At sixteen, she called at her stepmother's house seeking permission (readily granted out of economic necessity) and a small sum of money off her father with a promise of speedy reimbursement. She returned and with innumerable snotty and teary kisses said her good-byes to the godmother she was certain she'd never see again. Taking a terse and maternal tone, she parted from her brother with a word of warning about his asthma. He had already found his remedy, settled on his optimal spray, the intestinal inhaler.

She set off for Havana on the freight train, the one that makes every blessed stop along the entire wretched breadth of the island. Cuca Martinez does not recall her first impressions of that once most beautiful of Latin American capitals. She arrived, dying of hunger and exhaustion and heat, directly at the public house — that's how tenements, now called *solars,* were known in those days — in Old Havana, commended by Maria Andrea to a friend, the Asturiana, Concha, who lived on the Calle Conde. The fleshy lady at the door wanted to know Cuca's age posthaste and was staggered by the girl's extraordinary claim:

"I just turned twenty, it's just that I'm kinda slight."

Six years had elapsed between the averted rape and the triumphant attempt on her brother, and she was now sixteen.

"Kine off thlight!" In addition to having retained her native lisp, the Asturiana also swallowed her word endings the way they do in Havana. From between her breasts she produced a man-size handkerchief, weighted at the corners by the knots where she kept her money, and proceeded to redistribute the sweat that slicked her neck and forehead before refastening it to her bra strap. She shoved a broom handle into the Girl Cuca's hands and said: "Leth go! Hop thoo ith! There's everythin thoo be done here. I'll give you a cot in the room with La Methunguita and La Puthunguita. Lataah, I might thee about a job with Pepe in the cafeteria, but for thtarterth you'll get room and boarh in exthange for cleanin the bildin with theal and dedicathion: every thingle room, all the bathroomth, the thinkth and thtairwayth from landin to rooftop, and you'll leave them thwinkling like crythtal or I'll math you to minthe, and look tharp! my thlippers! (and she signaled for a pair of wooden flip-flops with black rubber straps). You will altho cook, run errandth, do the wath, iron, and carry out any human or divine tathk that thrikth my mind or holier regionth. And be well-advithed, I warn you! I will not thuffer dillydallyin, no fun and gameth with Methunga and her little frien La Puthunga. One hath to work here and mighty lon and har too!"

It goes without saying that Cuca Martinez was no exception. Just one more girl among the countless village girls who flocked to Havana in those years, without a stitch of experience or a penny to their name and in full adolescent bloom with the surefire prospect of becoming housemaids and not much of a crack at fame. In any case, Cuca Martinez sang so badly that even under the shower she didn't chance it. And then there was the problem of her feet, huge beyond compare, although later she'd learn how to roll her hips in step to the chachacha — and to any other rhythm that became all the rage. Still, she'd never really cut it as rhumba royalty. Cuca Martinez only knew how to serve, how to submit and love. Yet while the Girl loved everybody, no one loved her, and she was lavishly hungry for affection. A mother's love most of all.

She whizzed off to her dusting and sweeping, her scouring and cooking. To wash up the dishes, wash out the clothes, and starch and iron last week's bundle. Her chores done, she collapsed on the cot, without bathing or eating, quaking with a fever of 102. She'd felt too poorly earlier to take much notice of the room, but now, with hot and watery eyes, she took a hectic spin of the place. The walls were painted yellow and the door frames pale blue. A droopy lamp hung from the ceiling shedding crystal tears and bathing the walls in a phantasmagoric lament of shuffling shadows. The room was out-fitted in the Spanish Mortification style. Somewhere, a bed was thumping away to the beat of female groans. In her feverish state, she thought those oohs and aahs were rising from her chest. But no way, no, she wasn't the one blissfully plastering her naked body up against the cinnamon skin of an equally devastating body that could have belonged to a dancer from the Tropicana Nightclub. Just in case she was dreaming, Cuca dug her fists into her eyes and gave them a good rub. No, they were real. Those two heedless creatures could only be her roommates La Mechunguita and La Puchunguita. And the pair of them were whooping up some kind of omelette. You could practically smell the yolk. Tit to tit and clit to clit, they mashed so hard they gave off sparks. In a flash of cheap rings, fingers were strumming clits at the speed of light. Jumbo lips sucked on any protuberance that came their way. They also spanked each other's asses to a lurid pink and tweaked and pinched each others nipples until they set off a delirium of screeches. Cuquita thought she would die of shame. Why did life always place her before scenes intended for much more mature audiences? At a loss, she tried to call attention to herself by vigorously clearing her throat, but those two seemed not to notice. So she coughed and her anus went slack and honked. La Puchunguita's mahogany mane floated up in the air, her full tits stood at the ready and quaked like canons about to fire off balls of fire:

"Hey! Who farted? You?"

"Me! No way! Hey!" La Mechunguita protested, her reddish cap of wooly quadroon ironed hair bobbing on her head like an overturned basket.

Finally, they saw the Girl Cuca. Her back glued to the door, she looked on and trembled. La Mechunguita and La Puchunguita reached for their slips, which slid over them with the ease of nylon in one long stroke that stopped at the knee. As neither wore panties, their pubes pushed up against the sheer fabric and showed. Together, they turned on the weepy Cuca:

"Where did this ugly-ass face come from?"

"You asking me! You the one who farted?"

Cuquita nodded, her fear growing more and more as she imagined herself being raped by these hefty sirens. And as though the pair could read her mind, they immediately reassured her:

"Don't flatter yourself, we don't go in for the diaper set," said La Mechunguita. "We like our women and our men all grown up . . . so, you're the new one, so you're Cuquita Martinez. But child! you're much too young for this! . . . for how good the bad life can be!"

She breathed a little easier when she saw the pair of them flop on either side of the bed and light up Camel cigarettes in unison, and she explained that she was only there to cook and clean, to wash and help around the house . . . and to well, make a long story short, she was only there to make an honest living as the new maid.

"I don't know if the landlady mentioned that I'd be sharing your room . . . I'm a very polite person, I don't bother anyone, I respect others so as to be respected —"

At which point La Mechunguita cut her off with a sarcastic:

"Nobody's gonna do anything to you that you don't want done . . . am I right, Puchunguita?"

"No way! Hey!"

And the words were barely spoken, when Cuquita, with an upward bolt of the eyes, fell to the floor in a dead faint, inert as a throttled chicken, sapped by fever and too many emotions. The queen-size ladies hoisted up the frail girl and helped her on to the bed. Flat out on her back, she looked even more skinny and feeble and sick. La Puchunga rushed off for a basin of ice water, and both women gave her a good rubdown with cotton soaked first in alcohol then dipped in water. Some time later, Cuca's fever broke and she fell into a deep sleep. At ten o'clock that evening, she woke up refreshed and ready to sally forth and clean the whole building again if need be. La Mechunga handed her a bowl of chicken soup. She devoured it instantly, in slurpy spoonfuls, making a racket like a kitchen drain.

"Don't make this getting sick a habit. We're not the maids here — you are . . . and learn how to eat soup . . ."

"I'm so sorry . . . it'll never happen again . . . ," Cuquita Martinez promised, red with shame.

Meanwhile, La Puchunguita was cramming her statuesque body into a dress of scarlet lamé. She had already slipped into a pair of very high red patent leather heels and slathered her lips in a shade of Rioja Red. La Mechunga was also in full swing, adorning the body she had sheathed in gold lamé. Her sandals were steeples of gold; she applied yet another coat of vermilion to her harmonica of a mouth. Cleavages and napes and shoulders were dabbed with talcum pow-der — an absolute must in Havana, where women wouldn't think of leaving the house in the evening without a dusting of fat powdery flakes encircling their necks. Perfumed at last, they lit up more

Camel cigarettes. Standing before the mirror, they studied and pawed their bellies, adjusted fabric around rear ends and propped up their tits. For a finish, they used an eyebrow pencil to set off the beauty mark hovering above La Mechunga's lip and the one riding high on La Puchunguita's left breast, cresting just above the heart. Cuquita watched them in foolish wonder.

"Hey kiddo, maybe you should get up off your ass and come with us!" La Mechunguita teased.

Cuca swung her head in neat refusal, but she was wild with envy.

"Yes! come and have a little fun at the Momatter!" (She meant the Montmartre.) "Come on," La Puchunguita urged on between peals of laughter. "I'll find you an old dress from the days before these tits and ass took over."

In no time they had Cuca decked out in a black velvet number festooned with blue spangles. Her little tits were lost in the décolleté and danced about in a valley of whalebone. But her hips filled out the bottom part of the dress very nicely. La Mechunga stuffed the bra with padding, resolving the boob problem. She also produced a pair of black patent leather sandals.

"Hey girl! you got feet like nobody's business! You practically need a size ten, like me. Tractor tracks like that on a little girl like you!"

It was true: with feet like those, Cuquita could nap standing up, and she looked a ridiculous sight in that dress with her skinny hairy legs and feet enormous as a frogman's flippers. La Puchunga made up the adolescent's face as outrageously as possible. When Cuquita saw herself in the mirror, she thought herself beautiful. When a girl starts messing with makeup, you can just forget about it — her world will never be the same again, her days of feminine trauma and compromised freedom are here to stay. Too soon they came and took her by the arm, wresting her from her image in the mercurial glass and into the fresh Havana night in the direction of the Alameda de Paula, where their friend Ivo awaited them at the wheel of a Chevrolet to escort them to the Montmartre. At the sight of Cuquita, Ivo could not contain a Creole and unusual urge to poke a little fun and said: "And what hospital did the consumptive little floozy have in mind?"

With a mighty swing of her patent leather purse, La Puchunguita clobbered him one, chipping one of his teeth with the clasp. They waited at least an hour in all that darkness for Ivo to find his tiny piece of tooth for a dentist to glue back on the following day. At long last, he plucked something off the pavement and carefully laid it inside the folds of a linen handkerchief, then they all piled in the car and started driving in the direction of the cabaret. Cuquita's nerves were in a total state, because of Ivo's jab and of the purse-whacking La Puchunguita repaid him with, and her chin began to tremble and wobble and she gritted her teeth until she could hold back no more. "Ladies and gentlemen . . ." she began in a thick voice.

"Now what? Does she think she's a radio announcer!" La Mechunguita cut her off, and they all laughed hysterically, but Cuquita persisted:

"Ladies and gentlemen . . . I want to make it absolutely clear, here and now, and before all present that I am not a floozy or a whore or anything, and what's more, I'm a virgin . . . I can read and write, my godmother taught me, and when the opportunity presents itself, I intend to continue my studies . . ."

So thunderous was their laughter, passengers in adjacent cars strained their necks to see what was going on in the Chevrolet. Cuquita drew her mouth into a tight little pout and felt the urge to push the rear door open and hurl herself out of the moving car. In fact, she did, and had it not been for La Puchunga, who pulled her back with a hell of a yank, ripping the velvet dress in the process, Cuquita, today, would have been fossilized pussy in the asphalt of Malecón Avenue.

"Say! Girl! Don't you go crazy on us now! What the fuck is wrong with you? Nobody is a whore around here, and don't you go getting wild ideas about us. Mechunga and I are salesladies at El Encanto, the famous department store. . . . Hick that you are, you can't have the slightest idea what I'm talking about. We like a little fun in the evening . . . that's all. And we'll see how long all this virgin business lasts. And for your information, we, too, can read and write . . . because over here, where there's a will there's a way."

Apologies were made by one and all. A deadly silence fell over them, broken only by the immense blasts of waves crashing over the walls of the Malecón, sending water streaming well past the middle of the avenue to where the buildings stood. A saline mist draped the night in mystery. Only the yellow lights shining from the majestic and imposing lamps extending down the center of the avenue lit up the darkness. The wind funneled in the side window and dried Cuquita's tears as she sat lost in thought. She was thinking of her family and the desolate darkness of the countryside where they lived, which suddenly seemed so dark compared to the luminosity of Havana, so beautiful and new and radiant to her eyes. Ivo turned on the radio and the unparalleled voice of Ignacio Villa, Bola de Nieve, the Snowball, a voice leaning to hoarseness, came on singing a sad song in English. And even though she didn't know squat when it came to English, Cuquita immediately felt a tingling, as if some sainted or fetish-tainted thing was telling her that this was her song. At any rate, it was a tune singularly attuned to her mood at that time. *"Remember, it's my heart, my heart filled with old desires. . . . Be careful, it's my heart . . ."*

"What's he saying?" she asked in an anxious voice, her little twat already dewy, and she not knowing what to make of the vaginal affluence.

"Nothing, some foolishness about the heart." And La Mechunga started singing a poor Spanish rendition in her screechy voice: "*Recuerda, es mi corazón, mi corazón lleno de viejos deseos . . . Ten cuidado, es mi corazón, la, la, la . . .* I forgot the words."

Cuquita breathed out a deep and loud sigh, already in love with the proprietor of that diabolically melodic voice. It only took La Puchunguita, who had guessed her sentiments, a couple of pokes to bring her sand castle crashing down.

"That Bola de Nieve sure can sing. Plenty of tiger under that hood. Pity he's black and a swish to boot!" Seeing Cuquita's disconcerted expression she exclaimed, "I hope you're not going to go asking me what a swish is, are you? You'll find out soon enough. If you want to see him in the flesh, you can go to the El Monseñor Restaurant, or" — and her voice took a sarcastic turn — "hop the next plane to Paris. They say he's very famous over there."

The sea air mingled with the smell of grass and of two-for-a-penny colognes that filled the night. Cuquita hummed the song over and over again in the deepest reaches of her heart. Inside the very heart that she, even as a little girl, had wished someone would care for as they would for a bibelot or a bonbon. She was in dire need of a kindhearted, substantial type — substantial, as in man of substance, moneyed — who would spoil her with his attentions. Ivo put down the roof of the convertible. (My little eight-cylinder tribute to the gliding beauties in the novels of Cabrera Infante.) A gusting sea wind matted manes and vandalized makeup, licked the Ponds vanishing cream clean. Cuquita was thinking that maybe a man with hair on his chest, an everlasting highlander kind of lover, could give her just a little of the tenderness she'd never known in her turbulent childhood.

2

Waitress of my Dreams

In this bar we had our first heart to heart
delicious words were spoken from the start.
In this bar, we contemplated countless thoughts
which is why you'll always find me at my spot,
so make it rum for me and a beer for you
and come and drink here nearer my heart,
You, who are the waitress of my dreams.

By José Quiñones,
as sung by Beny Moré

THAT WAS HAVANA — SO VIVID, SO BRIGHT. God Almighty, what a city! Born too late, I missed out on all of it. The lushness of the women, with their taut fleshiness and their hearty thighs, long as bell towers, their shapely glossy legs, their tapered ankles and the consummate skill of their feet when they changed into a working girl's heels and broke into a rhumba. Their breasts, smallish and firm — sometimes plump and sweet — but small breasts and waspish waists and thumping hips are the norm around here. Scooped necklines and provocative cleavages gaping wider than the balconies and rooftops sporting the Cuban flag and awaiting José Martí. Heavy crimson lips woo and coo. Each and every thing, so I'm told, nearing the point of caramelization: a beauty mark here, the arch of an eyebrow there, a frisky fringe on that one's brow, that other one's perfumed ear, rearing rumps and rounded bellies, sashaying limbs and brass and sass. These were some of the happy codes of sexuality in the Pearl of the Antilles, *buena perlanga!*

Havana, saline, maritime city, clasping one and all in its clammy grasp. Havana, city of the freshly bathed and perfume doused and talcum powder dosed and eternally sweaty. Everywhere flesh perspires and glows, glows with pleasure, the pleasure of dancing the dance of love. Havana, city of eyes in heat and bump and grind and skin skimming skin like flames, city of the lewd come-on:

That's what I call a roomy backseat! Hope she don't fart in the talcum powder or there'll be snow for a month.

Hey, Mama, if you cook as good as you look, I'll lick your pot clean any day.

Bet your daddy makes his living by whittling, 'cause I never seen prettier curves!

Don't catch cold, Mamita, 'cause with those bongos one sneeze'll flatten you on your face!

Hey you! hey! Curucucucho de mamey! Hey! tutti-frutti in a sugar cone, vanilla custard and pumpkin flan, my cinammon-sprinkled rice pudding, come here, *tocinillo del cielo* . . .

It was the sugared city then, dipped in honey from head to toe — music and rum-ruffled voices, cabarets, parties, and dinner invitations and *cuisine typique* like roast pork *al mojo*. It's not so hard to make. You'll need about a six-pound picnic ham, a head of garlic, three-quarters of a cup of juiced Sevilla oranges, a tablespoon of oregano, two teaspoons of cumin, half a teaspoon of pepper, two tablespoons of salt, and a pound of onions. First, trim and wash the meat and with a sharp knife pierce it throughout. Then crush the garlic's noggin and mix it with the salt, oregano, cumin, pepper, and juice. With a brush, spread this marinade over the meat, and allow it to sit, covered by a layer of sliced onions, for at least twelve hours. Alongside, have a nice amount of chopped onions, the biggish white ones, and brown these together with the garlic and a pinch of pepper, making sure to keep the pan covered and that the onions are well wilted and the garlic doesn't burn. Add this mixture to the juiced oranges. In the meantime, roast the meat in a 325°F oven for four hours. If you use a meat thermometer, wait for the meat to reach a temperature of 185°F. And make sure you use a roaster with a lid. Place the roast on a shallow platter and don't stint on the onion *mojo*, drench it! Delicious! It should serve eight. Oh! and remember *masa frita*, pork chunks deep fried in loads of lard and finished off with a generous squeeze of lime. With plain rice, of course. There's nothing to get all worked up about. Easiest thing in the world. I know rice can be very temperamental. Not everyone has the touch. It turns out soupy for some and like mortar for others. To have it come out perfect, each grain separate and apart, do it like this: ingredients, well, rice, of course, let's say a pound, two cups of water, a tablespoon of salt, two cloves of garlic, and three tablespoons of oil. Heat the oil and brown the garlic cloves until they're golden, then discard them and remove the pot from the stove. Add the water and salt to the heated oil, and return it to the stove and wait for the water to boil. Now, pour in the well-washed rice all at once, and allow it to come to a second boil. Turn down the heat and let cook covered on a low flame for thirty minutes. This will feed six people. And black beans à la Valdés Fauly. Easiest thing in the world, let me tell you. Two and half pounds of black beans, a pound and a half of green peppers, two cups of olive oil, a pound and a half of onions, two jars of pimientos, half a cup of vinegar, four cloves of garlic, four teaspoonfuls of salt, half a teaspoon of pepper, a quarter teaspoon of oregano, a bay leaf, and two teaspoonfuls of sugar. The day before you're going to eat them, wash the beans and soak them together with the green peppers. In the morning, when the beans are all bloated, add enough water to cover them and let them boil. Grate the onions and green peppers but don't drain them. Pour this pulp, liquid and all, into a pot and cook it till all the liquid evaporates. Mash one jar of pimientos and add it to the peppers and onions together with half the oil. Let everything cook through before adding it to the beans along with the salt, the sugar, and the pepper. Allow the beans to simmer slowly over a low flame and, little by little, keep adding the remaining oil, vinegar, and the second jar of chopped pimientos, juices and all. In about three hours it should thicken nicely, or forty-five minutes if you use a pressure cooker. Remember to add bay leaf and blood sausage to taste. Of course, cooking time may vary, depending on the quality of the beans. If they are the American kind, those big, long, hard ones, then you'll need to cook them longer. But if they're the teensy-weensy round and soft Cuban or Brazilian kind, then three hours is plenty. Uncover them when they're cooked and turn up the heat and watch them closely till they thicken into a kind of puree. They'll taste even better the next day, when they'll become what people call slumbering beans, cause they'll look like mush, dead to the world. So many things to eat, so many things to smell! Ah for a taste of Havana with its mix of sweet and salty, rice and beans with a side of sweet fried plantains, or, for dessert, those preserved guayaba shells with white cheese. Ah, Havana and all its unfathomable pleasures of the palate, and . . . of the other thing too. So many immaculate young men in white twill suits (for those who could afford them. The other ones also had suits, of cheaper quality of course, but just as elegant). Because you have to admit — who'll dare contradict me? — that Havana was the city of learned college types gathering at the Plaza Cadenas with jackets nonchalantly draped over their shoulders to discuss a poem by Paul Valéry, the one that goes: *Ce toit tranquille, où marchent des colombes.* And it was the mean and not-so-lean metropolis of hyper-professional physicians who kept offices in the very elegant neighborhood of Vedado and of myopic scholars seated on the benches of the Parque Central dressed in their Sunday best . . . and let's not forget the pimps, which is how it should be. Because the richness of any city grows in direct proportion to the variety of characters that inhabit it. Yes, even the hustlers with their brilliantined hair and forced laughter. And the young ladies vying with the whores for prestige and fortune. And the assassins. And the assassinated.

The early morning air filled with the aroma of pricey perfumes (purchased at El Encanto, no doubt) mixing with the high, ripe bloom of toiletries from the Tencenes and the rancid smells of drunkenness. Ah, Havana! When the hour of kisses and caresses cannot abide delays. Ah, lush and humid city! City of hot nights and sweetness! Fuck! what sweetness! And every now and again, the sea air will break in, like a spell drawing with it, time and again, fragrant waves of a pot of beans or of *tortilla con chorizos* or simply, the smell of toast. Sometimes it might just be the immediacy of another body, the proximity of skin, the hasty feel and fondle in a doorway of the Malecón, and you'd have to know how to not hang back, but hang loose and party. And music, a furious stream of it coming from every terrace — the goblin genius of beating drums, and melancholy guitars, and audacious pianos, and the voices . . . All those voices, every single person in Havana, it seemed, was singing a *guaguancó* or a *filín*, a *guaracha,* a *son,* or a *danzonete!*

> Danzonete, lickety split
> let's dance, that's it
> to the music of a danzonete . . .

Neighborhoods intoned and resounded depending on the time of day. The thrum and hum of an early morning was a croon as gentle as any *danzón.* At noon sharp, entire streets were swallowed up by the sweltering heat, disappeared into shimmying air and the rattle of kettledrums. Afternoon, with its swishing and tossing, was a *son.* And night, night was a *filín* and a *guaracha.* And how could I forget the *chachacha!* The only anthem for a midday meal, with its dipping and breaking action, and the somnolent white sheets fanning themselves to sleep on the roof, and the clinkety-clink of each dish as it's carried in to delight the palate. And later, the smell — unmistakable — of coffee and tobacco . . . the flutter of ferns in the languorous hours of siesta . . . and in good time, much later: nightfall. Here, everyone sets out to find the night. Night is our altar. We give it our naked and sluttish all.

Cuquita Martinez was both fascinated and terrified by the city. From the car, she took notice of every little thing that went on in the streets, regardless of the velocity at which it sped past her eyes. Finally, they pulled up in front of the Montmartre. Her strange new girlfriends expertly darted out of the car, catapulting themselves one after the other. As I said, the car was a convertible and our good friend and chauffeur Ivo had put down the top *en route* — a maneuver that had not been lost on Cuquita, even though she didn't entirely

19

understand it. It was high time, or so she reasoned, for her to catch on to the bizarre and sophisticated ways of this place. In an effort to imitate her friends, she sprang out of the car like a shot and landed bottom first in a puddle of putrid, scummy water, busting her shoe straps and snapping off her heels, one of which settled in the toupee of an eighty-year-old who looked exactly like a Jesuit priest (and Jesuit priests look like moldy meringues). The other one disappeared inside the saxophone of a musician who happened to be checking in at that very moment. The old man never understood how that heel came to land on his head and he began to survey the balconies like some crazy damn fool intent on collaring the culprit. The saxophone player would find out only hours later, upon raising the instrument to his lips. Nobody saw Cuquita's dive, because she was back on her feet like a spring that had grazed the asphalt only to resurface pale and muddied, her face expressionless, with a powerful urge to rub her fanny and stroke her tailbone out of its misery. But she didn't do it out of shame. La Mechunga, La Puchunga, and Ivo saw her pop in and out like a hiccup. Between bafflement and hugging their sides, so as not to laugh themselves sick, they produced handkerchiefs and napkins and perfume bottles and gave Cuca a good cleanup. In any case, heel-less, Cuquita had lost stature. And as much as she furrowed her brow like La Puchunga had taught her, her piglet face with its little First Communion airs, her skinny knees and bony shoulders, betrayed her age. The patent leather sandals had now become slippers. The barman eyed her suspiciously:

"How old are you, young lady?"

La Mechunga, radiantly stuffed into her gold lamé casing, poised her colossal body between the terrified girl and the barman, who wished he had let things be. Her supremely perfumed and hitched-up breasts parked themselves directly beneath the man's nasal passages, provoking much sneezing.

"She's with me . . . my cousin . . . a dwarf, poor thing. There's no telling how cruel nature can be. Now, take me . . . I just grew and grew to an incorrigible degree, but if tiny, here, gets hasty, she can flush herself down the toilet, believe me!"

La Mechunga's joke brought down the house.

20

The barman, who was both confused and offended, showed them to one of the better tables. The client was still king in those days.

Tears started tumbling down Cuquita's rouged cheeks. In the dimly lit place she wept for everything that had happened, and also because she had never before in her life walked across a floor swanked in red carpets. She shed her slippers and dragged her flat feet back and forth on the downy warmth of the pile. Who would have thought it, in the days she tramped in her back-home dust, that a day would come when she would rest her feet on red carpets? Why! this was fit for queens, for heiresses, for . . .

"Whores, calling us whores! He better watch his mouth or he'll be needing a plastic surgeon next, after I'm done smacking him. 'Cause when my blood boils, forget it, I can't help myself, I need to mutilate . . ." La Puchunga fumed on and on about Ivo, who was making his way to a table where a busty blonde, who had been winking at him for some time now, sat presiding over her flesh.

"You're so jealous . . . I've known it all along, for months I've known it, you want him! Right down to your bones, you want him! Well, nobody's twisting your arm . . . don't hold back on my account . . . I'm not interested in him and anyway, I'm game for any camp . . . come to think of it, he's not so bad . . . But tonight is the night of the bottle blonde, she'll be getting a little sugar in her bowl, bringing the rooster home to roost."

"We'll see about that. What are you staring at? Find me attractive? Do I turn you on?" La Puchunga was shaking her mahogany mane at the Girl Cuca. "Go find yourself a boyfriend and leave me in peace! Did you see that! Stuck on me like a leech!"

The Girl's face went all pouty. Humiliated, she took off, dodging tables and bumping into people, in desperate search of the bathrooms. Customers grumbled about such rude and *stormy weather*. Dashing down a random hallway — she could've sworn there were at least a hundred — she ran straight into that *somebody's* arms.

He was young and slim but sturdily built. He caught her just in time to stop her headlong dive against the trim. His straight hair had been slicked back with brilliantine, and his swift lunge to save her

21

had loosened a strand that now fell right down the middle of his face. His eyes were pale as the sky (any sky you please) and his smile was very pretty, though his lower teeth straddled one another a bit. He took out a handkerchief and wiped her cheeks. He wasn't too tall and he wasn't too short, but just the right height to study up close from tippy-toe range.

"Dance with me," he said, his voice like salsa, and this was way before the days of salsa. The voice promised folly and augured safe harbors. A chill went through Cuquita, and she pulled away from his bony but steady grasp.

"Oh no, you can't mean that!" But she stayed right where she was, perched on her toes, ogling him and breathing in his aftershave, his Guerlain perfume and brilliantine.

In a split second, he had her by the waist and was pulling her toward the dance floor. The band began to play, and the planet was suddenly freed of its agonies — the power and politics, the *get outta my way or do I have to make you*, the *let's pull a dirty one on this one and a nasty one on that one*. Cuquita, for the first time, was experiencing the great Beny Moré wielding his baton and leading his extraordinary orchestra. His gray suit was much too large for him. Or maybe not, that's how they wore them then, with those billowy pants flapping like flags to the rhythms of his newfangled music. A voice, sweet as breeze in the sugarcane, started to sing the first bars of what would become the signature song of the first and only love story in the life of Cuquita Martinez.

> Here, in this bar, I saw you first
> and didn't think twice, I gave you all I had,
> We had a beer, maybe two
> and there was sadness in the air.

The ceiling spun round and round and round . . . the lights were spinning with it, the walls seemed as splendidly hung as the rooms of Versailles, mirror after mirror framed in silver and gold. Well, everything sparkly, whirling like a crystal labyrinth. Spotlights hurtled shooting stars by the hundreds, at an incredible speed. Cuca wished a thousand wishes. Hardly any would come true. She wished for her mother and father to get back together and move to Havana or Santa Clara and for them all to live together under one roof like a normal family. She said ten Hail Marys — for her mother to leave the theater, for her father to find a better-paying job, for her brother to be freed from asthma and delivered from buggery. She prayed for her other brother to regain use of his polio-stricken leg, for her sister's full recovery from the operation to remove the cyst from her brain, for her godmother's toothaches to ease up, for the damn-near-white mulatto to change his ways and leave her brother in peace. She wished for this man, with whom she was now dancing cheek to cheek, to stay right where he was, forever.

Waitress, darling waitress, you are the waitress of my dreams.

And then, he sighed, and Cuquita inhaled the foul effluvium of his breath.

"Oh! You've got bridgework?" she asked, wondering if he had false teeth.

"No, why?" and he pulled back, self-conscious all of a sudden.

"Because your mouth stinks a little, you know, bad breath. You should have a look around, 'cause what if a dog crawled in there and did his business under the bridge . . ." She was trying to be funny and sniffed the inside of her cupped hand.

"It must've been the onion omelette. I love raw onions." He smiled through pressed lips and spoke through clenched teeth but kept his fingertips pressed hard against the girl's backbone.

"You should wash out your mouth real well after eating onions and chew on a piece of paper bag or newspaper. So, what kind of work do you do? Do you work?"

One thing she had learned from her father was the importance of ascertaining a man's job situation.

"Who, me?" he said, fumbling.

"No! the man in the moon! Of course you! I'm talking to you aren't I?"

"Well . . . I'm . . . in sales at the moment. I sell whatever comes my way — books, furniture, sewing machines, washing machines, driving . . . cars, I mean. My mother, if she gets out of hand. I'm what they call a wheeler-dealer. Yup, I'd sell the old lady for a dollar if I had to."

She felt a damp shudder work up from her feet and out her neck and her skin went shivery all over.

"Don't say that! A mother is the most sacred —"

"It's just an expression. A joke . . ."

And in one full spin, he cut Cuca loose and forced her to fend for herself on the floor, urging her from the sidelines to really, really shake those bones. But she couldn't, because never in her life had she dared to dance with such an authority on local flavor and color. In fact, she had never danced at all, and strictly speaking, all she had done up to now was leave footprints all over her partner's two-toned shoes.

Left on her own, she could barely control her waist, she kept losing her balance, and not one of her moves was in sync, her body squirmed like flan on a tipping platter. He saw her for the klutz she was and took her by her tiny waist. With a gentle prod of his fingertips he steered her body and corrected her steps, readjusted the swinging motion of her hips and showed her how to display the elegance of shoulders. And Cuquita outdid herself. She learned her stuff like nobody's business. Before long she was rippling and swirling in the middle of the dance floor as if she'd come out squirming and dancing from her mother's stomach.

Her friends looked on in disbelief, drooling on their lamé gowns. La Puchunga only managed a mumble:

"Hey! What bit her? Did the spirit mount her or what!"

"I do believe she's found the man of her life," the sallow one replied.

Cuca was the absolute sensation of the evening! The band struck up a mambo and in a shake, she'd be arched up in that bitch-in-heat attitude suited to that dance:

> Mambo, how sweet the mambo
> Mambo, such a treat, the mambo

If a chachacha followed, she'd glance at her friend's feet and make a quick study of how he stepped to the beat and off she'd go again, with a one, two, three, chachacha and again, two, three, chachacha. La Puchunga amended each verse by putting Carauquita down:

> To Prado and Neptune, came a little lady. (A slut from the slums!)
> One you couldn't help but look at. (The guy should have his eyes checked!)
> She was so pleasant, so round (A bag of bones!)
> Born to astound. (No better than a spider monkey!)
> But the word was out (She's a hick from the sticks!)
> All over town and back (A backbiter!)
> There was mistaking (camel-back!)
> Her curves were all padding, she'd tricked us with wadding. (Flat as a boy's back!)
> Never are women such fools (thick-skulled)
> as when they try to fool us! (Wretch and thick lip!)

A *guaracha* was struck up and their bodies came together. Then a rhumba and they moved apart. She was drenched in sweat, her makeup running and her eyes shining from all the Martini & Rossi she had downed. Little Virgin of Charity have mercy! That poor girl had never tasted vermouth in her life! And she danced and she danced, over and over again, until, overcome by weariness, she once again went out like a light, collapsing in her partner's arms.

The Anointed King of Rhythm, Beny Moré, was back onstage with his consummate orchestra, and now his honeydew voice took off in a mighty bolero, the kind that makes you want to give up the ghost then and there, the kind that has you making a beeline for the cyanide. The young man pulled Cuquita to him, and she felt the nudge of his dowel against her scrawny thighs. She marveled at the twittery feeling set off by the tip of his stalk nuzzling her tufted pea. Pulling a white handkerchief from his back pocket, he mopped the sweat from her face and neck, and most of her makeup came off on the white cloth. She stood before him with her wavy hair, black as jet, and the perfect oval of her face and the slight stoop of her shoulders (hallmark of profound sensuality and a surefire signal of uterine blazes to come), with her wide brow and her gently slanted golden eyes, like honeysuckle, like rum, and her flat button of a nose and her rosy mouth much bolder than a bud and her pearly skin. Her face clean, bare, smooth, childlike. Her dripping hair revealing her for what she was, a schoolgirl, emerging from the sea or a river or simply the shower, as in Stanley Kubrick's *Lolita*.

"How old did you say you were?" he asked, holding her face in both his hands.

"And this is when the shit hits the fan . . . ," La Mechu, who hadn't stopped staring at them, remarked from across the room.

"I'm so sorry . . . I don't even know your name, nor you mine. I usually mind my manners . . . Caridad Martinez, but they call me the Girl or Cuquita or Caruquita. . . . Cuquita Martinez to serve his highness." He was far from amused.

"That little girl is splat on the windshield, now! She's dead mosquito . . .," responded La Puchu, who was busily lip-reading.

"You going to tell me how you old you are? My name is Juan Perez, but they call me Uan, you know as in Number One, because I always beat everyone hands down when it's time to deal, I'm always the first, I'm the best, yeah, the best and the most perfect, the One, here and everywhere. You're not underage are you?"

"He's not going to let himself be duped that easily . . ." La Mechu was still intently following their conversation and trying to decipher every syllable.

Cuquita nodded, where was she going to hide with that canary face of hers, and also, because above all else, she was terrified of losing this man, the one and only human being who had touched her with tenderness. Her first man. The one who taught her how to dance.

"How *young* are you, then?" His manly features were now crumpled by fear and doubt, but there was an edge of pride to his voice all the same.

La Mechu and La Puchu gave them up as a lost cause, especially as their habitual luck was now reappearing in the form of a pair of hefty fellows suited up like Sicilian mafiosi, asking them to dance.

"Not very, very young . . . I'm a little over sixteen . . ."

He leapt in paternalistic joy, Pygmalion visions already dancing in his head, crossed himself repeatedly, and hoisting her up in his arms, he swung her round and round before setting her down on the ground with the extreme wariness of a sales clerk in a toy shop.

"You've been putting me on, why you're almost ancient!" And . . . he kissed her on the lips.

And oh! was it good! delicious! But as much as she enjoyed it, she carefully pried his lips apart with her fingers and sniffed the inside of his mouth.

"It still stinks a little. Go chew some gum or drink something minty. Best thing for bad breath."

"That's all you can say about my kiss?"

"Well, with those onion and cavity fumes, how do you expect me to get what kissing is all about. That was my *first kiss*!" And the emphasis she gave to those words was much greater than any I could reproduce on this typewriter.

The Uan went off in the direction of the bar and disappeared among tables and faces. Cuquita suddenly recalled her new friends and began to scan the room for them. She found them knocking themselves out, or off, clinging like mad to those two George Raft bruisers. It was then she noticed the throb of her aching bunions and returned to the table. She stretched out her legs and rubbed her absolutely filthy feet against the red carpet, and gripping the longish carpet hairs between her toes, she fiddled away to her heart's content. The relief was unbelievable! It just about overcame her, and she even nodded off a couple of times.

She was startled out of her dream state by a racket of drumrolls. The place was dark except for a wide beam funneling down from a spotlight in the middle of the large room. Two men were cavorting inside the incandescent glade of light, exhibiting splendid bodies sheathed only in flesh-colored bodysuits and looking sure as hell buck naked. As they were very well endowed, their respective little parcels were packaged so nicely as to warm your heart. The Girl tried to avert her eyes, but she soon was locked into a sidelong study of that phenomenal duo on the verge of a jockstrap blowout. A woman, with a stiff smile and an American body — that is to say lacking an ass and with shoulders like a clothes hanger — appeared between the men. She wore a fringed bathing suit in a leopard print. The drums ceased, marking a silent beat, and the three of them moved as if in *slow mo* into their new positions. The drums resumed and the "Apache Dance" commenced. The choreography essentially consisted of the two men tossing the woman from one end of the room to the other, and catching her just as she was about to come crashing down. The well-built blond one with the mustache grabbed her by the wrist, and in a single motion pulled himself forward and sent her flying through the air like a peerless javelin toward a wall. The swarthy partner caught her in the nick of time, preventing her demise against the mirror-lined stucco walls. The drums played on with positively native abandon. Nothing had anything to do with anything else, not the music with its tribal persuasion, nor the violent contortions of the dance, nor the costumes, not even the title of the piece with its tribal pretensions.

In act two, the pretty but pathetic woman, her hyper-fabricated smile frozen in place so as not to show even a hint of fear, was once again hurled every which way, or prowled down tunnels of light into the farthest reaches of the room, as if to tryst with the Invisible Man minus his bandages. The light followed her into the shadows, only to reappear just in time to catch her as she was about to ream herself against yet another table, and again a hand would materialize to save her, then let go of her like a hot potato. Cuquita Martinez was fascinated, but most of all terrified by this new sport, though it did remind her a little of baseball, except the bat was missing. Or maybe soccer, but the half-naked cabaret fellows were nothing like the pictures of soccer players she had seen in the newspaper, nor basketball or volleyball players for that matter. In any case, the passivity of the female plaything and the violent tension on the playing field, as well as the extended absence of her escort, left her in a state of total confusion. She was a bag of nerves. She scanned the room again for her friends, and spotted their profiles in the semidarkness of the place. They were entranced by the performance, huddling and snuggling up to those two handsome Al Capone fellows, and maybe — who can tell — nursing a secret wish to find themselves catapulted in space, soaring past the field and all the way out of the ball park.

The dance drew to a close, and the all-but-disemboweled woman lay in a heap on the floor. She looked dead, but she never stopped smiling. The guys bowed in triumph and the audience rose in applause. A moment elapsed, the dancer sat up straight, looking much happier but still panting, and came to her feet in a single leap, then doubled over into a deep bow. The applause thundered to an ear-splitting pitch. Cuquita Martinez didn't understand a thing. She wept and joined her hands in a pious gesture, not because she had been overwhelmed by the quality of the show, but because she was relieved it had all finally come to an end.

An exhalation of mint and alcohol blew suddenly into her left ear. He was back, carrying tall glasses of crème de menthe on ice, and chewing gum, likewise mint-flavored. He pulled up a chair and handed her a glass. He stared at her ardently — with the tip of his moist penis — deep into the honeysuckle eyes. She held his obscene gaze. He emptied his glass to the last drop, and exhaled yet again, breathing right in his companion's face. Then, he tilted his head to inquire about any lingering odor. No, truly, no, she assured him that no, the sour fumes had vanished, not even a trace left. The mint had done a good job on the halitosis, no doubt disinfecting the cavity's rotted nerve.

He pulled up a different chair and sat very close to the Girl's vibrant and eloquent body. She lifted her glass to her mouth with both hands and bolted down the drink in one breath. Then, she reached for the ice cubes, noisily sucking and chomping on them one at a time. The music had started up in time to drown out the noise of teeth crunching ice. He couldn't stop looking at her; and as the last ice cube was about to vanish, he asked her to pass it from her mouth to his. She did, and the frozen delicacy immediately melted in a sea of saliva.

The kiss, which had begun innocently, as a little game of pass-the-ice-cube, now changed after the last ice cube had vanished and became a mess of coiling tongues, wrapping about each other like snakes, and ingenuousness found itself transformed into pornography. He nibbled her lips until they swelled, and she, somewhat more

29

shyly, nibbled him back. The kiss was as long as three back-to-back boleros: one was four minutes long, the other one, three minutes, and the third, four minutes and thirty-three seconds. All in all — eleven minutes and fifty-three seconds of sucking and tonguing. La Mechu, who clocked the kiss, was green with envy.

Cuquita Martinez heard the trombones blaring in another dimension, in rhythm with the blood now coursing toward her brain, her heart, and also, why not? toward the Uan's impenitent penis. The lights of the Montmartre, it seemed, were being snuffed out, one by one, to slowly reignite in her body, limb by limb, and light up every cubic inch of her desire. Cuquita Martinez closed her eyes and was about to open the whole kit and caboodle, when she remembered her resolution to arrive at her nuptials a maiden. And with a single push she broke from his embrace with a NOOO! as hysterical as in any one of those horror movies or thrillers that can be purchased for a song in discount stores everywhere — but in Cuba, of course. Like a flash, she bolted from the cabaret and its delectable vice, leaving only her howl stranded in the echoing hall.

She ran barefoot and so fast you couldn't even see her feet — not easy, given their spectacular size. She just about flew past the doorways of the Malecón, looking like the future track and field champ Ana Fidelia Quirot. She kept going, despite a stitch in her side, pounding through block after block and square after square and kilometer after kilometer. Before she knew it, she had arrived at the train station just a short step away from the Calle Conde. In a flash, she reached the Asturiana's doorway, her eyes ablaze, lathering at the mouth and dripping sweat. She started up the stairwell, looking for all the world like a woman who broke out of the Mazorra Asylum seconds after being administered shock treatment. She slammed the door behind her and flung herself on the cot to lament her fortune and misfortune. She was helplessly in love.

Before the half hour was up, in walked her bewildered roommates. They questioned her relentlessly. She could only shake her head and clutch her disheveled locks with both hands, completely incapable of stringing together a coherent sentence. Except for the ones she had learned by heart from the radio, spoken by actresses going through *similar* situations. A basin of cold water was fetched, and her friends placed cold rags on her temples and forced a carafe and a half of iced lemonade into her. The mock-white one dried her off with a towel, undressed her, and led her into the shared hallway bathroom. She turned the tap and released an imperious jet of water onto the middle of the girl's head. Inside her waterfall, the girl wailed, inconsolable:

"I love him, I love him, Mechunguita! I love him! I'm dying for him!" She sobbed so much that she almost choked on the soapy water she had inhaled. She gasped, and an immense bubble floated up from her lips.

"You're not normal, Girl! Why did you walk out on him?" La Puchunga asked as she leaned against the door frame, making the most of a mouthwatering opportunity to gaze at Caruquita's pink and perfect nipples.

"Because . . . because . . . ," and it dawned on her that she didn't know why, she had no idea why she had behaved in such an uncivilized manner, maybe some kind of aftereffect of that Apache Dance, maybe nerves . . . "You could say I got nervous, you know, it was my first time kissing someone on the mouth . . . Gosh!"

"Not bad at all for the first time!" said Lu Mechunga, teasing.

"Don't make fun . . . I left because, I don't know . . . Because that man will never marry me . . ." And again she clasped her hands to her face.

The other two could not believe their ears. Some unknown virus was clearly eating its way through the labyrinths of the Girl's brain. They didn't even feel like making fun of her. "Marry you? But why do you have to get married?" La Mechunga finished rinsing her off and copping a feel whenever she could. She lovingly took Cuca back yet again to the bedroom. Freshly bathed and powdered, Cuca got under the sheets and tried to sleep. But there he was. All she had to do was reach out and touch his face. She couldn't budge him from her mind. He was installed in her hypothalamus, his image fixed for eternity. La Puchunga brought her a glass of warm milk, which she had dosed with four Meprobamate sedatives. Cuquita drained the glass, her throat ticking as reliably as a convent clock with each swallow. Handing back the emptied glass, she wiped her mouth with the back of her hand and pulled the sheets up to her nose and closed her eyes with the certainty that tonight her dreams would bring her a José Angel Buesa, her very own second-rate Poet of the Heart — her Uan.

3

A Rose from France

A rose from France gave her sweet perfume,
her miracle to me on a May afternoon . . .

By Rodrigo Pratts,
as sung by Barbarito Díez

*T*HE DREAM WOULD LAST EIGHT YEARS. Not because of the four
sedatives but because she would not have it any other way. How did
she think she'd ever see him again without so much as lifting a finger? But she wouldn't yield an inch, insisting he was the man — the
one who had to track her down. Hound her. Succumb at her door.
She never again set foot outside Old Havana. Not once did she
accept to go along to the nightclubs with the inseparable La Mechu
and La Puchu, who hadn't seen hide or hair of him either. Uan's dis-
appearance had sent her desire soaring through the roof. What
began as love at first sight soon became obsessive passion, mute
devotion, and vehemence. Every night she'd be down on her knees
howling and pining like a half-starved bitch, or twittering over her
rosary in breathless ecstasy as if she were in the presence of Christ
at the Temple. For months on end, she worked herself to the bone
and waited for that man. The love of her life. The one to whom she
had neglected to give an address or the least clue to her whereabouts.

She ran herself so ragged that three years later the Asturiana finally came around to giving her a room of her own. And had Cuca been acquainted with Virginia Woolf, she most certainly would have lighted a small candle of thanksgiving to the lady. For years now, she had been expected to put up with her roommates and their acrobatic rounds of pleasure. And when they brought another man or woman along, she spent her nights in a panic of sobs, huddled in the crawl space beneath the stairwell with the cockroaches scrabbling all over (how was she to know that as an old woman she'd welcome one into her home as a member of the family) and the rats about to gnash her at any minute. On one such night, the Asturiana came into the communal bathroom to find Cuca fast asleep smack beneath the eternal leak that, just then, was pecking at her skull. The woman took pity and arranged to have her move into a little room that gave onto the roof. The heat was fierce up there, but at least it was private. La Mechunga and La Puchunga continued to pamper her, and she came to love them as one does a pair of sluttish aunts who are much too far gone for rehabilitation or redemption. Even though their daytime jobs as salesladies at El Encanto turned out to be God's truth, and they did, in fact, earn an honest living. There'd been no news of her real family, but that didn't stop her from religiously sending all her money to her godmother, Maria Andrea, who then parceled it out to the rest. Her mother earned next to nothing in the theater, and anyway, she always frittered it away in no time on the fancy boy of the hour.

One afternoon, another little scrap of a girl, fifteen and looking for work, came knocking at the door. True to form, wooden flip-flops in hand, Concha opened the door and took her in just as she had Cuquita those many years ago. Now that the household chores were shared with the new one, Cuca suddenly found herself with time to spare. The Asturiana set her up with a second job at Juanito's Cafetera Nacional around the corner, and she now spent her afternoons dispensing cups of coffee at three cents a pop. She also wanted to go to school. She tried hard to save the odd penny, and her new earnings, after she'd sent the tribe their regular cut, just barely covered her books and the rent the Asturiana expected her to pay, now

34

that she had a second job. But she met a teacher at the Chinese Laundry on Jesús María Street, who offered her lessons in exchange for help caring for her elderly mother over on Calle Merced. The teacher spent her weekends with her husband, who was a witch by vocation and lived in Matanzas, a town famous for its witches. And in this way, Cuquita Martinez furthered her education and, in time, took her high school exams, somewhat later than most, but then again, something is something. It's better than nothing.

This is a tale of love and woe much like the María Teresa Vera song — "sweet are the wounds of love . . ." It's a rose, like any other, with thorns. A melodrama with thistles, a cheap romance for penniless little country girls who come to Havana and get themselves a degree. Those girls who, if we are to believe the official accounts, all had to work as prostitutes and all learned to read and write after the revolution had triumphed. To this day, I still don't understand how they could all have had one and the same story and am beginning to think that the story is just cobbled together any which way to suit the needs of the teller. Many of them did manage to get an education; I know them. They worked themselves silly, going through books, not men, like wildfire. Much more difficult, that. And more stimulating. "Only the difficult stimulates," wrote Lezama Lima. Cuca Martinez was one of them, although she never did get her B.A., but almost. She was barred from the university because of a man, the one and only love of her life. And because of a dollar bill. The history of humanity is full of such stories of love and woe. And dough. Let's not forget that in 1626, the Dutchman and Protestant Huguenot Peter Minuit bought New York, New Amsterdam at the time, for twenty-four dollars' worth of glass beads.

But even mathematics could not cancel out the X (equaling Uan in this case) from Cuquita's heart. The as of yet unexplored cove of her vagina had not stopped throbbing since the night he had sucked and nibbled her tongue with his foul and minty mouth. She felt she was his, entirely his. She'd filled out in lovely ways since that fateful night. Not a knock-'em-dead beauty, you understand, but she could make you catch your breath just the same. She took a 36B, so her tits were to the taste of most, not exceedingly large or

35

exceedingly small, but respectable. She weighed 115 pounds, stood five feet six inches tall, had widish hips, a waspish waist, and an ass as insolent as any black woman's. She had long, strong thighs, nicely turned calves, slender ankles, and big feet. Nothing she could do about that — big feet are big feet everywhere, here and in Kuala Lumpur. They may well have been the toast of Paris in the 1920s, but here, in Havana, a woman's size ten foot is an abomination, an offense to the fine art of shoemaking. Cuquita did what she could, cramming her feet into shoes that were at least two sizes too small so that by evening she was ready to hack off her toes to ease the misery of her strangled feet. None the less, Cuca Martinez still stopped traffic on city streets and avenues, not when she was fifteen, but later — in her twenties. Which amounts to the same thing. She had a way of sashaying down a street, with a swish to the left and a swish to the right, of bobbing back and forth between Irish passion and Oriental patience, that could bring even the most languid penis to attention.

Alone, locked up in her sauna of a room, she spent sweaty hours admiring her shameless nakedness in the tall, mirrored doors of a Spanish Mortification–style armoire. Best of all, she liked to stroke her pubic hair and tell herself that it was Uan, himself, who was running his fingers through her thick, black bush, because in addition to being as meaty as a papaya, Cuquita's pudendum was as magnificently maned as her head. That jumble of hair and flesh, of mind and bone, was her. All of it her, and all for her man — her Uan. All those fixings of nerve and sinew and brains had become this precious creature with the body of a twenty-four-year-old virgin. A virgin in Havana, city of the eternally tousled and crumpled, which didn't take to virgins too kindly. The Girl, not that she could really pass for one anymore, was full of fine talk about saving herself for her Pipo, or her Papi, or better yet, her Papirriqui. Which is how women in Havana refer to their men, never mind if the guy's name is Guillaume or Fréderic or Andrés or John or Richard or Francisco, he is bound to end up as a Pipo or Papi or Papirriqui.

She stayed in her Old Havana cubbyhole and endured her self-imposed sentence like a beast. She never once went looking for him.

He would have to come for her and, failing that, fate would have to miraculously supply a second encounter. That's how she saw things . . . until that Saturday afternoon, when to put idle time to good use, she changed into her bathing suit and went out on the roof where she doused herself with a bucket of water, which she had remembered to dose with salt, and smoothed tanning lotion all over herself, and stretched out to sunbathe. *She whiled away a deep-felt hour under a heartless sun.* A good while later, a radio came on in one of the neighboring rooms and a male voice of unsurpassed elegance filled the air. Cuquita's breathing thickened, her chest swelled like a hot balloon, her pip twitched uncontrollably. The radio host was saying that the song was called "A Rose from France" and had been performed by Barbarito Díez in honor of a *grande dame of la chanson Française*, he said it like that, the divine Edith Piaf, to welcome her back to the Montmartre, so that she would:

> Charm us with the rough beauty of her songs, overwhelm and honor us with her presence and marvelous artistry. Three nights ago, the singer was met at Havana airport by Ramón Sabat, president of Panart Records, Miss Piaf's distributing company, and by Mario Garcia, social manager at the Montmartre. The singer was accompanied by Juan Perez, director of public relations, whose return to the island marks the end of an extended stay abroad, and who is said to be largely responsible for the singer's visit to our island. Miss Piaf was also accompanied by the photographer Eduard, whose last name we've finally managed to make out — it is Matussière. Immediately upon arriving, Miss Piaf sat for a card and shell reading — she wanted to know if luck would be on her side in our city. Her next order of business was to sit down with a French-Spanish dictionary and work on Spanish introductions to her new songs. Her Spanish is remarkably improved. But we are far more interested in the songs and the beautiful Parisian accent. Her two scheduled appearances are already sold out, and people have already started pressing for additional shows. She is a goddess of song in her plain little black dress and her simple flats. The only adornment she allows herself onstage is that marvelous voice that so moved Parisians more than twenty years ago, on the corner of the Rue Troyon and on countless other street corners of that most amorous of cities. Those who see her for

the first time are invariably surprised when she emerges onto the stage. How is it possible, those who know nothing about her will ask, how can this little woman, with her big head and her face like a cookie, and her dangling arms and those twisted little hands be such a famous singer? Your run-of-the-mill audience wants its stars bejeweled. So, where are her jewels, they'll want to know, this star who commands the world's highest fees? And then, the orchestra will strike up the first measures of a song, and Edith Piaf, *la grande mome* (I think it means *mummy*) of Paris, will ransack her memory for the right words and briefly introduce her next song in her picturesque Spanish and ready herself to sing. Those who are seeing her for the first time will still be trying to figure out the humility of that dress. The woman who likes to think she has a notion or two about elegance will take pity on her — that bared throat and those poor unadorned fingers. And then, she'll sing. Edith Piaf. And from the very first lines, the modest woman in her modest dress will forever be emblazoned in the ear of the orphaned multitude as splendor itself. In the room, the silence is palpable. A clause in her contracts stipulates that no meals or drinks may be served while she's singing. Nothing, not even a glass of water.

But the audience does not know or need to know about that clause to keep an absolute and expectant silence in the presence of this retiring girl. It's her voice that does the silencing. That anguished voice, with its street inflections and its sad songs about the chagrined and trodden. They listen without entirely understanding what she's saying. There are a few American tourists, but most are Cubans who may have traveled as far as Miami and back on some occasion. But none of that matters. When Edith Piaf sings, they all understand that they are in the presence of immense feelings. They can tell by the snag in her voice and the trouble in her faraway eyes and the slack and helpless arms that seem to have so little to do with the rest of the body.

Born to an acrobat and a washerwoman on the city's outer fringes, she ran away from home and made her way to those fortunate Paris street corners where she sang her first songs in a child's wavering voice. Even then she was dressed as she is now and went about barefoot, with the sepulchral black cloth hanging like a sack on her slight form. And when she turned her dark eyes up to the sky and threw her arms wide open, she looked like a crucifix that could have hung on any wall in any building. Someone once asked her to sing about happy things, because nightclubs are not so well suited to gloom. If she was listening, with that sad-girl smile of hers never leaving her face, she would have forgiven that person. And once a fashion designer — on the advice of film stars Arletty and Marlene Dietrich — concocted a luxurious and exclusive gown just for her. She was whisked to a beauty salon and, with colors from the latest palette, they made up her face, and pushed and pulled at her body, with a little help here and a little tuck there until they had her looking like a model. But when she appeared onstage, draped in her newfound elegance, the applause was scant and half-hearted. Courteous. The impresario, who saw everything from the wings, was waiting for her in her lodge when she returned, and without so much as an *excuse me*, he yanked the emerald crucifix from her neck. He tore off her luxurious and exclusive gown and covered her in a ratty black rag just like the one in which she had walked the streets of Paris, the city of love and song.

"Now, go Edith," he said, "you go and sing for them."

And she again became the Edith Piaf the whole world had come to love. A French rose like the one in the song Barbarito Díez sang in her honor on this great occasion:

"... The prettiest rose, the white petaled rose, she can put a spell on you, she's a rose from France, gave her soft perfume, her miracle to me, on a May afternoon ..."

The voice of the most elegant and sedated Negro (he didn't move a single muscle when he sang), the most beautiful, simple, and discreet man in the entire island, stopped singing, and the neighbor switched the radio off. Now, Cuca could only hear her own sobs, even though the huge tears evaporated in the hot sun before quite reaching her cheeks. She wept for everything at once, because of the song, an old *danzonete* like they don't make them anymore and this one was tailor-made for the aristocratic voice of Barbarito Díez. She wept for that French singer and her sad story and her shabby dress and her great melancholy and beautiful loyalty and mad desire to sing, despite all the heartbreak in her life. But above all else, she was weeping, bleating like a fool because of that name — Juan Perez, director of public relations at the Montmartre. The announcer had said that he'd been away from Cuba for a very long time, which could explain why he hadn't come looking for her, probably because of problems having to do with his work. But how had he done it? How had he become such an important man, so quickly? Last she knew him, he was selling whatever was at hand, odds and ends, even his mother if she got out of hand. How did he become so grand all of a sudden? The announcer had also said that the French woman agreed to come because of Juan Perez. What if he was in love with the singer, had forgotten her for another woman, and a French one to boot! She felt infernally jealous. She was not one to harbor false illusions, like those melodramatic characters in the radio serials, even though she knew thanks to her dictionary and her teacher that it was wrong and redundant to speak of false illusions, illusions are false by definition. Those who live off illusions shall perish from losing them, goes the saying. Hadn't she, until this very moment, been living off illusions? And what if this Juan Perez was not the real Juan Perez? There isn't exactly what you'd call a shortage of Juan Perezes in Havana and its surroundings. If this one turned out to be the real one, he was sure to come looking for her. But where would he start? Without even a picture to go by. And the island is filled with girls named Cuquita Martinez, they're as plentiful as daughters of Oshún, which means about 99 percent of the female population.

For the first time in eight years, Cuca was overtaken by the urge to change into an elegant dress, to put on makeup, lipstick, patent leather heels, to slip on a pair of stockings (suffocating in this heat, but they did wonders for the legs), to mantle her shoulders in a cloud of talcum powder and dab her breasts for good measure, to be womanly and worldly and go out into the night and head for the Montmartre. She thought all this while she continued to moan and wail with the best of them. With every new thought of Juan another round of snot came frothing from her nose. Suddenly, she flew to her feet, blotting tears and toweling off drool and making up her mind in a minute to do what she had not allowed herself to do for years on end. Tonight, she would catch the Uan.

Evening came quickly as she washed herself in the basin she had dragged into her room. She stepped out onto the cooling rooftop in a housedress with a towel wrapped around her head. Behind the buildings, a gigantic red sun was making a silent movie exit, falling in slow motion into the unknown depths of the ocean. Everywhere she looked Cuca could see the ocean, hence her love for living in high places, so close to the light and in command of the view. Someone else had switched on a radio, and a woman with the voice of a city sparrow was singing. It had to be that French woman. A ballad about a sad passion from another place on the planet hung above the buildings and quivered in the evening breeze. Cuquita was green as green when it came to French, but she was dead sure the song was about loving a man who had been snatched away. She wanted to go running after that voice, so very much like love, to be like the woman everyone admired. She even forgot about Juan Perez. She would have given anything to meet the woman behind that reckless melody. At least, she wanted to see her up close.

She darted toward the stairwell's black eye and taking the steps two at a time, burst into La Mechunga and La Puchunga's room:

"Well lookee here! The turtledove has flown the coop. This girl thinks we reside in a spa, you should've seen her earlier, crisping herself like a plantain or a morsel of pork . . . this is a tenement, sweetheart, so don't go mistaking it for the Ritz." La Puchu was in one of her bearish moods.

"What brings you to these parts looking so provocative in that flimsy little thing and your hair sopping wet?" As usual, La Mechunga didn't mince words.

Cuca hesitated, she didn't want them to make fun . . . she just needed to know if they had any plans for the evening, if they wouldn't mind coming with her to a certain place . . . could they spare a cigarette, imagine how nervous she must've felt to be asking for Camels out of the blue. She wouldn't want to inconvenience them, it's just that she was bored, needed a change of air, a change of scene, a little break in the routine. It was high time for her to be a woman again, desire was only human and so was being desirable. This life of hers had to change, she was tired of being a beast of burden, a toiling machine, a broomstick, a heap of ashes, a load of stale laundry. She was tired of waiting, of punishing her body. Something had to give or she would lose her mind, she had already started to bite her nails and chew her cuticles. Any love song on the radio, it didn't even have to be a bolero, sent her into fits of tears worthy of an idiotic heroine in a melodrama. Each song had marked her insipid life like a scar. She was starved for affection, for love, for —

"Cock, honey, what you need is cock and plenty of it." La Mechunga finished her sentence for her. "Who can live like that, all that sexless existence!"

"The girl is suffering from a deficiency, and I don't mean vitamins." La Puchunga put in her two cents' worth.

She only needed one thing — and it wasn't coffee or tea — she wanted a special favor, would they come with her tonight to a cabaret. "A cabaret!" they hooted in unison. "Yesterday she had a foot in the convent, and today she's raring for the cathouse!" She told them about everything that had happened, the radio program, and the name that had resurfaced, and its likely connection to her beloved, and most of all, she described the poignant sweetness of the song and all about Edith Piaf and her life, almost as sad as her own, and how a single life could be filled with so many twists and turns and tricks of fate, and how according to the radio host, the woman was totally insignificant physically, and how her own desire to rekindle her dwindling fires and appetites had been awakened. The women understood her perfectly. And they didn't need convincing, after all, in the intervening eight years, they hadn't spent a single evening at home. There was not a bar, restaurant, café, or cabaret they didn't know. They'd been everywhere, always escorted by Ivo, the most solicitous and highly solicited chauffeur in the entire island. They had toyed with him as an on-again, off-again lover to the point of tedium.

Just as night fell in a blaze of stars (those same stars I come back to in all my books as unique, sensational, marvelous, sublime, irreplaceable, in other words, as the cause of all my sparrows), precisely, at that moment of astral time, the three women stepped out of the building done up like a trio of carnival queens.

Ivo awaited them at the Alameda de Paula at the wheel of a gleaming Chevrolet. His renewed loyalty to Chevrolet, as attested to by this newest model, followed the five accidents that had befallen him after he had switched to Studebaker. The other fellows weren't half wrong when they jokingly called the Studebaker Ivo's Ball Breaker. The drive down the Malecón was even more wonderful than the first one. That's one thing about Havana, the more you walk it the more you love it. How can you tire of a city that surpasses its own beauty at every turn? There's a new adventure down every street, a new seduction to pulp your heart and whisk it into tropical nectar. Even if it is falling to pieces and languishing in disappointment, Havana will always be Havana. And if you've only walked her streets in the books where she looms like an apparition, if instead of walking actual city streets like the historian Eusebio Leal, you have only caressed the city as you would a sleepwalker dazed by suffering, if from the doubt and debt of exile, you have been tormented by the impossible, which, let me repeat, according to Lezama Lima, is reputed to be the only worthy stimulant, then you will realize that Havana is still the possible city and still the city of love, in spite of all the suffering.

The cabaret was filled to the gills. For all the rum and tobacco smells and the innumerable fine perfumes and loud colognes to seep in, you had to pause at the door for a long while and allow the senses to unclench like sponges. To tell the real gems apart from the fake ones or the merely scandalous ones, to study how one woman measured up to the next, to establish how a certain cleavage, though framed by an identical décolleté, had absolutely nothing to do with a certain other cleavage that was about to jump ship, to enter into the subtleties of a particular pair of fishnet stockings and be freed of the spell cast by a previous pair of silken ones, to appreciate a fine haircut and a well-groomed mustache, to know which chins had been splashed with Old Spice and which with Roger & Gallet, to review the neckties one by one and come up with a total of twenty pearl tie pins, a dozen minuscule diamonds, trifles and banalities galore, and too many unadorned knots to count, you had to stop for a long while, poised between fight and flight and take it all in, before succumbing to the juicy combo of rhythm and desire that is the be-all and end-all of being.

The three women entered, and all eyes landed on one. Inasmuch as La Mechunga and La Puchunga were regulars at the Montmartre, familiar as household goods, every eye in the place was turned on Cuca, who had had the inspired idea to dress in the yellow gingham she had purchased at the Fin de Siglo establishment. Gingham, as everyone knows, is the poor man's cloth, and when it's yellow gingham, then it's worn as a votive offering to the Virgen de la Caridad del Cobre. But Cuca's gingham had nothing to do with commonplace varieties, it had shimmer and chic and looked like chamomile. She had entreated a seamstress to whip up something nice, something snug at the waist with a deep V neckline branching from deep in her cleavage and a lower V in the back, dipping almost to her waistline, and little snaps, cleverly tucked beneath the shoulder pads, to keep her bra straps from slipsliding around. And it was in that dress and looking like the picture of loveliness that Cuquita Martinez turned up at the Montmartre. Her ten-inch heels had been covered with fabric to match, her legs were sheathed in flesh-toned gossamer stockings with a seam down the back (a ruse to make men cross-eyed), her waist was cinched in a wide yellow patent leather belt. The georgette shawl she had draped on her shoulder went from a snappy shade of yellow to a yellow so diluted it almost seemed white and sported an embroidered butterfly in one corner. A small medallion of the Virgen de la Caridad hung from the fine eighteen-karat bracelet on her left wrist. Her earrings, also eighteen-karat gold, were simple studs that her godmother, Maria Andrea, had handled incessantly and turned into love charms and amulets against the evil eye. La Puchunga had done Cuca's makeup, but a fine sweat had already broken on her upper lip and brow. She pulled out her lace handkerchief and dabbed at her young, hence succulent, sweat. She was nervous as a wet chicken, and all those men staring at her only made matters worse. Not that the women didn't rival the men in their scrutiny and assessment of her charms; they all looked her over, some with envy and others with repressed desire. Once she had gotten over how crowded the place was, she smiled and settled down into her chair, which, miracle of miracles, was the same one as that last exceptional time. She felt snug as a bug, as if she were among friends and the party in her honor, not Piaf's. Her friends ordered their crème de menthe on the rocks. Crème de menthe, it's not a secret, is purported to play swift havoc with the female mind. One had only to mention mint for her mind to fill with the exquisite bad breath of her tormentor. Oh, for a kiss, from those lips . . .

The bourgeois sensibilities of the gathered crowd were equally piqued by the goings-on at another table, where the famous painter Roberto García York was seated. His outrageousness rivaled Cuquita's, but whereas her extravagance was borne of poverty, his followed from an artistic temperament (well, if it's art, darling, even rags look sumptuous). He was wearing a silk top hat, black tails, and immense wings in homage of Marlene Dietrich's blue angel. His friend, a French woman known only as Janine, was dressed, or undressed, à la Josephine Baker. She was said to be on cozy terms with most everyone in the room. There was only one man in the whole company who dismissed the artist in his fantastic getup and glowered only at Cuquita, who rushed to look away. Had she returned the gaze of this man, who had a remotely Asian look about him and whose face was both sweet and sour, and who seemed short but wasn't really, well then, who knows, she may have ended up married to a Cuban writer living in exile in London.

The master of ceremonies, Bebo Alonso, shamelessly elegant, almost beribboned in his enormous mulberry bow tie, welcomed the audience in dockside English and airport French and keyed-up Spanish:

"Welcome! Divine Public! Is everything, *ça va? ça va?*" he repeated over and over again in his arrogant and execrable French, "Everything, *ça va?*"

Until a joker shouted, "*Ça fa, ça* good, but let's get going!"

The whole room was in stitches, and Bebo Alonso was left with no choice but to introduce the musical stars of the evening — the impeccable Barbarito Díez and the Parisian sparrow, the one and only Edith Piaf. A shaft of light followed Barbarito as he took his position center stage and embarked without ado on a sober rendition of "A Rose from France." He sang like a god, as always. Had Othello, the Moor of Venice, applied himself to a life of song, no doubt, he would have had the same talent to float a note forever, his voice the same timbre. Hearing is seeing. When he finished the song, Barbarito reached out a shiny, emaciated hand, so black as to be almost blue, and produced his Parisian rose out of the darkness. She was the strangest little woman, a girl grown old, with eyebrows like vaults in a cathedral and a touch of mischief in her honest eyes; she stood there, her feet planted far apart, like a thimble-size ballerina. Sweet Mother of God! she was fragile, an autumn leaf, diaphanous as onion paper from China. Barbarito Díez, like a true mythic god, bowed and touched her baby hand to his lips. She mumbled some nonsense in her rococo Spanish, and then she erupted, poured out her lungs, and the little ant became Artemis and Yemayá, Venus Aphrodite and Oshún. She was intelligence and sensuality rolled into one, and when those two things meet in one woman, you might as well kiss your ass good-bye, head for the exit quick or you're a goner. When that woman sang, she silenced the world and money held its tongue. Even love was different, when she was singing:

Tu me fais tourner la tête,
mon manège a moi c'est toi,
je suis toujours à la fête,
quand tu me tiens dans tes bras.
Je ferais le tour du monde,
ça ne tournerais pas plus que ça,
la terre n'est pas assez ronde,
mon manège à moi c'est toi . . .

The room was hushed with pleasure and expectation. Everyone there was in the thrall of that voice, its mystery, its wild trill, its enviable virtuosity, its *r*s (like the raspings of a demon about to mutate into an angel), *r*s like gongs, like echo chambers, *r*s like you'll never be able to reproduce, even if you attend the Alliance Française on the Boulevard Raspail in Paris for twenty years, even if you opt for tracheal surgery. And the fabulous lyrics that no one understood. But who needed a degree in French to know a thing or two about what she was saying; that voice could drum up love in anyone. Even Cuquita was busy wishing for her fantasy man, that is to say for any man who would fall in her lap, any man she could get her hands on. Edith Piaf has that effect, especially on women; they get all worked up, ready for avowals and betrothals, for love with extraterrestrials, for tragic endings. Those songs had made the night vast. Cuquita was now reduced to jelly, about to dissolve into tears of regret. Or was she just a hair away, a nail paring away, from forgetting instead of regretting and finding herself somebody else. What she needed was someone new, anyone, the first to come along would do. And then, she saw him, just like that, out of the blue.

He was at a VIP table, women engulfed in furs and minks were all about him. My goodness, what kind of riffraff had he taken up with! The men had on suits and hats à la Jean Gabin. Frivolity can be so divine, especially when it's so close to Greek tragedy; it's like an Attic video clip. His eyes, like everyone else's, were glued on the singer. He looked less handsome from that angle, in profile, his face completely still except for the little false smile he had glued to it, a crooked and tender and forced Roger Moore smile. Cuquita couldn't help feeling jealous of the voice that seemed to have such a power over him. But she quickly caught herself, Sweet Jesus, she could be just so silly, so quick to play the wife. She didn't dare sss, sss, siss him, have him turn around and see her there condemned to a whole damn life of heartache because of him, nor could she get his attention away from the singer by clearing her throat, nobody would forgive her that, and Frenchie would hate her for the rest of her life. Anyway, that was no way to behave. Then she remembered an infallible tactic, she would just stare at the back of his neck. As long as you didn't blink and took your time, all your time, it always worked. After a minute of her eyes boring into his neck, he would want to scratch it, and in another minute, he would be looking behind him and his eyes would meet hers. So, she did just that, stared and stared and stared, so fixedly at that man's ear, until her eyes were brimming with tears. Sure enough, he began to fiddle with his earlobe, scratching discreetly at first and then yanking it with savage gusto. He seemed set on tearing it off, when he turned and saw her. She was face to face with half his face, the other half was in the shadow. Like in a Hollywood movie, she zoomed in on the man and let the rest of the world go into soft focus. He was clearly uncomfortable, why didn't that girl stop staring at him?

In the intervening eight years, his nearsightedness had worsened considerably, and what he saw was somewhat blurry. Out came the glasses. And on they went, and boy, was he handsome, such an interesting face with those spectacles. It never fails and I don't know how they do it, but men always produce the right prop at the right moment. Those glasses suited him to a tee, as if he'd been born in them, he looked fit to eat, a tasty mouthful of coconut shavings. That girl reminded him of someone, maybe he had danced with her or someone who looked just like her. Now that he'd gotten a better look at her, through his bottle lenses, he was quite sure that he had pressed his cheek to that downy cheek. He smiled at her amiably, gently, and very methodically returned his attention to the stage. Sweet Mary Mother of God, he had recognized her! Of course he had recognized her! How was he not going to recognize her! Wasn't he the man of her dreams? But what if she was his woman from hell?

The cameras kept flashing throughout the concert. A very disheveled young man, in motorcycle gear and an unwieldy helmet slung on his shoulder, was taking more pictures than anyone. That must be Eduard Matussière, the Girl thought to herself, the photographer they had mentioned on the radio. Time passed, slowly when she looked at the Uan and quickly when she listened to the birdie-lady. Funny how time can be too short for one thing and too long for another. Still, she was afraid that the singing would stop and end the spell. The Parisian sparrow eventually began to make her farewells to those present and to those at home (there were many who were listening to her on the radio). So, she said good-bye for that night, she'd be singing again tomorrow. *A demain,* she said, and holding her sacred, twisted hands to her enormous heart, she said she loved them all. A murmur went round the room, her heart wasn't the only thing big enough to accommodate the entire planet as well as neighboring ones in the galaxy. There had been rumors, all the way from Paris, she was divinely huge, they said, there between her legs. It's what drove her lovers mad, and the reason she could shelter so many at any one time. She knew a lot about those things; she was an expert. They also talked about the extraordinary resin she secreted, finer than the best perfume bottled in the smallest vials, and so powerful that no matter how much you bathed you couldn't wash it off. She came back for nine curtain calls, there was sobbing, and the applause and bravos lasted fourteen minutes.

Bebo Alonso brought it all to an end by introducing the evening's dance band. The same people who five seconds before were weeping and languishing were now hell-bent on fun and laughter. That's how we are, we Cubans, while we pledge allegiance to the flag, there's a *guaguancó* playing in our heads. If we hear that a relation is laid out at the Funeral Home on Calzada and K Street, and that they're pitching a wang wang doodle all night long at the Tropical, we hesitate, going back and forth about what to do. But if you're placing bets, you'd be wise to put your money on the second choice, it's a sure winner 99 percent of the time. At daybreak, we'll drag our hungover asses over and shed a tear for the dead man, keep the poor sod happy. But hey! Give me electricity and long live progress! What's to be done? The place is a calamity. Must be the heat. It frazzles the neurons. And there's worse. After the heat and the sun that can blister stone come the downpours. So just picture the poor brain, bubbling like soup on a stove. At lunchtime, just crack an egg on your head and the sun will do the rest; and then, it'll rain like hell and that's when things get really bad, when neurons atrophy. How can people think like that, make decisions with atrophied neurons? And then, literary critics pipe up, from the lap of liberty and luxury, and dismiss the characters in Cuban novels as caricatures. And I'm sorry to have to agree with them, because on this caricature of an island we're all caricatures of ourselves. So why add insult to injury, when you've already added salt to the injury and we've already gone astray. And Máximo Gómez, may he rest in peace, regardless of whether or not he tore a page out of José Martí's diary (that's his problem, not mine), already said as much. "Cubans always fall short of the mark or overshoot it," he said. That's us all right, why we are the way we are. There's not a soul who agrees with the government, but when May first comes around, herds flock to the Plaza to shout and cheer on this one day of the year when they can buy their sodas in cans and pay for them in local currency. But never mind all that, let's rewind to the 1950s.

He walked toward the table, where with heavy, sinking heart, she sat waiting for him like sorry cabbage. La Mechu and La Puchu were out on the dance floor, dancing together. There were more than enough men to go around, but for fast results, all a woman has to do is dance by herself or with a friend and she'll land one in no time. It works like clockwork and beats waiting around. And this foxy twosome knew every trick in the book, look at them — carrying on like a pair of dead ducks, like crestfallen birds of paradise, like a double dose of heartache. And instantly, as if someone had heard or read me, a cloud of flies whirred in to dance with them. But haughty Hottentots that they were, they kept their hoity-toity airs. First, give the boys a run for their money, let them fight the good fight, take a few knocks, a couple of left hooks to the jaw, be pinned to the ropes and buckle to the floor and lick dust, kiss board. Make it hurt, make 'em drool at the sight of these free spirits in full swing, these two women who dance together now and will shift for themselves when the day is done.

He came closer to where she was feigning agony. From up close, he studied the situation cautiously.

Cuquita, forgetting the eight miserable years of waiting, dangled him a syrupy "Well?" that was almost flirty. He took her honeyed ways for a forwardness that was almost slutty.

Who was this girl who accosted him so boldly?

"Nothing. And you? How are you this evening?" He was already pleased with himself.

"Couldn't be better." She couldn't believe what she was hearing, where had she gotten the nerve! It didn't sound like her at all.

He sat down across from this charming woman and slowly studied her point by point: the oval face, the gently slanted royal jelly eyes, the soft fleshy lips, the easy laughter that played at now-you-have-me-now-you-don't, the black hair tumbling in hairspray-free waves. She smelled of vetiver, or some other perfume his mother may have used, Oriental sandalwood, perhaps, he couldn't say for sure . . .

She was pretty, without a doubt, *she so pleasant, so round, born to astound,* . . . he had no idea why that chachacha came to him just then.

"I think I know you from somewhere." He thought he'd hedge his bets. And the walls of Cuquita's romantic universe came tumbling down — that world where enamored princes win the hearts of loving princesses and eternal marital bliss is sealed with a kiss. But when Edith Piaf is singing, I've already said it, women are predisposed to anything, to Boris Yeltsin as their fairytale prince. And now, Cuquita thought she'd let him have his little game, let him pretend not to recognize her, she wasn't one to spoil anyone's fun:

"I don't believe I know you." She played right along.

"Really? Funny. You seem so familiar. Come, the night is young, let's dance . . ."

She rose up from behind that table like a spring blossom, hovering like a sleek Longines wristwatch, and the place grew as still as a snapshot. She stood there, lovely as a Coca-Cola, with that tight little waist and those hips and that uppity ass and thighs firm beneath shiny gingham and her firm tits and long neck and her ears like dainty cookies. He was overjoyed by the joy she produced in others. He was walking off with the prize — again. He was the envy of all. A doll, like that, took maintenance, the kind of upkeep that even the mechanics at Volkswagen were incapable of.

A smarm in a long-sleeved, starched guayabera — not a look one came across too often in this chichi joint — whispered "You're the hottest" in her ear as he walked past them.

In one smooth move, Uan jealously pulled her to him and raised an angry fist at his crass rival. The man beat a hasty retreat, dragging the drunken woman on his arm — another crème de menthe casualty — with him.

Cuca and Uan danced the first bolero like two people fused with Superglue. The familiarity of that downy cheek intensified his suspicions. He could've sworn that waist, those arms, had been with him since the day of his earliest and most precocious ejaculation. She was panting, her cleavage ebbing and swelling, her bosom heaving, ready to pop its stays, just like a heroine in a cloak and dagger movie with Errol Flynn or Alain Delon. Enough was enough, she could no longer put it off — oh to kiss that mouth. And kiss it she did. Exactly as she had imagined she would during eight long years of picturing this moment. She rammed her tongue into his throat, as deep as his tonsils, she inspected every tooth, she flicked and she licked. He did the manly thing and matched her slurp for slurp. They lapped each other up like cats. Then, they flew apart, sizing each other up, eyeing incisors and flaunting claws, until she said:

"You gave up onions, huh? Took care of that cavity, huh?"

"Excuse me?"

"Come on, cut the bullshit, you are the Uan."

"Yes, and you are . . . you are . . . Caruquita Martinez?"

"The same, in flesh and bone, and I've loved you for eight years, had you under my skin for eight years." There, she'd made a clean breast of it.

"Oh . . . well . . . after you took off like a bat out of hell, I thought maybe my breath was so bad . . . anyway, I gave up onions and uh, I did see a dentist, in Mexico, about my teeth . . ."

"You didn't have to go throwing money around on airplanes and dentists in Mexico, that cavity could've been diagnosed from across the room . . . I'm alone. And you?" She didn't hesitate for a minute. Tonight, she was a guerrilla, a terrorist of love.

"Alone as can be . . . not that I have much time . . . lots of work . . . so many pressures. I'm the public relations guy here, and if things work out, I'll soon be in charge of the Salon Rojo at the Capri."

"If things work out, I'm going to make you very happy for the rest of your life . . ." Fucking hell! Why do we always feel compelled to promise happiness to the unhappiest variety on earth — the male one? As if it were up to us to appoint them head of a company or a newspaper or to lead a party or an army or as chief of state of a very rich country. Is it ever going to sink in that their happiness is mostly about power and rarely about love? Even though they say men think with their dicks.

"Let's just start with tonight, make me happy tonight."

Cuquita consented by closing her eyes and opening up the rest.

Later, in his apartment, on the tenth floor of the Somellan Building, she would go all out. Virginity, be damned! Hymen! who cares about that scrappy piece of lace, the hell with it and with wedding bells! It happened on a terrace, large as a ballroom, facing the sea, way up high near the sky, the way she liked it — in command of the view like a night watchman. There was wind, there was salt on their lips, and when he entered her, there was thunder. Then came the rains, the heavy rains that go on and on for days. The whole country came to a standstill, as it usually does during hurricane season. (It seems that we've been having one for decades.) There hadn't been rain like that in a blue moon, with thunderclouds and lightning and tornadoes. It came in treacherous falls and blessed flows. And here, when the wet weather sets in, it doesn't let up and neither does the fucking. So they fucked morning, noon, and night for a week. In all the usual, and a few unusual, positions: on top, beneath, on the side, on the other side, standing, handstanding (the wheelbarrow), sitting, leaning on the balcony railing, on the bathroom sink, the toilet bowl, on the kitchen sink, in the rocker, on the U-shaped sofa, on the hard granite floor. Don't think that Cuquita didn't experience the occasional twinge of disgust at all that clubber sloshing around inside her, but nature would win the day. When the week was over, she returned to her dovecote. She was ten pounds lighter (the French, after all, keep slim on a steady diet of sex). No one had so much as noticed her absence; all businesses, except for those that sold hammers, nails, planks of wood, and everything else to board up doors and windows, had remained shut. Concha, the Asturiana, was the only one to fret, because La Mechunga and La Puchunga hadn't come home either. They were probably holed up somewhere, having the time of their lives, because no news is good news and bad news travels fast. When Cuquita turned up looking so gaunt, the Asturiana started in on her:

"Look ath you, you're thkin and boneth, you've been up to no good, I can tell, and what do I tell your godmother now? And who'th the thon of a bith, if I may athk?" And she pulled out the man-size

53

handkerchief, with its knotted corners, and redistributed the sweat on her neck, brow, nose, and armpits before refastening her coin purse to a grayish bra strap.

"The man of my life," answered Cuquita from the heights of Shangri-la.

"You don't thay! The man of your life! Ha! The man of her life! That'th what I thought the firth time, but now, I'm on the five hundred and fifty-fifth man of my life. Ha! Men! Do I ever know them! You go get thome reth, 'cauthe there'th all kindth of work waiting for you tomorrow."

On the following day, Cuca rang his office. He was glaringly absent. He had to leave on urgent business, a trip to Mexico. She wondered if he was having more problems with his teeth. This time, she wasn't afraid of losing him; she knew where he lived — on the tenth floor of the Somellán, and where he worked — at the Montmartre. Trips didn't bother her, sooner or later, he'd have to come back from trips. And he had sworn eternal love to her on sixty-nine different occasions. She was sure of the number, there had been sixty-nine orgasms and he renewed his vow of love after each one. He was dying of love — for her and for his city. As if a city and a woman were one and the same, as if cities had a uterus.

Days went by, weeks, a year and a half, and they were together. Well, together and not together. That is to say, rarely together. They would see each other for three days running, fuck like savages, and then, he would disappear. She'd immerse herself in her lessons, her job at the cafeteria, her housework. When a number of weeks had elapsed, he would return and honk his horn; she would signal him from the roof to wait ten minutes. Five to bathe, four for makeup, and one to run down the stairs. Off they'd go, first to dance at the Montmartre then to his apartment. Always in that order. From one pleasure to the next. And one good-bye to the next.

Twice, she was pregnant, and he had shelled out small fortunes for illegal abortions at the hands of Doctor Bandera on San Lázaro Street. After too many clinicopsychovarian risks, she finally learned how to insert a diaphragm. Whenever he'd leave, she'd take comfort in the works of Corín Tellado, the Danielle Steel of the day, which were easy to trade in at the all-purpose store on the corner of Cuba and Merced. She also listened to melodramatic radio plays and consumed romance magazines by the armload. That's how she found out about the visit of another famous French woman. This one was a writer, a girl really, and her name was Françoise Sagan; she had written a novel whose title instantly bowled Cuquita over; it was called *Bonjour Tristesse* and it expressed Cuquita's mood in a nutshell. She swore up and down that she had to read it. Miss Flora Lauten, the new (really, the last) Miss Cuba, welcomed Miss Sagan, as she stepped off her plane at Havana Airport, with a bouquet of gardenias.

After a year and a half of emotional and physical mayhem, Cuquita started becoming jealous. She couldn't stand to have people telling her he was cheating on her, that he must have a woman stashed away in Mexico and another in New York City — what else could be the reason for all his trips to these places? He tried to reason with her time and again until his jaw hurt. He explained that he only went away for his work. That he was completely faithful to her and she shouldn't doubt it for a minute. It was all for work, and extremely complicated and dangerous work, if she only knew the half of it. She wept and for the first time felt she didn't trust him — it wouldn't be the last time. Actually, she never quite got it — what kind of work was it, this public relations job? Why did he always have to be at someone's beck and call? His voice shook, and he explained to her that it had to do with representing local artists abroad and bringing artists from abroad here . . . like foreigners, like culture exchange.

"And why don't we get married?"

He blanched, looked fearfully into her honeysuckle eyes, and said, "No. Why the rush?" Rush? She'd been waiting for ten years. He was so nervous he didn't let go of the suitcase he was carrying. He didn't want to sit in the profusely patched damask-covered armchair:

"You hate this room, you won't even sit down. You never even spent a night here — always your place, your palatial apartment. You can't stand it here. It's me you can't stand . . ." He silenced her by clapping his mouth on hers, began undressing her with one hand, undressed himself with the same hand, never letting go of his suitcase, even when it became clear they would fuck. He unbuttoned his fly, pulled out his penis, and with somewhat more difficulty, liberated his balls. Later, while she was busy sucking, he told her he needed more time, there were problems she didn't know about, he was working for someone very rich, very powerful. He had to stash the suitcase in a safe place. Yes baby! That's good, that's good! Oh do it, do it. No, they weren't exactly government people, but almost. Oh, you mean Mafia, she looked up with his shlong gently clenched between her teeth like a fine cigar. Don't say that word, goddamn it! How dare you speak like that! Making wild statements like that. Shit, he never wanted to hear that word again. She promised it would never happen again. He made her swear by her love for him that she would never use that kind of movie diction again. She swore up and down. Never again. Never, and he shot his wad, bang in her eye.

He disappeared for fifteen days; when he came back, he had a new '58 Dodge, a sober, almost elegant car that reeked of expensive talcum powder. He produced a stack of bills from his wallet like she'd never seen in her life. Which is why she looked away, she didn't want to touch such an inordinate amount of money, not even with her eyes.

She had to pack her belongings, he said. Everything, the possessions of a lifetime that at some later date would become the bitter cargo of junked memories.

"We're leaving this place, you're going to live in the Vedado, across from the Malecón, not far from me —" He was more tentative than assertive, pretending that everything had been settled.

"Why not with you? We'll never live together, will we?" She wasn't wasting words.

"Not for now."

He handed out money all around, to Concha, to La Mechunga and La Puchunga, to the young girl who would replace Cuca. On her first night in the new place, he asked her to store some boxes of medicine under her bed. On the following day, one of his pals came to fetch them and leave a new batch of boxes. These contained red and black armbands. When he turned up, he found her in a rage:

"I don't want any political shit. I've never been interested in politics."

"Okay, okay, slow down, nothing happened. I am only trying to help some people out. Calm down, nobody is going to get you in trouble."

The rest happened very quickly, like an unbearable nightmare where you're falling and falling and falling. In a six-month span, he managed to get his hands on all kinds of money. Then, one day, he lost it all, he didn't have a penny. To complicate matters, the revolution triumphed. She was again pregnant. Again, he disappeared without leaving a trace; this time, he was gone longer than usual. Everything happened in less than six months; too many things happened, too much for her to handle. The apartment next door was vacated. She had her friends move in next door; she felt lost far from them. La Mechu and La Puchu were terribly thankful, couldn't believe the enormity of her gesture, money she had worked to save, saved by the sweat of her — they couldn't say brow, so they said nothing. In the middle of all this, her father died unexpectedly. Not so unexpectedly, of tuberculosis. Maria Andrea had also died, succumbed to a mysterious Clorox poisoning. Her mother and the rest of the crew had moved into a little house, also paid for by the sweat of her, you know, brow and ministrations to the Uan. Another trimester passed. After the revolution had triumphed, some men came looking for him. Bearded guys who looked like rebels. Other men came later, a couple of guys in suits and carrying suitcases that looked familiar. The suitcase fellows said they were the police and advised her to contact them as soon as he contacted her. She could reach them by phone; they handed her a card. Under no circumstances was she to tell him that they had come looking for him. Her lover (that's what they called him) was an extremely dangerous man, a terrorist bomber, and as long as he was on the loose, that son of a bitch was a public menace. She didn't believe a word they said.

He came back hiding behind a mustache and dark glasses, dressed like a militia man; it was funny and scary to see him in that disguise. His kiss was tender as always, and longer than usual, he wouldn't let her go, clung to her like he'd never, never let her go.

Clinging for dear life. Then, he stroked her belly and very softly, he whispered secrets that Cuca didn't hear to his beloved fetus. He finally looked at her:

"I am going. I have to get to an embassy tonight. Everything is ready. Don't be afraid. This won't last long. The government will fall soon. I'll be back in three months, we'll get married. I'll be with you for the birth. I'm flat broke, I have nothing to give you, but when I come back we'll have plenty, like before, more than before. There is one thing, here, take it . . ."

And he stuck his hand into the pocket of his militia pants and placed the crumpled thing in her ice cold hand. "Guard it with your life, as if it were me. If they find it on me, I could lose everything, even my life . . . don't cry, please don't cry. You'll see, this'll all be over soon. Take good care of yourself. Be sure to eat well. And, careful with that thing, don't lose it, our lives depend on it."

And he left, like men always leave, slamming a door in our heart. In her opened hand, she saw a 1935 dollar bill resting against her smooth, young palm. It was her first American dollar; she didn't give it much thought. What's the big deal? It wasn't all that different from our money, just a piece of paper in another language. She'd find a safe place for it, and she stuck it deep inside the flower-pot where her malanga flourished. He would come back, as he always did, money in his pockets and love in his heart. And she sat down in a chair to wait.

4

Party's Over

Party's over,
the Commandant is here
to put an end to the fun.

By Valera-Miranda.
All Carlos Puebla did was substitute
"Cabo Valera" for "Commandant."

*S*ITTING IN MY ROCKER FOR THIRTY-SOME YEARS, asking myself
the same question night after night — "What will I make for dinner tomorrow?" The sixty-four-million-dollar question. This, our
daily bread, which no one gives us. People now call Size Extra Extra
Large the onion; they say he's the reason Cuban women weep in their
kitchens. You will notice that at times Extra Extra Large (or XXL)
will be known simply as XL; his girth will vary to reflect the enormity of his response to a particular situation or responsibility. But I
have much weightier matters to attend to than all this political blah
blah — help me Sweet Mary, Mother of God! Help me pick this
day's pickings. What can I make for dinner? Sauté of samp, perhaps?
(Cornmeal casserole, perhaps? A course of coarse meal, perhaps?)
Take a package of cornmeal and sprinkle water over the contents;
then, season it with salt and vinegar, as lemons are a thing of the past,
add garlic and chopped onions, maybe you can procure these from

the country people who sell them on the side of the road to Güines. If you're not going in that direction, well, then, you're fucked. Brown everything in a frying pan and that's it — sauté of samp, the latest inedible thing on the Havana menu. Have several carafes of cold water on hand before sitting to eat, samp can make you real thirsty.

It gives me a rash just to think of it. What a fool! What a shit-eating goose I've been, sitting here perusing the horizon like a novice seaman, waiting for the ship that will bring him back to me. Or with my eyes clasped to the sky like a brooch, weak from night after night of searching the heavens for a light, other than starlight, that would reveal itself as the airplane delivering him to my arms. But there was to be no such thing. He never came back, never even wrote. The earth had swallowed him up. Months went by and I sat in my chair, rocking back and forth to the sound of his name: Juan Perez, Juan Perez, Juan Perez, over and over again, as if sheer supplication could summon him like magic, like witchcraft. I did all I could — wrote his name on a piece of paper, submerged it in a jar of honey together with the pubic hairs I had pounded into dust and a drop or two of blood from the second day of my period. Then, I said the Magic Phallus prayer: with my first, I name you, with my second, I draw you out, with my third, I bind you to me . . . And I lit the fat pink candle that could almost have passed for male genitals. I consulted all kinds — witches, spirit rappers, speaking wands, and talking drums and all manner of strange thing you can imagine. Did every humanly and divinely possible thing. I didn't get good results. Nothing, not even a postcard. My man was gone, bought himself a ticket long as my right arm, a political special that does not include a return. He was my heartache and my heartbreak, and he was never coming back. At least, that's what it looked like at the time.

Every single night of my life, I dreamed of kissing that man's mouth. I'd wake up with swollen lips from a night of gnawing and gnashing, my jaw sore from all the clenching. The chattering of my own teeth gave me nightmares, terrified me. I spent many nights grazing on my nostalgia. Some mornings, I'd find bite marks, blood even. So I protested, against that man's mouth and the kisses that had vanished from my life, I visited a dentist and had my teeth removed. All my teeth. In one sitting. The blood loss was something awful, pretty near sent me over to the other side. Don't think that the wholesale extraction happened just like that, there had been things, many things to break the camel's back, to overflow the cup. Aside from my nocturnal fits of self-mutilation, two events took place. First, I experienced a strange itch in my gums; I immediately took it for what it was — an unlucky sign. My darling Uan was dead, I knew it. My God, how I cried! Christ of the Cleansing Spirits, how I wept! I grew so thin my face seemed devoured from within. I was a widow wracked by fury and sorrow and dread. A death imagined is very hard to bear — how does an absent body go? And then, one afternoon, Ivo, the chauffeur, turned up in his famous convertible and told us that someone he knew had gotten word that Uan had left Argentina for Miami. And that was the second thing — saying that. Just that. No message, no nothing. I was fit to be tied and all the more determined to go ahead with the extraction. I had my Colgate smile removed by the roots; why not, when the brand, itself, had been banned? I had no desire to be beautiful; I wanted no one to think me pretty. When my gums healed, I thought to myself, well, at least he's alive. In time, I regretted and had myself fitted for dentures. I spared no cost, asked for three gold teeth, even. I would last a week, couldn't get used to the damn things, and now, my gums were more blistered than ever. And the gold teeth were untimely to say the least, unpopular in any circle — people mistook me for either a fancy schmance from Key West or for a Muscovite. Remember, this was way before *Moscow Doesn't Believe in Tears*, that movie about a group of women with troubles similar to mine. I decided to accept myself toothless. After all, I was the one who chose to have them pulled.

My daughter was born on September seventh, Day of Yemayá, Black Virgin of Regla, a stormy day of roaring waves crashing against the wall of the Malecón and wind that hissed and hummed against shutters and window panes. A storm ferocious enough to blow windows away, frame and all. The kind of Caribbean hurricane Europeans say they must experience at any cost, as if it were the eighth wonder of the world, as if it were as simple as picnicking on the Fiji Islands. Glass panes blew about like large razor blades, threatening to decapitate brave pedestrians.

A few weeks before giving birth, I went back to Santa Clara. I went to be near my family, but a family as remote as mine would have to be made to order. It didn't take long for me to regret my move to the provinces. I gave my daughter a simple name, Maria Regla, in honor of the birth, itself, which had been very simple. Later, I read in the paper that the hurricane had also been named Regla, an omen that put the fear of God in me.

I arrived at the hospital at one in the afternoon, and five minutes later, she was out. Incredibly ugly and incredibly beautiful. A bloodied, bleating creature. From the minute she was born, I knew she was going to be a pain in the ass, a rude and independent girl. Much too independent. I'll never forget that when they brought her to me, after they had bathed and dressed her, I didn't know what to do, where to put her . . . Then, she took my tit, herself, with the help of her little hand, guided my nipple into her mouth. She suckled until she was satiated, then, she turned her head away and fell asleep. That afternoon, they brought us blue lilies. They'd run out of pink ones; that day there were more girls than boys — the women of the future.

I gave myself, body and soul, to the radio. More in body than in soul, really, I converted the appliance into a physical extension of myself, carrying it with me everywhere and plugging it into the first electrical outlet I could find. The radio and I became friends, inseparable companions. The radio confided in me; it didn't work so well the other way around. I listened to speeches, heroic proclamations, political interviews, anthems, news bulletins. Radio Reloj Nacional, at the tone the time will be — pim! at the tone the time will be — pam! It was the first anniversary of XL's entrance to Havana — a time of celebration and festivities, of joy and fanfare and jubilation. How all that would change later, replaced by sacrifice and butchery and shortages. By wanton wanting. Do you know what they call the *período especial* in France? *La petite bouffe.* And in Brazil? *Um Carnaval sem samba!* And in China? I know this cabbage. And in Japanese? An aching yen. And in Arabic? Ali Baba ate all the babas!

And XXL went from being commander in chief to becoming comedian in chief.

It makes my skin crawl to think of everything we went through. I shudder in astonishment and shame. A rash of pyromania spread through Havana, saboteurs burned the El Encanto to the ground. Out of a job, La Mechunga and La Puchunga now offered to watch the Girl for me. That was when they all stopped calling me the Girl, and she came into the name. Now she was the Girl Reglita, and I was simply Cuca. Or Caruquita or Cuquita Martinez.

I took a waitressing job in a restaurant. Slowly but surely, they were nationalizing everything. "We are like the elephant," they chanted with good reason, "leisurely but lethal." I joined the Gastronomic Workers Union. For some reason, they called it the INIT, Institute of some Nationalized shit or other. Would you believe that a high-up cadre named his daughter Niarinit — INIT for the gastronomic workers and NIAR for the National Institute of Agrarian Reform. I'm not exaggerating when I say there's no name for what people do to names in this country. Only here would people think of naming a child Granma or Usnavy or Fatherland. My neighbor's little girl was named Fatherland! Thankfully, she went and had her name officially changed, except in her case, she may have jumped from the frying pan into the fire, from Baden to Baden-Baden. She changed it to Yocandra and no one understood that either. She tried to explain to me that it had something to do with Jocasta and Oedipus and whether Cassandra and the Trojans or the Achaeans I don't know what . . . all kinds of long ago stuff that I can never remember.

We weren't aware of how much things were changing, we accepted everything in earnest, we didn't dare joke or even offer constructive criticism. To do so was to be branded a counterrevolutionary, a turncoat, an archtraitor of the fatherland. My Uan was all those things, a wolf in sheep's clothing, a snake in the grass, a *gusano*. My man was the enemy. My daughter became the daughter of the fatherland, XXL was her stepfather, her daddy really. As far as they were concerned, her father ceased to exist when he left the country, as if by bolting out of here, he had departed the *mapa mundi*. Never mind that we were the ones he had left behind, my daughter and I didn't figure for much, but the new society — that was another story.

I remember that when Maria Regla was still in junior high, she came home one day and told me to my face that she was ashamed of her family: a father who had betrayed the revolution, a grandmother who was a slut, and a faggot uncle. At the time, I was vaguely involved with the Jehovah's Witnesses, not because I believed anything they said but because nothing could deflect them if they got it into their heads that they wanted to visit you and read you passages from the New Testament. They clung like barnacles in magnetic shoes. I joined out of pity, but I soon left the church, not just because of my daughter's nagging but also because I couldn't bring myself to accept the prohibition on blood transfusions, and most of all because it was a highly denounceable alliance, and if the police were to catch me running around in religious circles, they could deprive Reglita of her toy quota and would certainly pack me off to a forced labor camp. As the years went by, XXL went from being the nation's suitor to becoming the nation's father. We all got stuck with him as a dad. Not that I wasn't taken in, at first, with all the whatnot about building a future for our children, and I only cared about one thing, my daughter's future. So I signed up.

I would turn up for any campaign they would come up with. There were literacy campaigns followed by campaigns to train teachers in the Makarenko method, which simply meant making teachers out of the very people who had been illiterate six months earlier. I tell you, I didn't miss one. Always ready to volunteer, to do my bit for the betterment of all, to sweat and slave. A heroine from the rank and file, a mover and a shaker. And move and shake I did, to the point of wooziness, of nervous prostration. (Eventually, I learned to bide my time, take my friendly pills, sip my rum. Let someone else fight for a change.) I used to go around in pedal pushers with a small stool suspended from my waistband. (That was in the days of the Havana Belt Agricultural Project. There's a rumor going around that they're thinking of resuscitating it.) I would set my stool alongside the plowed gully and plant whatever it was we were planting, or weed, or pick whatever it was we were picking — tomatoes, potatoes, beets, coffee. Especially coffee, when XXL got it into his head to turn Havana into a coffee plantation and gave the order to clear any fertile patch of land of all fruit-bearing and woodland trees, to dig them up by the roots and sow coffee in their stead. In the end — no coffee, no trees. I even planted strawberries, when he got strawberry fever. We were supposed to grow them in microclimatic zones, we would've become the first tropical country to produce strawberries. I don't know, I never tasted one, not even a wild one. Then, we moved on to the artificial insemination of cattle. As we couldn't produce black gold (oil), we would produce red (meat). Dairy farms and cattle ranches went up all over the place. Everywhere, plungers filled with the semen of countless bulls (XXL included) were being emptied into bovine uteri. They say that Immaculate Mamelon, milk cow extraordinaire, is the daughter of XXL. The cows were crafty — not mad at all — and became super sacred, their stalls were now air-conditioned and furnished, their windows curtained in pinkish lace, and "Matilda the Cow" was the number one song on the hit parade: *Matilda steps forward, Matilda falls back, Matilda stands still and sighs moo, moo, moo.* They made a music video starring Immaculate Mamelon in the role of Matilda the Cow. The monthly publication *Opina* honored her with a Girasol Award for her performance. Mamelon was a star, hosted on the Sunday variety show *Para Bailar,* where she danced in a conga line and everything. In the end, so much inept experimentation finished off all the cattle in the land, and our beloved comedian in chief hit upon the idea of growing rice in seawater. That's when the Vietnamese lost all faith in us. Our methods, no doubt, bewildered them. We then moved into the world of medical breakthroughs. We had, it seemed, discovered a cancer cure — tannic acid. A simple banana peel milkshake and kiss your illness good-bye. Somehow, they didn't seem interested in patenting the cure internationally. Our attentions were soon diverted by a massive agrarian project to promote the microjet banana, a man-size banana that matured in under fifteen days. An intense agitprop campaign accompanied this latest vision; we could, they said, survive on a diet of bananas; they were preparing us for the simian days, for the hunger of the *período especial.* . . the time when Soviet aid would

also entail wanting to kill her mother? I finally just asked her, gently and in passing, why she would want to kill me? She didn't bat an eye:

"Because my father is the enemy. And the revolutionary children of the new society, the new children like me, cannot have fathers who are the enemy. I don't have a father because of you. You're the one who gave me a father who is the enemy."

La Mechu and La Puchu looked on with red and tearful eyes. I sat down across from her, took her hands in mine, and pleaded:

"Forgive me, I should have paid more attention. You should know that your father is not the enemy. Your father had to go away, but he'll come back to meet you someday . . . Who told you these things, my child? Who told you your father is the enemy and because of that you can't have a father?"

She didn't move a muscle, her thin, little face was completely still. She wouldn't even meet my eyes when she flatly and automatically answered:

"It's the opinion of the chief comrade of the Pioneer Youth."

I left my job at the restaurant and got work collecting access passes to the Nautico Beach. I never again took part in any volunteer campaigns; consequently, I would never earn the right to own an Aurika washing machine, or a Slava alarm clock, or an Orbita fan, which was really intended for the defrosting of Soviet refrigerators, but which also sold as a cooling appliance during the sweltering summers. Nor an Electron or Ruben television set. In short, I had to forego all my merit points; I didn't even get a badge for my efforts. Not that I cared whether they honored or blackened my name. All that mattered was my daughter. We would rise at dawn, I would take her to school, then ride, hanging off a route number 22 bus all the way to work. At five o'clock, I would pick her up. On weekends, I took her with me. Every day of her vacation was a beach day. She was proud to have a mother — she was finally calling me mommy again — who was, as she said, *assigned to the sea detail.* But she didn't want to hear a word about her father; she couldn't even bear to hear him mentioned.

In the evenings, we would sit on the wall of the Malecón, counting stars and wishing on them. We saw a shooting star once and wished to never be separated.

All this time, Havana had been filling up with rebels, militias, people from the countryside, scholarship students from everywhere. There was big talk about a monstrous sugarcane crop, about how we were going to bring this one in even if it meant our last drop of blood, even if it meant hell and high water. The harvest was lost in all the boasting. Many did give their last drop of blood in pointless wars, others went into the high waters and offered themselves up to the sharks or drowned, swimming after a better world. The world we had failed to build because they had tied our hands and dulled our minds, the world they had snatched from us with their madness, their folly for power and greatness. When they scored their first victory over Yankee Imperialism at Playa Girón, they offered to trade prisoners for baby food. Victory had the taste of things to come, we had been disproportionately blessed as winners, not by the gods but by the Soviet Union. They had us believing we were immortal.

Humiliation was becoming the order of the day. When Reglita was a little older, she walked in one day, plopped herself on the bed, propped her elbows on her knees, and rested her chin in her cupped hands. She was never going to set foot again in La Mechu and La Puchu's apartment. At school she had heard that they had been prostitutes, professional. A couple of days later, all the kids began to call them Fala and Fana — which meant something like the Phallus and its Fungus. How could my little girl, Sweet Mary Virgin of Us All, say such words? And so matter-of-factly? If La Mechu and La Puchu picked her up at school, the other kids would greet them with name calling and insults, horrible words in the mouths of babes. Reglita would dash off to avoid being seen with her pseudo-aunties. The whole thing began to take enormous proportions, tongues were wagging — they were a pair of dykes, they'd never had any children, they liked to do it with millionaires, with the filthy rich, they were bourgeois whores . . . Things were not looking good at all. Fortunately, or unfortunately, in our willy-nilly, tug-of-war existence, the Committees for the Defense of the Revolution were being formed. The Cuban Women's Federation would follow soon after . . . Meetings were now regularly held and the people's trials were gaining popularity. I was afraid of how bad things could get. So, I decided to raise my hand:

"I request the floor, Comrade. I think we should give Comrades Mechunga and Puchunga a chance to assimilate to the new society, and I propose that we put them in charge of Public Heath Care for both the Committee and the Federation."

An absolute silence fell on the room, until a man stood up shouting and flailing his arms:

"That just about fucking does it! So now the Revolution is going to dirty itself with whores and dykes. Why not invite the faggots while we're at it! You must be shitting me! Well, you can count me out!"

At which point, La Puchunga erupted like a caged tigress, and ordered him at the top of her lungs to:

"Pull out your cock right now. There's a tattoo on his cock, tell him to pull it out and you'll see. The nerve of him coming here and putting on saintly airs. La Mechu and I were there and saw him naked as a jaybird and in high feather at an orgy, an all-night bender of whoopee and buggery. Of buggery I tell you! Out with that cock, or I'll slay you like a dog!"

She was right. In happier times, the Comrade Secretary General of the Party had his sexual (not political) organ inscribed with the word *Benople*. They had done a very good job, because the penis had to be fully deployed for the whole message to unscroll, and then, it read, "Best Wishes from Constantinople."

And that's when the taunting started — it began with his block, then spread through the neighborhood and finally, all over the island, because this is a place where rumor flies and fast. Wherever he went, they would razz him with the song about:

> a girl so pleased, she was fit to bust,
> for carving her name on a tree
> and the tree, touched to the very core,
> dropped a blossom at her feet . . .

The meeting went on for days, we had a long, hard time of it. All kinds of experts were summoned to opine on tattoos, paleography, erections, and wanking. And to study the sexual organ of the Comrade Secretary General up close. They even brought a Soviet scientist from the KGB who specialized in penis microphones. When La Puchunga's allegation proved to be true, they stripped the miserable man of his party membership, and my friends were put in charge of Public Health for the CDR (Committee for the Defense of the Revolution) and for the Cuban Papayacratic Federation, the CPF. Foreign readers may not know that in addition to being a fruit in the shape of a grenade, in Cuba, the papaya also refers to female genitalia. To say of so and so she is a true papaya means she has been blessed with most excellently capacious parts; it can also mean she's brave — has balls. I once read that in the colonial period, a preparation of papaya sap and leaves was commonly used for its abortive properties by slave women who had been impregnated against their will. The practice was so widespread on the plantations that the female vulva simply became known as the papaya.

To make a long story short, my friends embarked on the life of social servitude exacted by the federations. And even though everyone still called them Comrade Fala and Comrade Fana, now they did it respectfully. Never again would Reglita feel ashamed to claim them as her aunts. People even contested the earlier interpretation of their names as the Phallus and its Fungus and made a good phonetic case for Fala and Fana as names that could have hailed from Rio de Janeiro or Lisboa. And life was on track again, back to a normality to which we were so poorly suited. Because when all is said and done, we're just too transcendental, abnormal.

I never stopped thinking about him, I hadn't forgotten him for a second. Others would come along, many in fact, none of whom seemed to object to my toothlessness. I never dared give any of them serious hope. I knew he was in the world; the hope of seeing someone alive again is hard to lose, even through inertia. Even Ivo wanted to marry me. He swore up and down what a good husband he'd be, what an excellent father for Reglita. I gave him serious thought, not because I found him attractive, but public transport was getting very

71

difficult, and he couldn't have taken better care of his Chevrolet, treasured it, kept it nice and shiny as an emerald pendant owned by Elizabeth Taylor. I thought marrying him could be a solution; I wouldn't have to worry about being late for work. He proposed to me at the final screening of the Novia del Mediodia drive-in; they shut down the place after that, abandoned it to the weeds. The screen where so many unforgettable movies had been shown disappeared into the jungle. Yes, ladies and gentlemen, I must confess Ivo had an immense crush on me, couldn't wait to see how I handled — as if I had a steering wheel for a pussy. He was ready to drive me to the Wedding Hall or to the Collective Buffet, whichever I preferred. The altar, of course, was out because church was in ill repute, high religiosity was punishable by law. He went so far as to steal a kiss from me, but Reglita, who was in the backseat, put a stop to it when she smacked him one to the head. She knuckled him so hard, she knocked the pleasure right out of him. I laughed so hard, I almost peed myself. The idea of a wedding and of owning a car didn't seem so bad, until I started thinking about the other one. What if he came back? All I had to show for myself were the years I had endured like a mule, kept my word, been faithful. I couldn't just toss my dignity to the floor and stomp all over it. So, I had to say no to Ivo. I wasn't so foolish as to not sleep with him now and again, because a body is a body and I had kept mine in very tip-top shape. You may not think so now, but there used to be an A1 body on these bones that could take your breath away. And a face like a movie star — toothless of course. I only did it with him for what you could say were physiological reasons — but why lie? I had my bit of pleasure.

None of it stopped Uan's ghost from following me everywhere. I often threw myself off moving vehicles in the absolute conviction it was he who had just rounded the corner. I walked and walked, looking for him in the crush of city streets. Always accompanied by the strange feeling that I was also seeing the city for him — on his behalf. Time was passing us by, countless buildings were fast becoming ruins, others were unrecognizably transformed as tenants added lofts and haphazard extensions to accommodate their growing families. Trees were trimmed with speedy regularity and eventually, completely felled. People continued to be happy — out of habit. There wasn't a thing to eat — surprise! surprise! But we had our dignity, didn't we? And, to top it all off, we had the future! Many (those of us with growing children, for example) didn't need to be told you couldn't make a meal out of dignity, and that the future is half-baked at best and, more often than not, unseasoned. Through it all, I walked and walked my city, street by street, rain or shine, always ending up at the Malecón and my sea blue sea. Face-to-face with the indigo blue of raging, loving waters, the sweet and salty to and fro, the abundant vastness with its sorrow and its kindness and its harshness. As absolute and erratic as any mother.

At least once a week, I tried to take Maria Regla to a different restaurant. I wanted her to see them before they disappeared for good. The Monseñor was her favorite; she even got to see Bola de Nieve there a couple of times. He'd always do that *Be careful, it's my heart* song for us. We'd sit there crying our eyes out like a pair of kids — well, she was a kid.

The Montmartre was now Le Moscou. Champagne had given way to vodka and *solianka* soup had replaced foie gras. Instead of Edith Piaf they played Edith Pilaf, a counterfeit Piaf from our sister countries in the East, and songs by Karel Got, Klary Katona, and La Lucia Atliera, who was probably very famous in her mother's living room. No one could ever understand how that tinseled, painted creature had ended up in Cuba. You'd have to be an ace on the workforce to even make it past the door at the Montmartre, and even then, a lunch or dinner reservation had to be arranged at least a week in advance. I had accumulated more than enough merit points to qualify, but I had made a solemn promise never again to set foot in that particular establishment, home to my first kiss.

Then one night, we were out on our shift, roaming the streets on what passed for guard duty, when I was suddenly floored by nostalgia, overtaken by a restless urge to see the place again. First thing the next morning, I set the process in motion, and as long as I was going to all the trouble, I was bringing everyone along. I invited La Mechu and La Puchu, and Reglita went with us everywhere as a matter of course. Our nerves were in a total state as we approached the door, we produced our National Workers Syndicate membership cards and a stack of certificates acknowledging my excellence in the workplace, and we were all asked to show a recent bill of clean health. Once inside, we realized that the dimmish lighting had less to do with ambiance and more to do with being down to two precious light bulbs. An hour elapsed before the Comrade Waitress finally ambled toward us in *slo mo*. As she finally reached for the stubby pencil behind her ear, a foul vapor seemed to stir from her body. Tonight's menu would have to wait for her to finish whining and moaning:

"Boy! Are my feet killing me tonight! My bunions are acting up again, betcha it'll rain, oh yeah, is it ever gonna rain! I hope you folks don't have your hearts set on anything special — like they say, if you live on illusions, you'll perish from losing them. So, we have *solianka* soup with pearl onions, *solianka* soup with vita nuova puree, *solianka* soup with potato cheese, water and sweet potato pudding. Don't forget, we send a part of the quota to our Chilean brothers and sisters. Bread and coffee come with the meal. Or you can have medicinal tea; it's not bad, but it is medicinal tea."

The caged-rhino stench persisted. She produced a repugnant, mildewy rag and went through the motions of wiping the vinyl doilies, and now, the grime was more evenly smeared.

We ate with primitive hunger and disgust from scummy bowls that bore the film of months of Fab shortages. We couldn't really finish the soup — not like we would have polished off a plate of rice and beans. For years, I'd been waiting for another chance to kick off my shoes and plunge my feet into the rich, red carpet. My bared toes were already groping for the luxuriant, hairy ground, when they hit bare cement as sharp and snaggled as the rocky shores of Cojímar.

"Where's the rug?" I asked, all out of joint.

"Honey, what planet you livin' on? Haven't you heard? The *bolos* got the rug, you know the Sovietunions. They took it to the *bolo* embassy to make coats for the scholarship people who go to Siberia. And good riddance too, that rug was an affliction, a dust trap that stunk of piss. The woman who cleans got so sick from it she went on medical leave. They could forget me, I told them, outta the question, I wasn't touching it. I don't do work on my hand and knees, slavery and exploitation have been abolished in this country, am I right or am I right! We are the first free territory of the Americas — Socialists as the day is long! Socialists By Any Means Necessary, and those who don't like it can Ship Out on the Ferry!"

She bopped away to a conga beat. La Mechu and La Puchu shed fat tears into the greasy remains of their unfinished soup. No amount of gulping could undo the knot lodged in my throat. Maria Regla was too busy licking her bowl to care about anything else:

"You're not eating? I'll take it if you don't want to finish it, I'm ravenous."

La Mechu, La Puchu, and I looked at one another, then we looked as the Comrade Waitress slipped a bottle of cooking oil under her skirt and secured it to her leg with her garter. We returned our gaze to the Girl, who was greedily eyeing our *soliankas*. I gave her mine. Her snuffling and slurping were an outrage.

"Reglita, learn how to eat soup."

We looked at one another again. What could we do, I ask you, but remember the day when we first met and how I had snorted down my soup, and we laughed so hard we almost fell off our chairs. Reglita didn't even look at us. We paid with coupons and got out of there. Money had lost all meaning, large bills were a rarity nowadays — value, supply, and demand had been consigned to oblivion.

An ocean breeze tunneled down O Street and moistened our faces. Havana smelled, as always, of decaying weeds and early corn, of petroleum and flame-extinguishing farts, of rotting eggs. Buses lumbered by spurting hot, black fumes and people went by in a haze of sweat. The weak wattage of the streetlights obscured the strolling forms, but we could make the most of a fat and teeming moon in all that darkness. Near La Rampa, we crossed a group of kids who were coming from the Malecón and moving toward the Coppelia Ice Cream Parlour, banging on drums they had fashioned out of tin cans as they happily chanted:

> Now that we are Communists
> and freedom rules the day,
> Nikita gives us oil
> for the sugar he takes away.

They meant Khrushchev. Soon after, Le Moscou was sabotaged, which meant that the counterrevolution continued the work begun by the revolution some years prior — the sure and steady destruction of all things. In the end, they decided to expedite things and burned the cabaret to the ground. It was closed for years of interminable repairs, to be reopened on further, further notice in the great hereafter that's become our daily lot. There's been talk about reopening it; about how it's jointly owned by some French guys now and how you'll have to pay through the nose, in U.S. dollars of course, just to get past the door. Maybe it'll get its old name back, it'll depend on the French guys, but still, I wouldn't put it past even them to turn it into a fast-food joint.

It was pitiful how much I walked. I walked as though my life depended on it, like a lunatic. I almost wore the soles of my plastic Kicos, the shoe of choice at the time, right off of my feet. Mine were the cheapest model — so boiling hot, people called them pressure cookers, so steamy, they softened calluses. White, once upon a time, they turned a pallid yellow from overuse, as if someone had poached them in lemon water or lightly browned them in hot oil. And despite being punched full of little holes, they were stifling. A muck of sweat collected in an impressive slick between heel and shoe. They stunk to high heaven and proved to be a superior breeding ground for fungi. Mine were thriving *champignon des bois,* and even all the Micocilene in the world, a medicinal powder for which one had to stand in line for up to five nights, was not worth a damn. Those were my shoes, my true-blues, for special days and for every day. All I had to do was whistle and they'd come panting like little circus dogs and curl themselves around my feet. When they became really old, I sawed off the heels with a Soviet-made Astra razor blade and dyed them black with China ink. There was no shoe polish to be found in those days. Later, you could find shoe polish but not China ink or typewriter ribbon, which meant we had to dip old ribbon in shoe polish. We also dipped into the polish tin when mascara dropped out of circulation. All those years of goop might be the reason I became squinty eyed and my vision got so poor. I am telling you it's a miracle we're still alive. Those were the years when just about anything you could think of would be considered contra-revo, as Fax used to say — at one point they even cracked down on potted plants like the malanga. I was listening to the Chilean Platters on the radio one morning (waiting for Vicentico Valdés's program), when a fumigator came knocking at my door. He came in, switched off my radio, and wagging one finger like an upside-down grandfather clock, he sang me a little ditty: *Malanga stalks in water are a no, no*. The campaign against mosquitoes and dengue fever was beginning, and I was within a hair's breadth of having my plant confiscated. Luckily, I had kept the certificate awarded by the Papayacratic Cuban Federation to the hardiest and most combative malanga shrub in the land. The malanga was spared; I, on the other hand, almost fell to my death while trying to train its long fronds around the poles with which I had propped up the ceiling. The building was in utter disrepair, because of neglect and crowded conditions and all the new additions that straddled its sagging structure. We lived in fear of imminent cave-in. At least, banning malangas was a health measure, but banning the Beatles! That was a wrong if I ever saw one! Tried to axe our youth at the root, they did! But we listened to the Beatles anyway, behind lock and key in bathrooms and rooms with hermetically sealed windows. For hours on end, we'd try to tune in to WSQMM, an American station that played everything. And sometimes we went to sit on the wall of the Malecón with our Soviet-made radios and listened to the Evening Gala Show from beginning to end. They would play all the Spanish groups: The Formulas, The Mustangs, and Juan & Junior. Even today, when I hear songs like "Anduriña" or "Globos Rojos" or "Una Carta" I get goose bumps. They also tried to hoodwink us with all those pipes-of-pan and all those morose South American flutes. Any street musician in a poncho seemed to end up on TV. I'm sorry, but a second into that stuff and I'd already be snoring. What the hell did all that Indian agony have to do with our easy exuberance, our extravagant music? What was a lament from Bolivia or Chile to us? Why all that sullenness instead of good cheer? Their twisted resolve to have us believing we had more to do with Quilapayun than with the Beatles just didn't wash. And isn't it the truth when they say you've got to make the most of youth, because when it goes, it's gone. And mine was going nowhere fast, and here I was still banking on slim chances and sick as a pup with love. Stuck to my false illusions, my life snuffed out by hope.

Then one day my mother showed up, claiming her share of tenderness. She met her granddaughter, they shared a moment of mutual admiration, which they both adored. She had come to rearrange my life, to derange me, in other words. To mess with my mess and impute repute, to meddle in every nook and cranny of my existence. She was very, but very, disapproving of my pint of rum and my frequent visits to the armoire where I kept it stashed. For a while there, I was always ready for a little pick-me-up. I got started on rum, and when there was no rum to be had, I moved on to the rotgut stuff, any kind of varnish mixed with a dash of lemonade. When people began referring to me as formaldehyde, I decided to watch myself a bit, but not too much. The booze and the tranquilizers helped mellow me out, but they didn't help me forget. At work, they had instituted a health-in-the-workplace policy, which meant that we had to stop whatever we were doing and exercise for ten or fifteen minutes. The minute our little workout was over, they'd advise us to pop a Valium or a Nembutol. Pills and liquor did wonders for me, I soared, I glowed, my sodium stayed nice and low. Now, cigarettes never did much for me — good thing too, seeing how expensive they became. When the going got really rough, Xerox Machine smoked the entire Bible, cover to cover — that onion paper is really good for rolling your own. I walked into her place one night and found it thick with smoke; she soon reassured me, however, she'd just been smoking her way through the Song of Songs. My mother viewed it all with a very jaundiced eye. She spoke from experience, she said, which we all knew she had plenty of, but hey, let her go get her own life in order first, and then we can see about mine. All my life I had put up with her excesses, her departures at the drop of a hat, her endless procession of lover boys. She abhorred La Mechu and La Puchu. Communist strumpets, she called them, and I was a union tart who had brought a fatherless squirt into the world. And that's when my mother and I finally went at each other and, boy, did the fur ever fly! But really, she did all the hollering because I never raised my voice

78

to my mother, never. After she'd told me her version of a thing or two, she whizzed off on the same ill wind that had blown her in and went to live with my sick sister. In the stairwell, she disowned me; I heard her cast me out of her life just like that.

I still supported them, I had made a decision to let bygones be bygones, to let well enough alone and begin anew. I didn't give a flying hoot about the fight and continued to visit them daily, always at a prearranged time. She was my mother after all, my one and only. My polio-stricken brother had married a woman who had borne him beautiful nut brown daughters with red hair and blue eyes like my mother. My other brother, the asthmatic and chronic Catholic, became an altar boy and official assistant to the village priest. In the ID card picture I saw of him, he looked exactly like my father, very Chinese and very sad and hollow-faced.

My daughter slipped away through my fingers. She grew up straitjacketed inside her starched and ironed uniform, which she carefully removed four hours before bedtime, and with a kerchief neatly and snugly knotted around her neck. At home, our motto was solidarity with all of creation, except between ourselves. Like everyone else, we sent sugar and coffee to Chile, clothes and toys to earthquake victims in Peru, shoes to Vietnam, teachers and doctors to Nicaragua, husbands, lovers, and brothers to the wars of Africa. Coffee, sugar, clothes, shoes, and toys were exceedingly rationed. One of the reasons, no doubt, that men signed up for wars in faraway climes — they needed a change of scene. My daughter was accumulating brownie points by assenting to any pointless task that came along. Only after night had fallen did we put aside our differences and climb onto the middle-size mattress that we shared, not because we wished it but because mattresses had disappeared out of stores like flying carpets. As if mattresses were yet another Imperialist conspiracy that had to be fought tooth and nail. I would make the most of those moments my daughter was sound asleep to kiss her softly on the forehead and hold her to me, wishing to save her.

Maria Regla was very busy with her afterschool activities; when it wasn't a workshop for labor education, it was a heat or a meet at the Pontón gymnasium or a rally in solidarity with anyone under the sun or an anthem sing-along or a practical training in this or that or a volunteer firefighter drill . . . Now, she was the one who was never home. When she was eleven, she emerged from the bathroom one day holding a pair of underpants smeared with a familiar coffee brown stain.

"Finally, I'm a young lady," she said.

I started telling her about Kotex, but she knew all there was to know. She was mostly concerned that her tits were not much to speak of, but her nipples, which were beginning to fill in, showed quite plainly when she wore her gym class T-shirt. I found her a little undervest on the black market, but she would have none of it, wouldn't be caught dead wearing such a ridiculous thing.

"Blue jeans is what I'd really like, Mommy, a pair of Caribus or of Li's." By which she didn't mean *little Li, little Li running through the trees,* but a Texan pair of Lee jeans.

I saved like a fiend. A pair of jeans, on the black market of course, was worth 150 pesos, and I was making 138 pesos a month. Not too long ago, a pair of blue jeans could cost you up to a thousand pesos. To make a long story short, I scraped and scrimped until I got her her Caribu, and she was as sweet and tender as could be.

Then came our first serious separation, our first real good-bye. She had to put in her forty-five days in the countryside, at the camp school. I had a wooden case made up for her, vinyl suitcases were useless, regularly slashed and robbed of their contents. By some miracle, I even managed to get my hands on a padlock with a working key. I got blisters on my fingers from so much darning and mending; I wanted her to have a good supply of work clothes to make up for the one inadequate outfit they gave each kid. I accompanied her to the appointed place, in Lovers' Park, where she would board her bus. I felt the lump in my throat and I could have fainted from my panic. What if anything were to happen to my darling girl? One heard of accidents, of overturned wagons and young lives nipped in the bud. She was less than pleased about having me along for the send-off; it was embarrassing and uncool and totally ridiculous. When we got to the boarding place, all the kids were being seen off by their parents, but she kept at it, insisting on my hasty exit, wanting me out of there. The minute she bumped into one of her friends her face lit up, became the picture of happiness. Then, she was suddenly pecking me on the cheek and running off to join a line of bubbly girls being swallowed up by the bus. The buses took off and I stood there like a zombie as my baby rode away in a monotonous singsong of children's voices:

> We're off to the country and won't be back again,
> We're off to the country and won't be back again . . .

I never missed a Sunday, every week I visited her in the dorms. The first year, the camp was all girls, but later, they'd have boys there too. At 5 A.M. I'd be posted there like Mrs. Jesus Christ, carrying a bag of groceries in each hand. The food they gave them was such shit that I would spend the whole week chasing after all those foods so dear to my daughter and her friends, the croquette generation. I brought them only the best, the finest things I could find: croquettes, of course, and shortbread cookies and pizzas and bread and pound cake and condensed milk and chocolate bars and any delicacy that turned up on the black market. I even brought them breaded turtle fillets on more than one occasion. It broke my heart every time I saw my daughter so sunburnt, with her hands all calloused and her feet in a state of similar neglect (they didn't have workboots her size), and her hair damaged and brittle and so thin, God Almighty, so thin. After all the trouble I'd gone to to find a pharmacist who could get me five packets of Ciproectadina and three jars of vitamin B to increase the appetite. Not that her appetite needed increasing; those miserable camp food rations were what needed increasing. Even if she had chosen to come home early, not that she would have, the stipulation was that all those who did not volunteer for the rural camps were by definition apathetic to the revolutionary project and would be barred from entering the university regardless of the excellence of their grades and character. Kids who couldn't take it anymore and asked to go back to their homes were pelted with obscenities, insults, even stones; teachers and supervisors not only looked the other way but went out of their way to bless the rough stuff. They labeled those kids the deserters. Didn't matter if they

81

were the brainiest kids to walk the earth, deserters had a record for life. Maria Regla would never be a deserter; or rather, she'd only want to desert her home, which she did soon enough, at a very young age. An apple never falls far from the tree. So at fourteen, she was given a scholarship to Turibacoa II, a country school as opposed to schooling in the countryside. The subtleties of language in Cuba today are such that a preposition can make all the difference.

This new separation was killing me. Reglita, who was well behaved and never got detentions, spent every weekend at home, but that still left all the other numbing and tedious days of the week. Until I finally hit on a brilliant way to fill my days, aside from my job of course. I began to stock fabric, save thread, collect old shoes. I started saving money again, selling odds and ends, any old thing I could get my hands on. I had a goal, a dream. I was going to give my daughter what no one had ever given me — a grand event, a celebration, a sweet sixteen party.

Naturally, La Mechu and La Puchu were the first to know. You'd think it was their daughter, they were so thrilled, flying into a frenzy of unpacking old dresses, old shoes, fabrics purchased at El Encanto once upon a time. They dusted off phone books and dug up the names of old friends, old pals, the kind of people who had landed jobs managing ritzy restaurants and who could solve the beer problem and the little buns for sandwiches problem and the cake and the sodas and all the other many problems. They remembered spending a week in a house in Guanabo with a fellow who now managed the Santa Fe Beach Resort. I knew him too from my job at the Nautico. And then it came to us in a flash, "The Spanish Casino!" We were all shouting at once, "The Spanish Casino! So classy! We'll have the party at the Spanish Casino!"

I closed my eyes and imagined Reglita in long, blue tulle waltzing in the pink room with its marbled floors, and it was too much, I could have died then and there from the excitement. But, wait a minute, who would she waltz with? Girls were usually escorted by their fathers for the first whirl around the room. I needed a someone to fill a father's shoes, a stand-in at any cost.

"I know a choreographer who is a specialist in these things. Oh, he's very famous, and his name is Cuquito! Ah, what a funny coincidence! He won't charge much, don't worry, and darling, his choreography is tops, just like in that Spanish movie *The Virgin Wax,* you know, with Carmen Sevilla. I must've seen it about forty-five times, at the Jigüe Cinema with stereophonic sound and everything. I never get tired of it, and if they ever let us travel again I know where I'm going, straight to Spain. Because aside from their funny way of lisping when they talk, they have everything you could want over there: cider and olives and sausages and lovely nougats and bean soups and Spanish omelettes two meters tall . . . Oh, yes, Cuquito the choreographer! Oh by the time he's finished, you'll be calling him Maestro, believe you me! He can get a little carried away sometimes, with the costume changes, but it's because he's very professional, you see . . . Come on, Sister-Girl, cheer up, get rid of the hangdog face! Don't worry, even Ivo can be the father, he loves any kind of sentimental ooing and cooing." La Mechunga was deliriously happy. "We'll have to film it of course, and I imagine, Cuca, that you'll want to have a lot of pictures, 'cause it's a once-in-a-lifetime kind of thing . . . Tell you what, the pictures are on me. They'll be my present to you."

I didn't know how to begin expressing my thanks to my friends who were so enthusiastic about my plan, so determined to see it through. They were right; Ivo was the perfect solution. I worried what Uan would say if he ever found out about his beautiful daughter and how she celebrated her Sweet Sixteen in high style. I worried about everything and everyone, except for the birthday girl, herself — what would she think?

"Over my dead body. You can forget it. I don't need your bourgeois silliness, I don't want parties or complications or any other shit of the kind you like to wallow in. You can forget me, I'll just stay at school that weekend. Why're you killing yourself over this, Mom? And what's all the business about *Virgin Wax*? Is Aunt Mechu losing it or what!"

Was she a virgin? I stopped stacking the brand-new towels I had collected over the years for the Girl's trousseau. We stared at each other. My eyes began to fill with tears. I very much wanted her to be a virgin until she married, to have what I hadn't had because I blew it. I locked myself up in the bathroom and sobbed like Joan Crawford in *Mildred Pierce*. I could hear her going round and round in circles, and then, she stopped just outside the bathroom door:

"Don't worry, Mom, I'm on the pill, nothing will happen."

We ate dinner in silence. I wanted to ask her how it happened, who was the boy, did they love each other . . . But I didn't dare. I, too, would have been incapable of telling when it happened to me, of confiding in anyone. But I had no one, and she had me. I studied her face for signs of love, proof of joy or suffering. Nothing. She just sat there devouring her food as she always did, the way they eat in those dining halls — bolting it all down in time to have seconds and still escape the shame and agony of being late for class or work in the fields. I never found out how it happened. *There's no explaining what it was, I couldn't tell you if I tried* . . . At any rate, she wasn't in love, far from it. It happened like these things happen. I like to imagine it was under a starry sky in a fragrant tobacco field filled with the song of crickets and the glow of lightning bugs with the Evening Gala Show playing on the radio. I like to think he's a good boy who loves her and will someday come ask me for her hand in marriage. Good God! She wasn't even sixteen!

The party was everything we had expected it to be; it was held at the Spanish Casino with choreography from *The Virgin Wax*. She looked stunning in her long, blue tulle and her white Primor pumps (these shoes were exclusively reserved for girls who were celebrating their Sweet Sixteen and could only be purchased with coupons at a special store. They were very expensive, and I had managed to buy off enough coupons from other girls who couldn't afford them). Oh yes, my daughter had four pairs of Primor pumps, her de rigueur maxiskirt with a slit up the side, fine mesh stockings, and ten new outfits that included three babydoll minidresses. We also had to produce ID cards and coupon books ahead of time in order to qualify for an appointment at the Kou Yam Beauty Shop where they did her makeup. She was utterly beautiful and found it all completely unenjoyable. After her waltz with Ivo, she put her head down on the table and went to sleep; it couldn't have been more than nine o'clock. Her friends, on the other hand, had the time of their life; the party was a great success, a gem. We had 352 guests. I spent a fortune, let me tell you, but it was worth every penny. I felt so rewarded, as though I was the one turning sixteen. Well, I always say, if you're going to do something you might as well do it right or not at all. Did you hear about that party in Old Havana for one of Reglita's classmates? Right in the middle of the "Blue Danube" the whole building collapsed, everything — the sixteen couples in the choreographed piece, the birthday cake, everything ended up on the ground floor. Well, that tenement was condemned, but the girl's mother got it into her thick head to have her party no matter what, and she couldn't afford to rent a hall. And, to make matters worse, all kinds of people who weren't even on the guest list showed up and the sheer weight of the dancers brought the place crashing down. It was a terrible mayhem, people got injured and a pregnant woman ended up dangling from the rafters, it's a miracle she didn't give birth on the spot. The firemen had to come, it was a total chaos, an unforgettable evening all around!

Three days after the party, Maria Regla went out very early with one of her girlfriends and didn't return till evening. She came back looking haggard, with dark rings under her eyes and a small bruise already forming in the crook of her arm. Then I understood why she had been so sleepy: she had been pregnant. She had just had an abortion and was clinging to me in a swoon.

"Oh, Mom," she cried and cried with her head in my lap until she was spent. I felt this big, like a splat of shit. Where had I gone wrong? Why didn't she tell me, talk to me? Why did she always keep me at bay, at arm's length? It has always been like that. And now, she's slipping from me, I'm losing her, and it will have been my fault. I didn't know how to keep her.

She studied journalism. I was in the dark about her grades, her hard times, of course I knew she had them. Studying journalism in this country is like making a pact with Mephistopheles during a heat wave, the contract can stipulate all sorts of crazy conditions. And she didn't have the sense to keep her mouth shut, she could back talk with the best, and they tried to shut her up in a thousand ways, and they did. By promising her her own cultural program on TV, for example, or by dangling a prime slot on NTV (the Not (fit) To View national news program).

She's just like him, just like her father. The two great loves of my life have abandoned me as they would a mangy dog. Thank God for La Mechunga and La Puchunga, they're fast and true. And thank God for my beloved cockroach, my Nadezhda Common Itch, and for Mr. Perez the Rat, who queues up for me at the stands and shops. Good thing that Fax and Yocandra take such good care of me and give me little gifts of aspirin and tranquilizers. Even Xerox worries herself about my health, and when all is said and done, she's a good soul despite being a gossip. I thank the Lord for them, because Reglita doesn't even call to ask if my sugar is up or down, if my migraines are acting up, if I had my blood pressure checked, if I went for my pap smear. I'm not going to tell her about the little lump in my tit. So there!

When the phone rings, Nadezhda Common Itch is ironing a safari shirt for her husband, Mr. Perez the Rat. I'm about to pick up the receiver, but she's closer to the phone and gets it for me. I hear her say a tender hello, and immediately guess she must be talking to Reglita. She pushes the heavy black Kellog telephone toward me. I barely have time to say hello, dear heart, and she's off, talking a mile a minute, like a cart careening down a hill:

"Hello, Mom, hello! I'm very busy, Mom. How are you? Real soon, if all goes well, I might have a surprise for you. . . . Yeah, I'm gonna be on TV on Channel Six. No, Channel Two is sports and official speeches. Yeah, I'll tell you all about it. No, silly, I didn't have to go to bed with anyone. Don't say stupid things. Big kiss. Bye."

I can't stop busting my brains to figure it out: what's the point of all this effort? this constant struggle? Look at how my mother died, with a vibrator that an ex-sister-in-law prostitute sent her from Manila wedged between her legs. I can't go on with this litany, this suffering, this sweet and bitter suffering. All I need to be happy is bread, love, and chachacha. But I can't be happy. Easy as it may seem.

5

A Cuban in New York

Hey, fellow Cubano,
time to get tough now,
this is New York now.
I, too, left my Havana,
was new to this city,
lost my heart
to the first passerby.
"I don't know speak to you,
Cubano," she said.

By J. Aparicio and M. Sánchez,
as sung by the Trío Oriental

I NEVER SAW HER AGAIN, NEVER EVEN WROTE HER. Rumor has it I fathered a beautiful daughter with pinko pretensions, a red love child who is ashamed of me because someone's been pumping her full of snake-in-the-grass dirt. Her mother must've had a hand in it, raised her like that. To get back at me, of course, but get back at what for pity's sake? Let's face it, she hardly knew me. I never even took her to meet the old lady, may she rest in peace. My mother, bless her soul, wrote letter after letter, wanting to know about the buzz going around the neighborhood about some pregnant girl I'd left behind. And I always answered that it was just idle talk, Ma, just folks trying to scare ya and get me into even deeper trouble. Still, she wouldn't let go, wanted to get to the bottom of it. So she undertook an investigation more thorough than Holmes and Watson, Marple and Poirot, Derrick and Colombo taken together ever would have. Luckily, she never tracked down the address in Havana, because she suddenly had to relocate to Matanzas, midcase. Once I was gone, you can imagine how they harried her out of home, neighborhood, and county. They made her life one long draught of castor oil, with all the stuff about her son the traitor.

The old lady, my saintly mother, may she rest in peace, kicked the bucket on the day of my daughter's fifth birthday. Which is to say, she lasted about as long as meringues among schoolchildren, not long at all. She couldn't take the separation. People we knew from there — they came in dribs, at eyedropper intervals, all of them were political prisoners and they weren't going to let them go just like that, gratis — told me she suffered horribly, life without me was hell on earth for her. Me, her only son, the one she sent to the best schools and who, in the end, turned out to be more crooked than a barrel of snakes — a fancy hooligan. When father went into the hospital, I had a feeling right here, a bitter knot in the middle of my chest, I could've told you he was marked for the cemetery and sure enough, he was. The minute the funeral was over, I saw my chance, let your grandmother take up lawyering, 'cause I was on my way. And I walked out on everything my father had scraped together by the sweat of his brow to set me up for the future, which, frankly, didn't amount to much, and headed straight to the other extreme, to all those things that were more to my liking: the swindling came first, then the uglier deals, and finally, the Mafia. But, can't complain I didn't make a living; can't say I'm not pleased with how things worked out. I'm one of those Cubans who made it here in the Mecca of success. Not that it's been easy street all the way, I slaved like a brute, but a little work never scared off a Cuban as long as he's being paid for it, which makes sense. This thing about Cubans being lazy is news to me, and it's only over there, 'cause the Cubans I've known don't stop till the job is done. I mean, who built Miami, for Christ's sake? Self-denying and hardworking Cubans is who, 'cause there was nothing there but a wasteland of weeds till we came along and raised the glossy mirror that is Miami from the ground up, gossip capital of the world bad-mouthing the present and missing alike.

Once I arrived in this country, it didn't take me long to get super well connected. I came highly recommended by my good buddies at the Capri, you understand. And, to help matters, my old boss from over there had beaten me to it, managed to get here first. There's a strange one for you, the old buzzard must be a thousand years old by now and fit as an ox. There've only been two tough customers of his caliber in the history of the earth. Lucky for me, the other one is ninety miles offshore. This one, the stateside one, has informed me in no uncertain terms that he intends to stick around till I give him his dollar bill. What could I've been thinking? How could I have given it to her for safekeeping? I can't believe I didn't bring it with me. Well, I was scared shitless for one, and I thought if they found it on me I'd be in a whole lot more trouble than if they caught me with a suitcase of hundreds. Who would've thought all this was going to last? I figured that before too long I'd be coming back to her and to my dollar bill. And now it's been thirty-six years with the old creep giving me a bad name, tormenting me with his blasted dollar bill, blackmailing me through the teeth. If it hadn't been for him, I could have gone the distance, swung bigger, better deals, been a real somebody, but that old son of a bitch is always carping in front of the others, making an issue of my loyalty, warning them to watch their step with me because thirty-six years ago, I lost a dollar bill. So much crap for a dollar bill! Not that he didn't warn me from the start:

"Guard it like gold," he had said, sucking the butt end of his cigar. "Our future depends on it."

I more or less said the same thing to her — guard it like gold, our future depends on it. I palmed it off on her 'cause I was shitting bricks. I mean, who was going to believe a single dollar bill? They were going to think it was a code, they were going to get me on smuggling military or economic intelligence. That's why I gave it to her — I thought it wouldn't last long. Once I landed in this country, without even two nickels to rub together, who should meet me at the airport but the Old Man. Later, I'd hear about all the others who were also looking for me because of the dollar bill, but the Old

you think he wrote that straight? And wouldn't he have been tickled to know about his grandson, the Hollywood actor César Romero, who played the Joker in the old *Batman*? And wouldn't he have laughed himself silly if he'd heard people tell about his son, Ismaelillo, singing, "Father shouldn't have died, have died, have died," over and over again in the shower? I mean, shit, even a National Hero is a man beneath it all!

It's colder than Alaska out here, and the Old Man insisting we always meet in this godforsaken place, buffeted by the elements, for security reasons, he says. He still thinks we're a 1940s Mafia. He could've invited me to Victor's Café, but he's so tightfisted he'd rather crawl on his elbows than use up his shoes. Damn, does he ever have me by the short hairs! And where the hell is he? I'm freezing here, if he doesn't show up soon I'll be as stiff as José Martí, minus the horse. Everyone will stop to pee on me. Pee, pee, pee. There's the cellular. It's the Old Man insisting I return his call. He's on his way, another ten or fifteen minutes. He's delayed because of a girl, he says, a coconut flan of a girl. Another skinny wonder, no doubt; bulimic girls are his curse and downfall. My wife and daughter are also bulimic. It's fashionable these days, the way it used to be with TB. Can you picture Marguerite Gauthier bulimic? Nowadays, a woman can't even make the cut as a real woman unless she's had a brush with the bulimia. It all began when Jane Fonda came out with her bulimia, stirring up a lot of good publicity for CNN. The point is, I share my life with a pair of monsters, skeletons who never stop eating and vomiting. I put in a special bathroom for them, with separate stalls and special bowls that won't back up from all the puking. Their friends were green with envy, and they all had their own vomitoriums built, usually somewhere in the vicinity of the swimming pool. It's the age of puking. Those who don't are disgusting tubs of flesh who wouldn't presume to dream of fame or Hollywood. Well, the subject wouldn't be worth a second of my time, if it weren't for the psychosis. My wife and daughter both suffer from serious depression, they claim they're having identity crises, their psychoanalyst confirmed it, long after I had diagnosed it, of course. Anyone can see that they don't want to be who they are. They'd rather be just about anybody but themselves. I don't know — Pamela Anderson, Sharon Stone, Madonna, for example. They're dying to join a sect and spend their days reading promotional brochures that all promise new paths to self-knowledge and success. My wife is also Cuban, but nobody knows it. She passes herself off as American, American born. She doesn't want to hear about back home. She's not the least bit interested. I had never seen her before, in Cuba I mean. Although, it could have easily happened, I knew her brother.

Toward the end there, her brother and I were tight buddies. A great guy, straightforward, on the up-and-up. He was in a bad way on the night we met at the Montmartre; his cousin had been taken down to the police station because of some political shit. He came to see me, sent by a mutual acquaintance to whom I owed a favor. He was desperate for someone to intervene, before the cousin disappeared for good only to resurface early some morning at the bottom of a ditch with his balls stuffed down his throat. He knew of my contacts in the police because of my line of work in public relations. I got the cousin released, they'd roughed up his face pretty badly, and handed him his finger and toe nails in a little paper bag. I got him out and never regretted it. I did it 'cause I liked him, he seemed like an all right guy. Not that I didn't keep my eyes open: there was that cousin, after all. One of those wolves in sheep's clothing, a revolutionary who talked a pretty line but could be hell on wheels with a machine gun, a rebel with lofty affectations, he may even have had good intentions.

Luis, my would-be brother-in-law — not that I knew it at the time — dropped in to see me now and again and we became good friends. Cabaret friends. The police station business was never mentioned again. Once he showed up with boxes of medicines he needed to stash someplace until the guy who was taking them up into the mountains turned up. It was just for a couple of days and I hid them in Cuca's apartment. Another time it was armbands, and again, I helped him out. And even though I never meant to, I ended up helping a cause that didn't interest me in the least. In fact, it should have interested me more because it had very adverse effects on people like me, people who lived and breathed for the love of money, but I helped out anyway. I don't know why. I know why, 'cause he was my friend, and if there's a good thing about me it's my loyalty to my pals. Also, I had a sense that when it came to money, to the cash bonanza, they weren't any less entranced than we were.

Early one morning, Luis and I were walking by the doors of the Manzana de Gómez, we had just come from a quickie motel in Tejadillo and a night of voracious sucking and nibbling with a pair of fabulous prostitutes with a Tibetan aura about them. They smelled of patchouli and vanilla, they burned incense, wore Chinese silk kimonos, and did their hair up high, Pagoda-style. Their penile rubs were just out of this world and they took polymorphous perversion to new heights. They said they were geishas who had left theatrical careers in Shanghai to start their own business, which they ran with impeccable professionalism.

We were level with the pharmacy that had an immense aquarium as one of its window displays when we heard the screech of car tires rounding the corner at breakneck speed. The car slowed down alongside us, a hand holding a machine gun materialized and shot two rounds. At the first sound of gunfire, I went for the ground, pretending I was dead or had taken a bad hit. All the bullets lodged in Luis's body, he had been walking closer to the curb. His brains and blood were all over me, my eyes, my lips. The second round struck the aquarium, blowing it up into a thousand pieces, the spurting water rinsed off the blood, the fishes were jumping all over me, trying to swim. My flesh was stinging, splinters of glass were sticking to my face, my arms, my back, my legs . . .

Given the delicate nature of my line of work, I had to leave Luis lying there and get away as fast as I could. Nonetheless, I did go ahead with my own inquest. There was nothing to pin his killing on the police, and the Mafia didn't have its hooks into this one — so, by all indications, it had nothing to do with me. The crime remained unsolved, the perpetrators unknown. My wife — his sister — suspects his cronies; she thinks they tagged him as unreliable when he got involved with the Mafia, in other words, with me . . . I don't know. I don't think so, but it's a good enough argument to keep me feeling guilty for the rest of my life. I'm sure that's what she's after, she hasn't lost much sleep over her dead brother for a long time now. When I had no choice but to get out of there, it was none other than the cousin whom I had rescued from the police who supplied me with the militia disguise. Ain't life rock and roll! The cousin didn't shed any light on the killing, maybe he didn't want to, afraid to really blow it and find himself trapped between two camps.

I've witnessed hundreds of killings, people dropping like flies, routine. But always with good reason, for amounts of money I don't dare repeat, even to myself. In the world I moved in, those murders made sense. But I could never make heads nor tails of what happened to Luis. Who's to say he's not the reason I became a setter of bombs, a terrorist. Blowing up or burning down a cinema became child's play to me. Like playing a stupid and dangerous game. I can't get over the feeling that they're the ones who pumped Luis full of bullets. They, themselves.

Not long after I settled in New York, I met my wife. She adapted to this country in no time, a couple of months and she was strolling up and down Fifth Avenue like she'd been born and raised there. Still, I picked her out in the crazed herd of hundreds just then charging down the opposite sidewalk. Those tits and ass on the move, all that plenty twitching like store-bought Jell-O could not have hailed from these parts. I fell for her "too sexy for you, too sexy for me, too sexy as far as the eye can see" way of flouncing down the street. She had me going with her rolling tits and ass, all charged up with Oedipal longing. I thought of my mother and almost came. My blessed mother naked as a jaybird and dancing the mambo in front of the mirror of her dressing table. And a mother is a mother! And a pair of Cuban buttocks is a pair of Cuban buttocks, even if it steals past in the crush of a multitude following orders to *walk, don't walk*. As I still spoke broken English, I went for it in Spanish:

"*Oye, tú eres cubana, no me digas que no.*" — "Hey, there, you're Cuban, right? Don't tell me you're not." We were right in front of the Empire State Building.

"I don't know speak to you, *Cubano*," she said, and there was a momentary hardness in her eyes. But the recognition had been mutual, and we both started laughing. We met frequently after that.

I always took her for an afternoon ice cream in the Village. We still had good laughs then. She would tell me in great detail how her hairdresser in Havana had concocted a mile-high hairdo for her to smuggle out the family's jewelry. She talked about her brother as though he were still living, and she mentioned a cousin who had stayed behind in a high government post.

When she finally came around to telling about the tragic way in which her brother had died, I had the sinking feeling she was talking about Luis. She was. I was ready to marry her then and there, because for all these years I felt I owed him something and marrying his sister seemed like a good place to start. God must have had his mysterious reasons for putting this girl on my path. Plus, I had the hots for her in a big way. When she walked that way, that *I don't cut sugarcane, let the wind do it, let Lola do it* way, I knew I was headed for years of intensive therapy. This didn't mean that I had, for a minute, forgotten Cuquita. But three months, no three years, had elapsed, and the new Communist society gave no signs of falling. Because of my filthy line of work, I had been advised to send as little mail as possible to the home territory. Each time I wrote my mother, I did it under a different name and address and at long and irregular intervals. I wasn't sure if Cuquita would have been up to all those multiple, changing identities. At any rate, I've always been a man of few words and fewer letters. I don't like to fuel illusions. If it wasn't meant to be, then it wasn't meant to be and the hell with it. Why open old wounds? But Cuca Martinez is a thorn in my side and so is that unknown and unclaimed girl, my daughter. I don't think my wounds'll heal anytime soon. Not that I'm in any hurry.

There's still no sign of the Old Man. The fewer signs the better as far as I'm concerned. In my book, finding his name in the obituaries or chalked on a board outside a funeral home will go down easy as whiskey. I'm going to get sick sitting out here; as soon as I'm over one cold the next one is already on its way. The minute I start to feel better, the Old Man calls, wanting to meet me at the usual place. There goes Madonna with her gorilla patrol, people say she fucks them. We, too, had our Madonna, our Martha Sánchez Abreu, she was so rich she had her own private zoo, the *Quinta de los Monos*. People also said about her that she did it with the chimps. Her property still stands over there, and a Sicilian fellow interested in investing in Cuba told me he was looking into it as a location for movie shoots. The French and Spanish TV are there as we speak, paying cash dollars to make *period* films, from God knows what period, like *Tierra Indigo*, for example, that is set in 1920s Cuba and features Indians with plastic pet parrots clamped to their shoulders and speaking Yoruba no less. It's the kind of movie with ecological pretensions they show on international flights during takeoff and landing to make people yawn so their ears will pop. Martha Sánchez Abreu did collect monkeys, it is true, and malicious gossip had it that she cozied up to them. Her niece was Rosalía, La Lilita, the stranger of Saint-John Perse's poem. I'm not erudite, just informed. This must be the tenth time Madonna has gone by, exercising half-naked in this ball-breaking cold. If my daughter hears I bumped into Madonna, she'll kill me for not buying her and bringing her home.

At long last the Old Man's unbelievably long limousine appears. This entrance begs for background music, don't rack your brains, just reach for the classics, you can't do better than the track to *The Godfather*.

We are the miracle of love, tralala, la la la la . . .

Don't think for a minute that the Old Man will step out of the car to greet or meet me; that's not his style. I, on the other hand, given the rules of hierarchy, have to stir my stumps, jump up on legs that feel more like ice columns propping up the Winter Palace, and dart, faster than Carl Lewis, than Michael Johnson, toward the car's half-opened door. I scoot in and before I'm even done grazing his shriveled hand with my lips, his secretary is already handing him alcohol-soaked swabs as a precaution against the imagined miasma of my offending mouth. I stretch my legs and inadvertently bump into the cadaverous little whore who is spitting up a purplish scum all over herself and convulsing like a throttled chicken.

"It's nothing," the Old Man explains, "she helped herself to the wrong batch."

Batch of cocaine, he means. And skipping preambles, he lays out his plan with the guttural velocity of a machine gun:

"Everything is ready. We've studied the case with utmost care. This is it. They called themselves, they need us. You'll be on the next flight. Here is your passport and your travel permit. Your record's been wiped clean, with us and with them."

"Who is them? Where am I being sent?"

"To bring back the dollar bill. They, the ones over there, are expecting you, you'll get a fine reception. Their one condition is that they want a cut, but I'll be handling that. That's between me and them."

"I can't believe we're back to the shitty dollar bill again."

"Don't be stupid now. We need the serial number, it corresponds to our most important account in Switzerland. The account has been off-limits for thirty-six years, there are nine gold threads, each in a different karat, woven into that dollar bill. We need the code to get to the account. Look, I don't have to give explanations, you've been democratically elected to carry out this mission. You'd better do as you're told, my advice to you is come back with the dollar bill or don't bother coming back. Your family will be well provided for," and he snickered, "there are plenty of coffins to go around. I've made very important contacts . . . They are waiting for you."

"Who is they?"

He turns his full fury on me, I can't tell if his flailing hands mean to hit me or if rage has triggered one of his sporadic fits of palsy and brought on the mad fluttering of his hands:

"You've been in our family for nearly fifty years, and you still don't get it. There are certain *theys*, who must never be mentioned by name, for security reasons! Do you want me to wring your neck, you brainless piece of shit. The least we can do is try to be discreet if we're ever going to get our dollar bill back. Nothing else interests me. We need the money for a complete overhaul, we can't go on being a 1940s Mafia forever. Either we get on the Net, like Commandant Marcos did in Chiapas — on Internet and CD-ROM, Régis Debray donated all the equipment — or we're history.

And getting electronically hooked up costs money! Ah, my heart, my heart, there's a pain in my heart, I must be becoming sentimental in my old age."

To him, pain in the chest area never means a potential heart attack in the near future. He has long since dismissed any notion of his own mortality. He attributes all aches and pains to his overly sensitive nature, to his magnanimous spirit — a ruse for him to be an even bigger miser and an even greater son of a bitch. He makes God look human. What the hell is he trying to pull with this sudden interest in computers? Unless cyberspace is a by-product of senility? Something is not adding up here. But what choice do I have? They've already informed my family that I had to leave on an urgent humanitarian mission to Kenya. With their new plastic surgery techniques they remake my face in fifteen minutes. I heal in five. Medical advances, these days, just boggle the mind. They hand me a sealed briefcase. One of their goons is traveling with me as far as Miami. He spends the whole three-hour flight updating me on the thousand and one new names given to the dollar in Cuba today: Dracula, Mongo, Juanikiki. Almost four hours of training and I'm ready to infiltrate Havana's underworld after an absence of thirty-some years. This time, I'll be licensed, well, let's hope so — 'cause you never know.

The goon has orders to take me all the way to my seat on the plane to Havana. I still haven't had a chance to digest any of this. I open the briefcase and review the documents. They inform me that I'm visiting Cuba to research possibilities for a rum distillery. I'm supposedly returning, sorry I ever left. That might even be the truth. Nothing is clear. Everything is clear. I'll just have to go with my gut feeling. My whole life, I've had to follow orders, like a soldier or worse, so adjusting to this new twist of events will only take a second. I take a deep breath and rest my head on the small square of fabric that covers the headrest. But what about the bombings, the acts of sabotage? Have they forgotten about them? I doubt it. The minute I settle down, I'm overcome by a mad urge to jump from my seat. I'm peeing and shitting myself, probably nerves. I hate shitting on airplanes. Sitting on the john, I think of my mother. I'll visit her tomb first thing. I hate not knowing where my turds are landing — in what country, on whose head? Then I'll go see them — my wife and daughter. To solve the fucking dollar bill problem once and for all. The Dracula problem, I mean.

6

Cuban Blues

Oh Cuba, beautiful, so fine
you've grown sad beyond recall.
Who could've known
you'd be so blue beneath blue skies.

By Eliseo Grenet,
as sung by Guillermo Portables

I AM NOT THE AUTHOR OF THIS BOOK. I said so at the beginning. I am the corpse. I dictate and that one, the one who is very much alive and kicking, writes it all down. There's no need to look so crestfallen. It's always been an aspiration of mine to run with rowdy spirits — dead or alive. And especially if I'm going to be dead, then this strutting skeleton of mine had better shine in the conga line. Come, come, skip the tears. It's a minor detail, but I thought you had a right to know. This is how it works: I supply the goods, the true-to-life facts, and she writes them down, embellishing a little as she goes along. If I had it my way, I'd go for the truth straight up, but she's another story, she won't even leave her perch — that narrow, humid balcony she built herself on the moon. Don't come blaming me if you haven't understood a word of what's being said, the fault lies with the scribe. She's the designated scribbler, I'm putting all my trust in her. Well, not all, I've been dead long enough to know better than that when it comes to the living. I'm now free of conscience and consciousness. She has too much of everything, a conscience and two kinds of consciousness — the valid one and the false one. We'll have to see how it goes.

They're going to make a writer out of me if it kills them. People tell me stories that make me itchy, they get me going and I can't stop scratching till I start writing. Tormented souls are the worst, when they turn up with an assignment, I never know how to turn them down. 'Cause who's to say they won't come into my room at night and drag me kicking and screaming into the next world, which, as far as we know, is no world at all. I hear her whispering in my ear now, she tells me everything more or less happened in the following, corny manner:

On a pretentious, musical island, there lived a woman, who was lonelier than the numeral 1 and a thousand times poorer than Cinderella. Whenever the woman heard even a snippet of a bolero, she would fall into a dreamy trance and imagine her Prince Charming with his requisite heavy purse. Apologies to Jane Austen for the rewrite, and many thanks to Guillermo Cabrera Infante for setting me, via a reference in one of his books, on the trail of *Pride and Prejudice*, a work I have to unearth this very minute so as to avoid inadvertent plagiarism and expose my ignorance. I won't sleep a wink until I've read it cover to cover.

The truth is, I haven't the slightest idea how to be true to the damned truth. Is drama the better vehicle, I wonder? The ex-Soviets always adapted children's stories into little playlets that never made a bit of sense but always wound up in a great moral finale. Or maybe, porn movies are the way to go — the characters don't need to have ideas, just as long as they have cocks and cunts, and fucking is the moral of the story. All things considered, this country is not entirely unlike a pirated porn video that's gone through umpteen generations of copies and blurry from overuse, before a Greek sailor, returning from a lengthy journey, smuggled it in at great peril to himself. Besides, our story starts out pretty much like a porn movie: once upon a time, there was a woman who loved passionately, a great tragic wretch of a woman like they don't make them anymore. A woman, enchanted by the sea, by palm trees and streets and shadows in doorways, by the uninterrupted 365 days a year of sunshine and all the other familiar tunes of Cubanality (sounds like a venereal disease: *he gave her a heavy case of Cubanality and no penicillin in the world is gonna do the trick*). True or false?

As I was saying, she paid much too much attention to matters of the heart, she had a good ear for such things. Too much loving and too much listening did our heroine, no, no, scratch that, forget heroine, we've had heroes and heroines up the ass. Our protagonist, that's what she is, even if it sounds more magazinish and less like structuralist criticism. But that's the approximate truth of the matter, ladies and gentlemen, and wouldn't you rather be here than lining up for bread.

(Listen you, don't you get me started with your literary airs. First, we line up for bread, okay? Novellas and pretty poems are for the birds, all this high-flown banter does not put food on the table and can only get us in trouble . . .)

Political trouble . . .

(You said that, I didn't, so don't go laying it on me. This is me speaking, Lady Jane Cricket, your conscience, so listen closely and don't get us thrown in jail. At my age, I can't very well see myself taking up lesbian love behind bars at the New Dawn Prison for Women. How do you like that — New Dawn, indeed! Try to write without making mistakes, I don't want problems with the secret police. Be careful or you'll find yourself with every door closed to you, every single door, even the doors to the country.)

I know, those are the first to close, I know, but not the doors of the heart.

(Lord save us, child, what kind of bolero drivel is that, you better be quick and get real now. *Get off that cloud and step on down to reality.* And remember, the state is not guided by songs.)

But it's all about songs, Godmother . . .

(Shut your mouth, you half-wit, I'm not your godmother! I am your revolutionary conscience and that's all anybody knows, so drop the godmother . . . I haven't taken leave of my senses, yet! I'm nobody's godmother, do you hear, I don't bring, give, or grant wishes. Don't mix me up with that *santero* stuff! I'm not about to believe that from one day to the next they decided to go soft on it. I don't care how many reports I have to write for them — they want a report on every bloody person that comes in for a consultation. They're gonna make a writer out of me if it kills them.)

Hey! That's my line! I'm copyrighting it right now!

(Your line, my line, who cares! You, me, it's the same thing. I'm your conscience aren't I? They have me writing reports by the cart load and what do I get for all my efforts? Nothing, not even half a pencil as an offering or payment for my disinterested services . . . All they've ever given me is a free hand — rope and rope and more rope — and there I am, writing like there's no tomorrow about this and that patient, I mean client, I mean disciple . . . They'll hang me with all that rope. Did you know that they've given me the go-ahead to work in dollars, so now I also get the tourist trade. A quick session at the cowrie board has those tourists making a clean breast of their itineraries. They don't miss a single one, I'm telling you! They say that one of these days I'm going to get a medal . . . or a kick in the pants . . . Where did they ever get the idea that medals can do the trick? I'd be much happier if they pinned a pork chop on my lapel. Medals, my ass! You know what I did with my godfather's medal? I went all the way to the sanctuary in El Cobre and just like that old American fisherman, that Jemimbuey, the one who gave her his Nobel Prize medal, I offered it up to the Virgin of Charity. He knew what was what, that one. They gave him the Nobel Prize for telling about all the things he saw here and there — in Paris, in the Spanish Civil War, in the fisheries and brothels. If they only knew the half of what Xerox Machine has heard and seen, they would give her at least a thousand of those Nobels. Not to mention everything I've heard and seen, plus, it's not like I don't have a way with words — even Corin Tellado can't hold a candle to me. But I keep my lips zipped up, 'cause a closed mouth doesn't catch flies. And you should do likewise if you want to keep out of trouble.)

But it's just an innocent story, very innocent, one of those truly simple stories like the ones Marguerite Duras writes: characters going around in circles, not saying much and doing even less and the ending is exactly like the beginning. So that when they option it for the movies they can make it for a song, a song they could've spared themselves, 'cause in the end only two people will attend the screening — myself and Rufo Caballero, the last film critic on the island. And neither one of us will have purchased a ticket because we'll both have press passes. Nothing could be more innocent than what I have in mind.

(Brrrr, I feel the spirit riding me, Eleguá is at the doorstep, girl, gonna enter me any minute now! Do you have your heart set on prison or what? There are no innocent stories. Don't you ever believe that crap!)

My story is innocent, I tell you. It's a story about a woman . . .

(Oh! Sweet Mother of God! not again, not another story about a bold and daring woman, you never learn, do you!)

This woman is very calm, more peaceful than Saint Placid, a saint, whose life is turned upside down by any song she happens to hear. In her life, songs called the shots. Her fate hung on radio and TV programs, on singers, on cabarets . . .

(That's terrible! And what kind of songs did the poor wretch listen to?)

Boleros mostly.

(This gets worse and worse. So where did they bury the poor soul? Is there still room in Colón? 'Cause I'll bet my bottom dollar she must be mouldering or smoldering by now.)

No, not at all, she's alive and well and lining up for bread as we speak. So, put that in your pipe and smoke it! As I was saying earlier, this is the story of the protagonist, I emphasize, the protagonist . . .

(Don't be thick! Of course it's the story of the protagonist! Whose story do you expect it to be?)

Fine, fine! The long and short of it is this is the story of a woman who loved only one man, one lone man, which is not the same as loving a lonely man, ahem . . . Her whole life, she waited for him, whiling away the time listening to boleros. She also listened to *guarachas, sones, fílines,* and just about any kind of romantic dance music. She liked dancing well enough, but she loved the love songs best, the more grimly perverse the better. Lest you've forgotten, allow me to remind you that our protagonist is Cuban. She's not Danish or Finnish or Swiss. Even if, in order to survive here in Fairest Cuba, going Swiss (putting up an unruffled front and remaining calm while witnessing your own funeral) may not be such a bad idea. And maybe, just maybe, that's the reason I keep having the same dream over and over again. I dream I'm the inventor of a small pill that can, when ingested, transform you into a Dane or a Swede — finally make a Finn of you or turn you into a resident of one of those countries where people don't cry when they listen to boleros, and what's more, are delighted by the news of moving to distant places, far from the ones registered on their birth certificates. But that story has more to do with the schism between Doctrinaires and Apocalyptics; a story I'll probably never end up writing because I spend my days sniveling and listening to boleros. Much like our protagonist. Because this book, ladies and gentlemen, is unabashedly X-rated material for marginals, crackpots, and housewives. No, housewives won't do — Dependently Unemployed Household Monitors —that's good, it has a ring of solidarity about it. If XXL were to have a change of heart and grant me an exit visa, I'm ready to join a delegation on its way to an NGO caucus. As I was saying earlier, this is one of those stories where people swing on the draperies and scale the walls like in Humberto Solás's movie *Lucía* or better yet, in Visconti's *Senso.* It is no more and no less than I've said. So prick up your ears, dear listeners, and tune in and tune out . . .

(If you say so, but where's the escape in this tedious deluge, this humiliating lack of balls, this pap that turns the soul to mush? You may as well hand yourself over on a platter to the comrades and ass lickers!)

Shut up, Lady J., no one asked you. What do you know about living on illusions? It's a novel full of gags and gagging. At least, that's how I imagine it. The critics will have the last word anyway.

(Talk about living on illusions. Listen, precious, you know who has the last word, the very last word? The immigration officer, that's who! The fellow who won't let you exit or enter the country, depending on what side of the border you happen to find yourself.)

Anyway, it's a shaggy yarn, a romance — I couldn't help myself. Don't give me that look. I did it for . . . for . . . for the hell of it. I did it because my mother loves a romance.

Cuca Martinez pricked up her ears. She had been suffering from sporadic deafness lately, or, to put it precisely, more and more she heard only what she chose to hear. She indulged in aural hallucination, phantom sounds that could drown out real sounds, real conversations, real speeches. But this, she wanted to hear. She stuck her pinky into her ear, poked around, scratching her eardrum. No, she hadn't misheard; a sad and pretty bolero by María Teresa Vera was playing, yet again, on the radio:

> What can my love be to you
> if you have stopped loving me?
> if love past is love forgotten?
> I was your joy once but
> that was long ago.
> Now, I am your past,
> and that I cannot bear.

Cuca Martinez listens to boleros the way people do at her age, or at any age, as though every time is the first. The listening does not interrupt the chore she has come to perform with increasing love and speculative anticipation — throwing out the garbage. For her, throwing out the garbage is like attending a reception at the Spanish Embassy. Well, maybe not the Spanish Embassy — they're so stingy they don't even hand out thank-yous. Better at the French Embassy, outside which on Bastille Day a twenty-kilometer line forms for the snacks and croissants filled with ham and cheese. They've come to cheer *liberté, fraternité, egalité* so long as the queen will *let them eat cake*. They'll take her untimely *brioche* any day over a king whose diary entry for July 14, 1789, reads: *Rien à signaler* — nothing to report.

107

For Cuca Martinez throwing out the garbage is like winning the lottery. She discards pure shit and always gets a slightly better thing in return, a give-and-take made possible by the untold number of people in her neighborhood who shop on the black market or have ties to foreigners and who toss out sumptuous leftovers: bright, colorful tins, delicate candy wrappers, empty milk cartons perfect for storing spools of thread. Unattainable, forbidden fineries not covered by her coupon book. She's retired now, living on eighty pesos a month. Her neighbor, Xerox Machine, refers to the Dumpster as the gift exchange — you leave your shit and pick up someone else's, every now and then it's vaguely superior. There are neighborhoods where the garbage is of higher quality, in Miramar, for example, where there are many foreign currency diplo-shops. Which is why, in recent months, people started lining up around the Dumpsters on Fifth and Forty-second and on Fifth and Seventieth. The refuse is so good there and the crowds so large that you have to take a number; measures were taken by the Revolutionary Government in conjunction with the Ministry of Foreign Affairs and State Security Branches (I need to take a breath) and the Workers Syndicate of Cayo Cruz (Cayo Cruz is the cemetery of shit) to issue tickets and ticket vouchers through the various neighborhood Committees for the Defense of the Revolution so as to prevent disorderly public behavior and all hell from breaking loose in the lines and to ensure every citizen's right to a fair share of the dung heap, as we live, or rather belong, to a society that knows no privilege.

Luckily, in Cuca's neighborhood the garbage doesn't incite such furor, because there are no diplo-shops on her block. Still, she always manages to come home with a little something. Today, it's a bit of elastic. She snatches it quickly before someone else grabs it. She's already thinking how it'll come in handy for the underpants she's been hitching up with a couple of safety pins from the days when her daughter was still in diapers. She thinks and then, in a plaintive voice, she says:

"And to say I had him on a pedestal!"

Suddenly, the women are on her, pelting her with sticks and stones, insisting she fess up and wanting to know who it is she had on a pedestal, and what changed her mind from one minute to the next to make her topple him just like that.

"Who is it you had and no longer have on a pedestal?" the spies want to know.

"You know, you know who . . . no one . . . it's an expression."

"An expression, eh? Listen here, you delinquent bag of bones, scum of the earth, you sewer rat, you better put a leash on that tongue of yours or we'll feed it to the dogs."

She goes Swiss on them, plays the fool. Now she's whistling the "Internationale," they decide to let her be. Finally, they relent and allow her to dump her garbage. You need permission for everything here, even to shit you need a special dispensation. They give her back the plastic bag, with the Cubalse logo on it; for a year now she has used it to transport her garbage; she washes it out very carefully after each trip to the Dumpster. Everything is redeemable in this country: jar lids, plastic packaging, cartons, even coffins . . . How many times has she not dreamt of finding a bright plastic detergent container to store boiled water or to put on top of the refrigerator or the table at mealtimes as decoration. But every time she catches one out of the corner of her eye, someone else always beats her to it. Also, her daughter has scolded her for hours on end about the dangers of drinking water stored in those containers, it could make you sick, it could be toxic.

The old woman crosses the street, trying to avoid the puddles on which a rotten olive green film has settled. Now and again, she misjudges, her wooden flip-flops make a clacking sound as they splatter her stick thin legs with muck. Untroubled, she continues whistling her off-key rendition of the anthem until she gets across the street. Weeds have pushed through, cracking the cement. The roaring sea suddenly sends up a gusting wind and a thick cloud of dust races down the sidewalk. The filth of an entire century floats up above the asphalt. The women spies make a dash for doors and stairwells, shouting, cursing the Holy Mother of God and the Mother of Socialism, cursing the wrenching birth by forceps that befell this wretched island. They curse XXL and the Gods and Saints of Turbid and Limpid Olympus. Cuca Martinez doesn't even flinch. Nothing surprises her anymore. Her body blows about like a sugarcane husk, she is blinded by the sand, her hair is greasier than parchment paper on which banana chips have been left to drain. Her Cubalse plastic bag is gone, swept by the wind from her raw hands, but she presses on, looking straight before her or searching deep within her. She tries to remember what she ate yesterday. Yesterday, she ate nothing. She fed on sliced air and fried wind. Maybe today she'll fix herself a nice steak out of the old floor mop she's been marinating for fifteen days. Or maybe, she won't eat; her appetite isn't what it used to be. Every now and then, she smiles. Her varicose veins are killing her and her bunions and calluses and ingrown toenails and the lumps in the armpits that have really been bothering her lately and the annoying beadlike thing in her breast. The pebble in her boob. Could be cancer, not that she gives a hoot, it's all the same to her. At this pass in her chaotic life, it's not cancer that's going to scare her. One of these days, she'll just take herself to the Hermanos Ameijeiras Hospital, and if they haven't run out of anaesthetic, she'll have them excise the tumor, and good-bye lump. *There's a lump bouncing inside of me, rising and sinking inside of me.* Just like the song. Cuca Martinez knows that when it came to hospitals, the revolution outdid itself, building hospitals to hoodwink the people: there may be no aspirin, or inhalers for asthmatics, or cotton, or alcohol, or sheets, or dishes, or light bulbs, but as for hospitals, there are plenty. Once they even donated one to Vietnam. There were stories about our Vietnamese brethren using the sterilizing equipment to process yeast. They turned the damn place into a brewery, how about that! But you can't blame them, if anyone is to blame, it's Yankee Imperialism — good old reliable Yankee Imperialism. Come to think of it, the clinics for medical tourism never seem to run out of anything — yeah, like they're gonna run out of anything. Just goes to show how dough can be a palliative for woe and how the woe-dough syndrome got started in the first place.

She's at the intersection of M and Calzada, in front of the ghostly headquarters of U.S. Affairs — the ugliest, most insipid, and most closely watched building in the world. Scrutinized by the police and besieged by the covetous crowds who dream of consular interviews the way other people dream about the lottery. Indeed, there is a visa lottery. And if you're granted entry or a travel permit to Úrsula Sánchez Abreu (a code in the case the phone is bugged), well then — thine is the kingdom. Getting a U.S. visa is very hard, harder than freedom for Angela Davis, for whom we chanted every day at school. The sea is up in arms today, in a snarly, raging mood. Again this year, Yemayá will get more than his share of blood, he'll have to come ashore to perform his ablutions, to cleanse himself with dirt. Waves flood the horizon, lapping up the light. A salt mist rushes into the city, thrashed on by a brawling wind, wind like a veritable fury, like an evil . . . eye. Knocking off shutters and bringing down windows, frame and all. TV antennae hurtle through the sky, snagging and gashing clouds in their flight. Satellite dishes, the latest thing in blooms, give way less easily, but they too hightail it out of there, pack up like that revolution in the 1930s and the other one — or what's left of it. If there's anything left to speak of.

Cuca Martinez suddenly stops in her tracks, she looks like she's walking on a rolling mat, like Michael Jackson doing the moonwalk. She thinks she's moving forward but her legs don't budge. She's having a face-off with the wind, a confrontation, a *mano a mano.* The old woman holds her ground — *come what may I'm here to stay* . . . And the double-dealing wind counters her weak, bent form with double furor. She summons up strength from forty-year-old vitamin reserves. Those who ate well as children are not going to be bamboozled by judo kicks or karate chops or the *período especial.* Juicy steaks and Gerber compotes in the first year of life are as good as a black belt in martial arts. Something is flying at her — a leaf, a flower, a dead butterfly, a piece of beshitted toilet paper? It lands on her face, smack in her eyes. Cuca Martinez bats her lashes, the thing is still caught in her wrinkled squint. She can barely lift her hands to her face, her arm twists back at the elbow, jerked by the twister. She forces her eyes wide open, like a chicken, like an alien. The tempest suddenly stops, the sea settles, calm and hot as a bowl of soup. The sun glints like a Hatuey beer cap embedded in asphalt. Poor Chief Hatuey, that Indian has died a thousand deaths — every time a drunken boot pounds a beer cap into the asphalt. She keeps walking, *it* sits on her face like a pair of glasses. Squinching her eyes, Cuca Martinez sees that *it* filters the light and is made of some kind of paper. She makes out large and pleasing letters, but these are framed and adorned by other signs that stump her understanding of that word — *ONE* — and the language in which it's written.

She might be an old lady, but she's not that old (even though she may feel old as Methuselah sometimes) and sharp as a tack. She moves her eyes side to side and back and forth and traps the fluttering green bill as it grazes the bone that used to be her cleavage. A dollar bill! God Almighty! Sweet Miracle of Lazarus, what'll she buy herself? What'll she buy?

"How about a lollipop! No, no, no — a Coca-Cola? Oh come on! What'll XXL say if he hears I'm gaga for the drink of the enemy. Maybe . . . I'll buy a stick of butter, or maybe . . . maybe . . . Yes, why not? A small box of face powder, a compact. I haven't worn makeup in years . . ."

The flights of stairs seem endless to a woman her age. She crosses Fax, who is running down the stairs. Fax is young, not a day over twenty. She spends all her time at the Hotel Nacional — no, she's not a hustler. She's just mad, lost her mind because of those two deaths (one physical and the other mental, I'll explain it in a later chapter). And when she heard about the machines in the hotels that could communicate in seconds with the most obscure corners of the earth, she lost it even further. She claims they stole her idea, that she's the champ, the Communication Queen. She can fax up any spirit you choose to name, in no time. Excuse me, in less than no time! She has communicated with Lenin, Marx, Engels, Rosa Luxemburg — funny, all her ghosts are Communists. Maybe because of the shock treatment they give to those who have left their wits behind. She goes from hotel to hotel in search of the millionaire who will patent her project. See, she thinks that in the very near future every living being will be a Fax Medium. We can all be pen pals with Christ, Cervantes, Sor Juana Inés de la Cruz, Napoleon, Pascal, Goethe, Nijinsky, Marilyn Monroe, JFK, Saint-John Perse, Lilita, Che Guevara, James Dean, John Lennon, Marlene Dietrich: and all the other legends who have enriched or fucked up our lives.

Fax believes that in the future we'll have a brand-spanking-new society — not communism, of course, but a kind of hodgepodge, the best of commu and the tip-top of capi, a kind of commu-capi. This was communicated to her by no less than Marxy and Rosie Lux, as she calls them, as though they were brands of soap. Cuca Martinez is in too much of a hurry to want to greet the girl, but there's no getting past the girl's ecstatic hugs and kisses:

"I've just received a message from Engels . . . Capitalism is at the edge of the abyss!"

"Yeah! to get a good look at the dinosaur of socialism hitting bottom!" yells down Xerox Machine, who lives to dish the dirt.

"This is black magic speaking, this girl's possessed. There's nobody but her in this whole damn country still talking about communism, aside from XXL, who, as we all know, is *non compos* and a nincompoop."

Xerox Machine slithers down the handrail, leaving the fishy whiff and white track of her sweaty, stinky cunt behind her. In addition to being a gossip, she never wears underwear. She can afford not to, she's never had her period. When she was a girl, she went to have her tonsils removed; the nurse misread the form and they took out her ovaries. Well, periods, like underwear, are becoming more extinct and anachronistic with every passing day.

"Don't get duped by the enemy, Caruquita, sweetheart. We have no other option but option zero. Option zero in time of peace. Very soon, we'll pass through a long capitalist phase, and then we shall at last enter a Communist phase. Later, when we get tired of communism, we'll invent capi-commu. It's the law of recurring cycles. The cycle in the cycle, amen."

"Have you ever heard such nonsense in your life! She expects to live for all eternity!" Xerox was fit to be tied.

"I am not the only immortal one. The revo — *lotion* — will make us all eternal!" Fax admonishes with absolute certainty.

Cuca Martinez feels trapped by these two women, her head moves back and forth between them like a spectator in the middle of a match between Monica Seles and Steffi Graf at the French Open. The same old arguments after thirty-some years. The compulsory quarrels, the pettiness. People don't live things as they really are. They live on dreams of immortality. Even Xerox Machine, with all her pessimism, spoke in that transcendental tone, in platitudes. Everyone so ready to make decisions, so hungry for power. Finally, the aspiration of every Cuban is to be like XXL. And there's the root of all our misfortune, the obsessive need to become Martí's dream. We're all fucked by our fixation on XXL, by the malefic, hypnotic power he still has over all of us; we go to bed at night and wake up in the morning speaking of him.

"Are you hearing what I'm hearing, Cuquita? Can you believe we have to put up with a lifetime of this shit to end up with communism again? I sure fucking hope that the coming capitalist phase will last a real long time. Let God take me feet first if we're in for another dose of communism!"

"With all due respect, the conversation is very interesting, but *other parts of the earth are calling for my modest assistance . . .*" Cuca quotes what XXL reported el Che wrote in his last letter. Putting the words to good and decorous effect, Cuca opens a path for herself with her spotty, knotted hands. She climbs the stairs slowly and at long last reaches her door. The door she has opened and closed so many times in the past thirty-some years; she studies it closely. It could do with a coat of paint, a coat of oil-based white. She reaches in her bra for the key and sneaks in a touch of the folded bill. The key dances around in the lock. She hears Xerox Machine still at it:

"Poor thing, she's coming back from the Dumpsters, they almost made bean paste out of her 'cause she said something against XXL, they almost killed her . . . she didn't even flinch. Did you see that lump, Fax, sticking out of her skinny chest? Cancer must be eating her up or else she's hiding something in that disgusting bra she never washes because it's the only one she has and she doesn't want it to fray even more. Anyway, she can't even afford soap."

The door to the apartment finally opens; the streaming light blinds her. All the sunshine in the universe seems to pour itself into this narrow room at this hour of the day. Cuca Martinez goes first to the kitchen; she opens the rusted and ruined refrigerator she sometimes uses as a cupboard. In her coffee-cup-bed, Nadezhda

Common Itch, the Russian cockroach, sleeps; she is blonde and blue-eyed — the frightful heat emanating from the irreparable 1950s General Electric refrigerator has transformed her into an albino for life. The old woman nostalgically remembers the glasses of ice water she used to drink. Still, she can count herself lucky the thing worked for more than forty hard years before giving out. The Soviet refrigerator Reglita bought her didn't even last five years before going to the repair shop for intensive therapy.

The story of how the old woman and roach became friends is a complicated one that shows how hate can turn to love. At the end of the 1980s, a plague of flying cockroaches befell Havana. After turning out the lights and going to bed, Cuca would often soon wake up thirsty. Upon reaching the kitchen and switching on the light, she'd find the table and both fridges under a living carpet of cockroaches. She used every kind of poison known to man; she battled the roaches with technology, ideology, and even psychology, but they always won. Finally, she came to the conclusion that they were stronger, had more power. Faced with her inability to exterminate them, she decided she had no option but to love them. In the 1990s, the plague abated, the cockroaches disappeared. Except for one, who got stuck in the butter dish. The old woman washed her off with great care, and baptized her with a sonorous and extravagant name in honor of the Queen of the Balance Beam.

In the 1990s, there came a plague of rats. And the same battles were fought again. Cuca was about to have a heart attack (or ask to have a recycled pacemaker inserted) from chasing rats with a baseball bat and all the grief they gave her. But, lo and behold, the mysteries of the species — Nadezhda Common Itch fell hopelessly in love with a squalid, black rat, an Ethiope who returned her feelings and more. Cuca Martinez had no choice but to give her blessing to the union. On the appointed wedding day, she baptized him Juan Perez, as an homage to the one and only man of her life. The wedding was a grand affair; the bill footed by Cuca, the matron of honor. Nadezhda Common Itch went straight to the Gonzalez Coro Hospital and had herself fitted with an IUD; these weren't times to be having children. And that's how all three came to live together happily. At the beginning, it wasn't exactly easy; what with the Papayacratic Cuban Federation accusing Cuca of sheltering foreigners in her home. It didn't matter that the foreigners in question belonged to friendly peoples, to our sister eastern and African countries. Cuca had a very close shave with the secret police, she came this close to being tortured, to finding herself in the cold room at Villamarista. But just around then they authorized possession of foreign currencies and took a more lenient view of contact with tourists. And everything went back to that abnormal normality to which we've grown so accustomed.

"Are you there, Nadezhda Common Itch? It's me, Cuca. Is Perez here?"

"He's lining up for me at the grocery store. They have cabbage today. I came home to rest, my legs are killing me from the pizza line. Those slices are for you. We already had our lunch." Nadezhda takes off the scratched Karel Gott record. "Make sure you eat, Cuquita," she scolds, "you've gotten too skinny."

Good thing that Perez the Rat is standing in line, because even though she's on the Working Woman Plan (a plan whereby working women stand in a shorter line) it doesn't mean she's on the Full Belly Plan. Anyway, it's just another gimmick, sometimes the Working Women lines are longer than the lines for the Dependently Unemployed Household Monitors. And it's not because the number of working women has increased but because anyone can get a piece of paper certifying that they work in this or that office and end of story.

Cuca is not hungry, her appetite is not what it used to be. She reaches for the rust-colored Soviet radio and turns it on:

The Passion of Silvia Eugenia — the third-rate tenor voice of the announcer for the *Enemy Broadcast*, the most listened to frequency on the whole island — fills the room. Then and there, the actress begins to weep. Her lamentations, together with the occasional mumbling and yelling, last about five minutes. Cuca identifies, by inertia, and sobs along with the radio. People don't only applaud by inertia; they also do all the rest — they survive, by inertia. In tempo with her whining, Cuca introduces her knotty fingers into what was once her cleavage and pulls out the bill. A real dollar, so lovely, so green.

Yes, I think I'll buy myself a compact.

She looks past the fly shit at her face in the mirror, at the thick tracks of her brownish tears, at the grime that coats her brows, her lashes, her hair, her clothes, at the dirt she brought home from the storm.

God Almighty, I'm so old! There are warts where there used to be beauty marks, and the worst of it is that I got used to it, I don't even notice. I'm sixty-two years old and look every bit of it . . .

The room is full of mismatched furniture. Art deco chairs together with vinyl armchairs from the 1950s. The mirror is art nouveau. On the Creole-style sideboard there is a blue crystal vase in the shape of a fish, immense plastic sunflowers emerge from the gaping mouth. On the biggest wall hangs a splendid altar to Obatalá, the Virgin of Mercies. Cuca gets up from her chair and seems to float toward the altar. She raises the pearly white cloth and with the utmost respect hides the dollar bill between the goddess's thighs. She stands there fixing her hair and notices a toppled picture off to a corner of the sideboard. She picks it up carefully and wipes the glass with her sleeve. It's the bad faith picture, the hollow memento for the sake of appearances. It's a tinted photograph of XXL as a young man. It's XXL, it's *You Know Who, Ruth,* it's the Evil Sister from the Brazilian soap opera, it's That Girl, it's María Cristina:

> María Cristina wants to run my life,
> and I play, play, play along
> 'cause I don't want people to say
> María Cristina wants to run my life . . .

It's all the nicknames that everybody knows and that haven't brought him down. The old woman speaks to him in a whisper, wags a finger in reprimand:

"Don't expect me to forgive you, you SOB. I want to be very clear: if I still keep you in a gilt frame, it's because I don't want to get on the bad side of the troublemakers. Today, for the seven hundredth

117

time the bread didn't come. The milk soured in transit. The special chicken ration for the elderly and the sick has been conspicuous by its absence. If things go on like this, we will not be able to give you a revolution larger than ourselves . . . Tsk, tsk, tsk . . . Okay. I'm going to put you back on your altar, 'cause I don't want to blemish my record. We'll see if you've learned your lesson, old man . . . Nah, you'll never learn, you SOB. You make me want to spit, to push you facedown in the dirt, to dump you in the garbage. Life really sucks, 'cause in the end, you're the one who'll come out looking good in the history books. I'll come out looking like shit, like the villainess in the movie, the shrew, like La Lupe says — *they'll tell the story however they please, make everyone believe whatever they please* . . .

Cuca Martinez is pleased with herself for remembering La Lupe so clearly and with such affection. La Lupe with her honky-tonk voice and long teeth. The next instant, tears come, washing the smug expression off her face, infuriating her. She works up a good phlegmy mouthful and lands a nice glob right in the middle of XXL's phony face. All at once, there's fear all over her face, she wets the corner of a handkerchief with alcohol and makes a great to-do of cleaning the picture. On the radio, they're saying that Silvia Eugenia has to marry a man she does not love.

2

A Woman's Loneliness

At long last, the main theme of the movie *La Flor de mi Secreto* has appeared, and it is not unlike the theme of the movie I would have made from my mother's byword — loneliness.

— PEDRO ALMODÓVAR

7

An Amorous Encounter

Where is it now, our first tête-à-tête?
Remember the night when we first met?
Gone like the faded violet
In yesterday's book of memories.

By Gabriel Ruiz,
as sung by Freddy

A *YAM, LADIES AND GENTLEMEN, A YAM* — makes my mouth water just to think of one! And today, what the blazes am I to cook, today? I'll have to go soon, for a bit of foraging, go see what luck the streets will blow my way . . . who's to say I won't bump into Chicho, the clandestine greengrocer? Who's to say he won't have a small plantain or even a yam, imagine! Wouldn't that be a miracle to bump into him just when I could curl up and die, my gut so empty it gets in the way of my thinking. Like thinking ever did me any good. Chicho's prices aren't so bad, and sometimes he gives me a break. He knows that those exorbitant rural free market prices are not for me. I'd have to put down half my monthly pension for a pound of pork. So they can just skip it. Damn peddlers better stay away from me! Well, I'd better get along, see what there is to scare up; if nothing else, the walking could be a diversion, keep my mind off my belly. Nadezhda Common Itch, the sweet-tempered and thoughtful

Russian cockroach who lives with me, and Perez the Ethiop Rat are sleeping the sleep of the innocent. It's common knowledge that food can go a long way with those little critters, their digestive systems are very sluggish and they can eat just about anything. Wish the same went for me, but there isn't a single thing in that ration booklet that wouldn't turn my stomach right now, ugh! I'd rather die than touch the stuff! Still, I've got to put something in this stomach. I'm so hungry, I'm seeing double; so hungry, I'm doubled over. And so thin, I don't know what to wear. There's not a dress in the world that wouldn't end up looking like a rag. So thin I don't know where I went to. Oh, my bones are weary, I'm all out of joint, can't even find myself in this body, look at me — what a frightful, flapping mess, like a boat lost at sea.

In the blink of an eye, Cuca Martinez throws on her tatters, washes her face and limbs with a sliver of laundry soap, runs a comb through her graying locks, rubs a drop of violet water behind each ear. She remembers the friend who many years ago had warned her against violet scents, telling her they drove men off. Well, her man had certainly cleared out beyond yonder — all men, for that matter. She unhooks her errand bag from the latch where it hangs behind the door. Before leaving, she writes her beloved animal friends a note. She wouldn't want them worrying for her; they're so good-hearted, so noble, so loyal. Just the other day, she sat telling them how she wanted to sign the apartment over to them, so that in the event of her demise the urban reform would not turn them out on the street. They were her real family, when all was said and done. And Fala and Fana, of course, how could she forget them; I mean La Mechu and La Puchu, no slouches in times of trouble. And yes, the Girl.

The building appears deserted, silent as a tomb, which is unusual in a place where blaring televisions and radios are the main and most apparent signs of life, a reliable index of demographic explosions even. In the twinkling of an eye, she reaches the end of the corridor and starts her descent down the stairwell; she doesn't see any lights (candlelight) coming from her friends' apartment. She emerges into the midday sun and gives up her tired body to its blinding warmth. A white intensity pulses everywhere outside. She walks in search of shade, but almost every doorway she comes to is a crumbling ruin, sunlight spilling through the gaps where columns once stood. She turns down Calla Línea in the direction of the sea; a large crowd seems to be moving from somewhere near the Hotel Nacional toward the wall of the Malecón. It couldn't be the May Day parade because there are still two months to go. People are dressed in funny clothes, like extras in a movie on the French Riviera, like guests at the Cannes Film Festival. They're wearing veils and feathers, turbans and straw hats, jewels in their cleavages and wigs. Cuca rubs her eyes, wondering if her hunger is responsible for these absurdities. On top of the fake *green how I love you green* lawn, which couldn't look more like plastic, tables have been set up, spread with lacy white tablecloths, paper imitations of the elaborate embroideries of Bruges. Spotless plates rival the impeccable whiteness of the waiters' jackets. White seems to rule the day. Cuca Martinez expects blood. Because wherever there's an excess of purity, violence is sure to follow. But no. The rich, we're talking millionaire rich, are lording and boozing it up like ancient Romans. Saliva trickles out of Cuca's mouth and she suffers a mild vertigo, preceded by rumblings from a digestive tract that is emptier than a stadium in a downpour. Wealthy tourists and wealthy party bureaucrats are living it up in their colorful party hats, their gaudy Lycra outfits, their starched guayaberas and their pink palm tree–printed shirts. On the wall of the Malecón, a thousand spectators bake in the eternal summer sun and look on like Cuca in a stupor of hunger and thirst and heat. Our kind of heat, giving us the feeling that here days are more profound, more intense, more tiring, and supremely histrionic. Cuca walks slowly, for fear of slipping and breaking her hip. She approaches a fellow gawker and asks:

"Tell me, sweetie, am I having fantastic visions?"

"No, Granny, not visions, fantastic divisions. I thought I was seeing things, too, but they're holding a speedboat race, a world championship for people with tons of money . . . I only came for the food. I wanted to see what they'd be eating, to see in order not to forget."

Cuca wanders off, veering this way and that like a Barbie on rollerblades, strangely coquettish in an old lady kind of way. The avenue is crawling with the well-to-do. Not even before this, our era, the era that birthed a heart (as the song says), had she seen so many millionaires in one place. The hill, where the Hotel Nacional nestles, doubles as a tribune overlooking the Malecón. Size Extra Extra Large, in his vomit greens, smiles yet again, contorting his mouth like a dimwit or someone whose brain has gone softer than a soft coconut from arteriosclerosis. One could venture (or misventure) that there's no happiness like his, that he's within range of Paradise (or his demise). He's surrounded by foreign impresarios and members of the triumphant team from the Arab Emirates. Cuca's stomach churns its juices as she squints at platters of nicely roasted chicken making the rounds in the tribune. XXL suddenly bolts to his feet, exits amid applause, his own and that of others, and gets into his Mercedes for a little spin around what he denominates as *the glorious, triumphant quarter of the Malecón,* where, he informs us in his raspy voice, once again we gave Yankee Imperialism another lesson, won another Battle for the proletariat, and defeated the fifth columnists (a 1960s expression that he stole from his little sister Chinese Rosa) in the murky events of August '94. It makes my skin crawl to hear myself described as the proletariat by politicians. Eventually, one of those millionaires, who can't get it on with his honey without first impersonating Julio Iglesias to a particular karaoke number, rises to his feet, raising a can of Coca-Cola in a toast to the comedian in chief, I mean Maria Christina, I mean you know who. Autographs fly out of XXL's hand and into the hands of the clamoring crowd. A check in the amount of twenty-five thousand dollars is donated to the children of Cuba, which means that each child, if they allot it fairly, would end up getting a piddling half dollar. I love millionaires, the splendor of them, the way they spend all their days pining for their coffers. Cheers and half-remembered hymns soar in memory of Che, whom they clearly don't remember well at all. And then, as usual, someone requests the favorite conscience-cleansing anthem of the well-heeled — you've guessed it, the same old, same old: *The pure and cherished clarity of your dearly beloved presence shall remain with us, Commandant Che Guevara.* Overexposure has made me allergic to that Carlos Puebla tune. Finally, and to no one's surprise, XXL is disposed to impose a speech on all present. His reputation as orator and demented ranter is universally acknowledged. Before long, he begins amorously to stroke his right breast pocket, and a thousand white doves take off in mass flight; then he starts fiddling with his left pocket, but nothing happens this time. He's fidgeting in earnest now, trying to get the special pen to release its precise frequency — audible only to doves — and trigger the small contraption that has been fastened to a dove's leg and that will steer it, in a bit of technological rather than supernatural wizardry, to touch down on XXL's shoulder. This shoddy mechanism was inaugurated in the early days of the revo, when the whole world took it as a sign from the beyond pointing to XXL as the chosen one, when, in fact, he was none other than the reincarnation of the same character who years earlier had kidnapped Fangio, the Argentine race car driver, on orders from the 26th of July Movement. Maria Christina, I mean XXL, keeps fiddling with his left pocket, but instead of lighting on his shoulder, the dove flits by and thumps a stream of shit down his face all the way to his graying beard. There isn't even the hint of a titter, because our historico-magico legacy is the one thing we never joke about. The luminaries on the podium are all thinking bad omen, but not a one of them is laughing. A dread hush spreads through the crowd. Only his disaffected and impotent voice (not just the voice), with its intermittent squawk, can be heard coursing from loudspeaker to loudspeaker through the streets of Havana. He begins by citing every economic statistic in the book, beginning with the year one and bringing us up to the glorious pres-ent of the *período especial;* he stresses the importance of sacrifice in these times of crisis and economic reform, when the ex-socialist camp blah, blah, blah, and again, he bad-mouths the Russians. Our glorious nation will resist to the bitter end, and even when not a soul is left standing, it will continue to resist, and we shall turn the very bones of our dead into . . . and he loses his train of thought. We shall turn the very bones of our dead into . . . and he looks this way and that for assistance and comes up empty-handed. What, what shall become of the bones of our dead? The crowd is rapt, attentive to the last cuticle, deeply concerned for the tragic fate and uncertain outcome that may be awaiting our femurs, tibias, and fibulas, our tailbones and funny bones, our shin and collarbones, our craniums, our spines—very concerned, in short, for our osteodestinies. Finally, he snaps his thumb and middle finger, a sign that the solution is at hand. We shall turn the very bones of our dead into a giant marimba on which to play our glorious national anthem. A collective sigh of relief drowns out the waves crashing against the wall of the Malecón. A musical instrument, thank goodness. It could've been worse: he could've just as easily donated our internationalist carcasses to a museum of natural history, or shipped us off as rattles for the amusement of lion cubs in a European zoo or fashioned us into earrings to be exported to a world fair for new inventions. He stresses the necessity for increased ideological work and renewed revolutionary consciousness and a strengthened spirit of struggle to put an end to corruption and to rout the bloodied jaw of the imperialist Yankee foe, and he reminds us how proud we should be to live in the *período especial,* because our heroism has made us greater revolutionaries, has made us stronger and more free . . . The rich people can't make head nor tails of what he's saying and keep toasting him with Dom Pérignon. We are stronger, he repeats, and a roar goes through the crowd, and someone yells for help and a stretcher for an old lady who just collapsed . . .

La Puchu and La Mechu, caked in a milky sweat (the habit of powdering one's body from head to toe is hard to lose, and pulverized eggshells almost do the trick; and in these times, when the evil eye is on the loose, each one clenches a fleshy palm frond in her right hand), turn their attention to the crushing melee around the old lady who just keeled over. Next to them, also baking in the sun, are Fax and Xerox Machine. Xerox Machine chews on a piece of gum she managed to intercept before it hit the ground after some bigwig on the tribune spat it out. Fax is feeling extremely perplexed; she's completely stumped by the goings-on; none of this mumbo jumbo has anything to do with the new brand of communism being communicated to her at that very instant by the infinitesimally small mummy of Vladimir Ilyich. So, she decides to make contact, tele-pathic of course, with Nikita Khrushchev, but she misdials the area code and gets the purgatorial headquarters of JFK. The president, not the airport, who didn't have a stupid bone in his body and whose jaw, if you look closely, is exactly like Clinton's. While he advises and opines, Fax listens pleased as punch, delighted to be engaged with Nikita himself. But when it's time to say good-bye, she real-izes she's been talking to the assassinated ex-president of the USA and falls into an epileptic swoon and her brain swivels 180 degrees in favor of capitalism. Together with Cuca Martinez, she is ur-gently carried off to the Hermanos Ameijeiras Hospital by a State (of putrefaction) Security agent, who orders, not mouth-to-mouth resuscitation or aspirin or a wad of alcohol-soaked cotton wedged beneath the nostrils, but a double round of electroshock for the pair of them. The doctor almost carries out the good agent's bidding, not out of professional conviction, but because electroshock is all he has to offer. It's a good thing La Mechu, La Puchu, and Xerox Machine are on hand to follow longingly the copper's ciga-rette (oh, to cop a puff!) as he moves toward the exit, and to con-vince the kind doctor that what the old lady really needs is a crust of bread, a sip of sugared water, that her problem is that her stom-ach is cleaved to her spine and emptier than an Olympic-size pool in a downpour. They hasten to assure him he need not worry with the young one, they'll take care of her. And the minute he goes off in search of chicken broth and a bit of bread, Xerox Machine jumps up onto the stretcher, squats with lifted skirt, and exhales through her cunt, right up Fax's nose. Fax comes to life in a haze of rotting squid, hailing Rockefeller. Then she sees Cuca all laid out on a stretcher, bluer than a cadaver in a Siberian camp, and screams bloody murder:

"They've killed her! To hell with communism! They've killed her!"

Xerox Machine plugs up her mouth with the chewing gum, while La Mechu and La Puchu restrain her by the arms and legs. Fearing the worst, they do what they can to calm her, speaking in soothing voices and admonishing her in whispers to:

"Think what you like but watch what you broadcast!"

She opens her eyes wider than a madwoman and sobs as she howls:

"Long Live XXL! Socialism or Death!"

The doctor couldn't turn up any bread, but he hands them a grimy plastic glass of water into which a spoonful of sugar swept up from the refinery floors, the same sugar they sell by the coupon book, has been stirred. Semi-comatose patients on other cots are being solicited by black marketeers offering a wider selection than a Wal-Mart in Miami or a Carrefour in France: chocolate ice cream by the pint and boxes of fake Cohibas or Montecristos and potatoes stuffed with rat or cat meat. A woman, just out of surgery, holds her wound and screeches:

"A painkiller, somebody, bring me a painkiller!"

The lady in the adjoining bed explains that she's just had a growth removed with a new Chinese method that induces amnesia in lieu of anesthesia.

"Could anyone spare a painkiller?" The embarrassed doctor addresses himself to the patients and their visitors.

Cuca Martinez drinks up her tonic and feels much restored. She digs around in her bag and comes up with a Dipirona, purchased in the 1980s. It's somewhat yellowed, but it should still work. The woman takes the pill and swallows it as if it were the flesh and sinew of the risen Christ. With blessings aplenty, Fax, Xerox Machine, Cuca, La Puchu, and La Mechu thank the doctor for his first-rate first aid and begin to take their leave only to find themselves in a blind alley, blocked by Mister State Security. Once he's made the most of his rank as an official bully and intimidated them to his satisfaction, he steps aside in a mockery of courtesy and bids them to the door. But before leaving them in peace, if without prosperity, he jumps on Xerox Machine, who's the last to exit, and inserting his hand beneath her skirt like a libidinous devil, he sticks his finger in her crack. His aim is not to misuse her as a female but to ensure she hasn't made off with a medical instrument or a bottle of medication nestled inside her twat to resell at some later date. Xerox Machine doesn't even make a peep; she knows full well that she's deposited a wicked strain of syphilis (eradicated from the island, according to our glorious statistics) on his fingertip.

The Five Musketeers find themselves in the now desolate avenue. The festivities are over, the tribune dismantled, and there's not a soul in sight, but signs of the banquet are everywhere in the flashing heaps of plastic cups and paper plates that have been not scraped but gnawed clean. They cross to the other side of the wall and sit with their backs to the city to look at the pale sea, which even now is overwhelmingly beautiful and vast. They pay their silent respects to those who disappeared. There isn't a person in this entire country who doesn't have someone who left on a raft. Fax weeps: she's inconsolable, confused. Feelings she's kept under lock and key for an entire lifetime emerge. People begin to gather at the wall. Our weakness for gossip is no secret, and people are coming, dribbling in to form an impromptu audience to listen to her story. There's Hernia, who lives on the ground floor and whose house has been turned by the sea and other misfortunes into a ruin with a rocky floor and spiky reefs and stalagmites and brilliant stalactites overhead and walls soft with algae and moss. There she comes draggling her misery. And there's Yocandra with her two husbands, come to see what the tearful commotion is about; everyone knows that two-bit intellectual fucks like a mule and shares her bed with two men — or maybe they rotate — but hey, if she wants to pass her ass around like a drum and give it to the best drummer, I say more power to her. The other neighbors in the building are joining in, and gradually the whole neighborhood shows up. Then they start coming from the municipality and from the surrounding provinces and from the whole county and the city outskirts and adjoining rural areas, until the entire island has come to stand by the wall of the Malecón to hear the sad, sad story Fax has to tell.

As it so happens, Fax had a brother and a lover. Needless to say, she loved them both to distraction. When her brother and lover decided not to enroll at the university, where their only options were to study construction and veterinary teaching, they were, naturally, automatically drafted by the army. So they decided to give it a whirl; after all, they didn't have much choice. And one morning, they got

129

again allowed him to speak his piece while they whistled and fixed their eyes on a spot somewhere behind him and above his head. In all honesty, they had shown extraordinary patience, remarkable for men so unfamiliar with such sentimental stuff and nonsense. Show me a soldier who is. They refuted every argument. His friend was the guilty party and that was that. But wouldn't there be a hearing, a chance for the defense? No, no . . . it was an open-and-shut case, and now, it was closed. Fax's brother pulled out his gun and aimed it at the big guns. He would bury the lot of them first. Just like that, he lost it; you could say he was hot-tempered, choleric. There were too many of them against him; there was a struggle, and they eventually managed to disarm him. They tied him up and tossed him in the back of a truck; they stuffed a typewritten note in his breast pocket that diagnosed him as a dangerous maniac. The truck took a while to get started; it wasn't a very good truck because of all the potholes, boulders, and surprise attacks on the roadways. Ten minutes after they took off, he heard the sound of gunfire and a brief, childish cry. The cry that would send him forever beyond the pale, the death cry of his blameless friend.

They moved him from unit to unit, hospital to hospital, town to town, until they forgot the reasons why they had brought him there in the first place. He didn't utter a word. He pretended he had lost track of reality, of his mind even, though he was really only half lost. They came up with a new diagnosis — total amnesia — and he was returned to Havana posthaste. A Lada, ministerial blue with white license plates, delivered him to his family — a sick man bedecked in medals and weighted down with certificates of valor attesting to his bravery as an internationalist warrior. When they were finally alone, Fax knelt before him and asked like one who already knows:

"They killed him, didn't they?" She meant her beloved.

He closed his eyes in acknowledgment; when he opened them and looked up at the ceiling, tears streamed down his cheeks, rolling past the throbbing veins in his neck. She spent a week sobbing inside the armoire. She didn't eat a thing and even stopped answering nature's call. I'm not kidding, her insides went on a long silent lament that would leave them scarred forever. He didn't go back to work. In time, he became a professional turn keeper in the line that formed outside the Centro Market (in the days when you could still go with Cuban pesos and queue up for weeks and months to shop at the famous food store). He helped to keep order in the line; he saved and sold places and made more money in this semilegal way than any state employee. The hours, long and round-the-clock, were a kind of solution for his insomnia, the sleepless nights he spent tossing and turning and unable to forget. All was going very smoothly until the early morning police roundup that pulled professional turn keepers out of the queue to trundle them off in a paddy wagon packed to capacity. Before the van had even reached the jail, they had already registered the detainees, confiscated all ID's and seized everything down to pocket combs. As bad luck would have it, Fax's brother was found holding a suspicious bill, an enemy bill smeared in blood, not the glorious blood of martyrs that laps the island's every shore, but menstrual fluid from the prostitute who had changed his pesos for the bills she kept hidden between the meaty lips of her pubis. A dollar bill, in short, infected with candidiasis and reeking of period. His first black market dollar, which must have run him a mere fifteen pesos at the time and for which he would be sent up for a mere fifteen years. In the end, they reduced it to five for good conduct. I won't luxuriate in the details of his incarceration, the tortures and humiliations he was subjected to — atrocity makes me squeamish. Suffice it to say that he emerged from the tank with a long seam across his cheek à la Scarface, Al Pacino style, as well as 165 traumas occasioned by repeated rapes. Fax ended up in a clinic and in the hands of a psychiatrist who determined that her madness, her loss of faith, identity crisis, and ideological confusion could only be taken on with electroshock and plenty of it. They stormed her with round-the-clock electric zaps to the brain and up the ass, and good-bye capitalist melancholy. The poor girl went completely haywire by the time she got out of there, thinking she was an appliance, a new electronic invention — a Communist fax machine. This condition persisted until the fateful dialing error that hooked her up to Jayef-kay instead of Khrushchev and all hell broke loose in her subconscious.

She was transformed into a fax with liberal or left-of-center tendencies, or whatever the right term is these days for such left-handed, ambidextrous politics, which I bet even Konstantine (of pamphlet fame), if we were to resuscitate him, wouldn't know.

And in this way, and mighty the worse for wear, our dear Fax ends her public auto-psychoanalysis. An entire nation grieves, openly wailing by the wall of the Malecón, the wall of lamentations. Before they know it, the raspy, abrasive voice of XXL is upon them again, announcing that the ban on Carnival has been lifted. This doesn't come as much of a surprise, everybody knows that firing squads and carnivals go together. Mutually apt diversions. And then, as soon as people are drunk and past all recollection, they will again prohibit pageantry and conga lines. Our forgetfulness could floor you, and when our already feeble cells are further impaired by home-made rum and barrel beer, which we soak up like there's no tomorrow so that we need to pee then and there, we pass our memory together with our kidney stones and when we can't flush it down (because of water cuts) we wash it down with the handy water bucket, if we haven't spilled it in our inebriation. This is our fate, our cross to bear. And before you know it, tears are dry and Fax's tragic tale has become a conga lyric and an entire nation dances off, tagging behind the Building-works Float and escorting the Scorpion Players.

Only the aforementioned few who live in the building stay behind; the others are off shimmying and drumming their memory into oblivion. La Mechu and La Puchu along with Xerox Machine are trying to keep Fax, who has succumbed to a violent epileptic seizure, from swallowing her tongue. It's already evening and Cuca Martinez cocks an ear to better hear the odd drone coming from on high, as if someone had motorized the moon. She raises her eyes and sees an airplane twinkle by, followed by a white wake in the darkened sky. And as always, when she spots a plane, which is almost never, she harbors a hope for the long-awaited return of her beloved man. Her savior, her destroyer. She has a sudden urge to preen and thinks she must absolutely, by hook or by crook, get herself some teeth and touch up her graying hair with gentian violet — or tincture of iodine, or Mercurochrome, maybe buy herself a compact with the dollar bill that is still hidden under the mantle of the Virgin of Mercies. These thoughts leave her mind as quickly as they came. She pulls a crocheted handkerchief from between her breasts and mops up the sweat on Fax's brow. And she's suddenly moved to sing in a contralto clear as Clara's, the Clara from Clara and Mario, the famous duo who perform on *Together at Nine,* the TV program hosted by Eva Rodríguez and Héctor Fraga, or in earlier, happier days on *Buenas Tardes* with Mirta and Rául:

> Only the sea, true mirror of my heart,
> knows the tears I shed
> on your treacherous love . . .

She studies the immensity of the sky, and a cloud swallows the plane. The lump in her tit throbs like a streetlight on the blink; she thinks it must be a sign of rain or good news or bad. She pokes around in her bag, comes up with a small bottle of home brew, and tosses back a couple. She offers it around and is gladly taken up. A fellow approaches proffering lines, pick-me-up not pick-up, cocaine for dollars, as though it were business as usual. When no one pays him any mind, he quietly disappears into a white Nissan full of whores of both sexes and progressive Italians. The women cross the avenue, moving toward Rampa; the young one still chilled and shuddering, clacking her jaw like a castanet. They've walked no more than a handful of blocks and are near the Yara Cinema when Xerox Machine is intercepted by a man with extravagantly long, bleached ringlets à la Shirley Temple.

"Xerox? Is that you? My, you've gotten skinny! What's the matter darling? You look terrible!"

"Well, well, if it ain't the Bureau with Ringlets! How you doin? Wow! you look swell. And where in God's name did you get the peroxide? I can't even remember the last time I got my hands on the stuff. Look at this matty mess, five-inch roots and show me the iron that's going to keep these hackles down! The hairdressers have gone out of business in despair. Who's your supplier, you better tell me, Bureau with Ringlets." 'Cause that was the nickname everyone knew him by, this hip functionary with a hoop in his ear and the mannerisms to go with it and a cutting-edge apparatus piping music into his ears that must have cost someone a whole commissary full of foodstuffs.

"I got it at the Union of Cuban Artists and Writers outlet, let me tell you that shipment disappeared in a flash. They had a couple of bottles of peroxide, three jars of deodorant, you know the cake kind, a bag of rollers, five boxes of talcum powder, and tons of post-cards of a painting of Bone Apart from the Napoleonic Collection. There was no paper and no ribbon, the typing not tying kind — not that we'll be getting new typewriters anytime soon. They've been glaringly absent. Anyway, tell me, tell me about yourself, darling. What's your news? Just the legal stuff, now! And who are your friends? Oh, but the pleasure is all mine. Yes, Bureau with Ringlets. I work for an INSTITUTE," he says, caressing the word and so impressed with himself. "Xerox and I have known each other since the beginning of time, from our days at the Academy of Sciences. Remember, when we had to cross the black mosquitoes with the red ones and those red racist vermin just wouldn't go for it!"

Cuca Martinez is so disgusted she's gagging; she takes a deep breath and holds it, waits for the feeling to pass. La Mechu and La Puchu are settled on the stoop, facing the cinema; Fax is propped up between them. They're both holding on to her for fear she will faint and sneaking in a feel every now and again; they may be old but they're not indifferent. The Bureau with Ringlets is still gesticulating, big as you please, like a fly swatter glimpsed in a box at La Scala during a performance by the Peking Opera, and producing one juicy bit of gossip after the next. Finally, he unkindly asks them if they have plans for the tedious hours that lie ahead.

"We're going home to watch the Saturday night movie, the one on Omnivideo," Xerox answers him.

"Girls! girls! how utterly boring! I won't allow it! You're coming with me to my friend's. Believe it or not, he, too, is called Omnivideo, and every Saturday night, he organizes fabulous extravaganzas that put Carlos Otero to shame. They're the hottest thing in town, marvelous transvestite soirees like you've never seen. An

136

absolute must-see! You'll have loads of fun; you must come, you just have to come to the Hoi Polloi. The cover charge is ten dollars, but tonight you'll be my guests. It's the latest thing, girls! Forget the Tropicana! Even tourists don't go there anymore, so passé, with those overweight mulattas in their fishnets full of holes! The horror! We've stolen the swankiest clientele in town, you'll see. There's even a runway number for transvestite fashions. You just have to see it. And don't worry about the police, they half look the other way; after all, we have to promote ourselves to the outside."

"Where, outside?" Cuca asks, thinking of an outdoor patio.

"Over there, girl, in the great U. S. of A. We're going to do like Sotomayor, put our country on the map, with or without a pole, we're going to set some world records around here."

"And what do you mean, they half look the other way? Is it semishadowy?"

"Come on, Grandma, enough with the questions. I don't know what I mean and I don't care. The only important thing here is not to die, to catch the flow and ride the wave, okay?"

The Five Horsewomen of the Apocalypse roundly refuse but find themselves reluctantly accepting before such insistence. It's true that they're not particularly thrilled at the thought of spending another mind-numbing Saturday night watching the feature on Channel Six — twenty-four buckets of blood per second flooding the screen. Fax, whose antennae are picking up new social democratic whisperings, thinks of the promising networking possibilities the evening may bring. Who knows? By evening's end, she may walk out with a six-figure contract to write her autobiography for an American publishing house. She may even feel inspired to open her own semilicensed family restaurant, one of those *Paladars* that are just about impossible to run given the exorbitant taxes. The important thing is to make money any which way, and she's already cooking up a scheme for tax evasion. For their part, La Mechu and La Puchu would give anything, their large and small intestines as well as their fallopian tubes, to have their old lives back — with all the romance and cabaret outings and orgies, their diddlies have been buzzing for months. Xerox Machine needs to have another go at it, give the old reproductive system one more chance, despite the missing ovaries and her nonexistent periods. For years now, she's had to put up with a minor but annoying problem — a jack-in-the-box that pops out of her vagina each time she opens her legs. More than once she's been slapped around by fellows who thought she was mocking their prowess. And slapped around is the least of it. At one time, she was in love with an intellectual, an essayist with a dinky dick who was an agent for Internal Affairs. She couldn't bring herself to do it with him, go all the way I mean; she knew what was coming, and sure enough, it was exactly as she had anticipated: she opened her legs and out popped the clown, standing a full head taller than the intellectual's minuscule member. It is still a mystery why, on that same afternoon, the militant masses came to jerk her by the hair and drive her from her house with blows and kicks to the tits. They shipped her off with a group of Jehovah's Witnesses, delinquents, and homosexuals to a forced labor camp. Of course, all this happened a long time ago, in the years of her youth. No one seems to understand that she can't help it if a clown burgeons from her clit — it's her unfortunate nature is all. The Bureau with Ringlets promises them a good time, assuring them that plenty of curious heteros turn up at these homo happenings, and that they are often more than happy euphorically to forget themselves in the arms of the so-called riffraff. Cuca Martinez gapes at the heavens and a twinkling plane again catches her eye. At any rate, there's nothing normal about so many planes in the sky all of a sudden, so many flashing lights, and so as to distract herself from her aeronautical fixation, she accepts the invitation to go to the Hoi Polloi.

The semiclandestine nightclub is directly opposite the Colón Cemetery. This does not bode well with Cuca Martinez, who has always shown the utmost respect, not to say servility, toward the dead and who always remembers to leave small vases of white blooms on the ledge and frosted crystal glasses filled with water to placate the spirits on high so they won't make a hash of her life, soy yogurt out of everything. Omnivideo, their host, is a builder of tombstones, unlicensed, of course, and because marble is scarce, he pays a gang of thieves to go and steal his old handiwork. At night, he smooths the stone, polishing off the name of the deceased, and tomorrow is a new day with its new dead and tombstones and floral urns.

The Hoi Polloi proved an exotic sight, indeed. A transvestite fluttered by in blowsy finery; she had made up her face with chicken shit, thickened her lashes with broom cuttings, and then brushed the lot with shoe polish; extended her nails with melted toothbrushes, and donned a wig she bought off a hairdresser at the National Institute for Radio and Television (and which had once belonged to Mirta Medina, a variety singer who managed to splash her way from Mexico to Miami, where she now resides). The month's growth on her face, because of the razor blade shortage, has earned her the name of bearded lady, and her sweeping tutu once belonged to Alicia Alonso, who traded it for a picnic ham for a clandestine Christmas dinner — the transvestite still had country connections in the sleepy town of San Tranquilino in Pinar del Río, where she was born and raised. Foregoing all niceties, she launches into a recital drawn from a repertoire of her making, but it's the finale that has everyone on the edge of their seats in anticipation; they're all waiting for the last song, the one that sends gay audiences through the roof, her signature song, the one she named herself after. Her name used to be Profirio Esmenegildo Barranco, and you can understand that with such a hick mouthful she could have kissed stardom good-bye. Now, both she and the song are known as Paloma Pantera, the Panther Dove. Among the hundred or so people who have huddled into the room to be utterly riveted by her make-believe tits fashioned from today's crumpled edition of *Granma* are Argolla, Laca, and Arete, members of the selection committee for the international festival of the old latin american cinema (I expressly left out the capital letters because they're apparently carcinogenic when used to excess). The handicapped queens, Optical Neuropathy and Peripheral Neuropathy, one blind and the other maimed because of historical malnutrition and bathtub rum, are also present. The Red Witch (a dyed-in-the-wool queen who is a cross between Little Red Riding Hood, the Big Bad Wolf, and the Witch from Snow White, and who before becoming a censor and opportunist used to seduce draftees and recruits so she could then build her dossier by denouncing them) is here with his wife (yes, he's married, a queen who married for the form), Leonarda da Vinci, who got her name for all the times she beat her husband to a pulp and landed him in the hospital when he failed to bring home a prize — any prize: a Coral Award, a Sunflower, a Sickle and Hammer, or even a measly Perlana, which is nothing more than a penis wrapped in wool. The other VIPs include His Ex-Superfluous Excellency, yes, you read correctly, the ex-National Lyrical Pansy Ass of Latin American Cinema. What is a lyrical pansy ass, you'll want to know? Well, it's just what it sounds like — a dreamy ass redolent of pansies. (The image is even more hermetic than a Yale lock, I know.) But they don't even want him anymore now that a whole new generation of pansy asses has cropped up. Also present, as though it were possible to overlook them, are Desequilibrium Crespo, the Cubo-Venezuelo-Hungarian film producer, and Francaspa, the enthusiast of Cuban Imperfect Anti-Cinema and chronic chewer of gum, and his wife, Lila Escuela Medieval, as well as the very well known Abad Tamaño, who is both the right hand and the left hand of all ecologically correct, that is green, international film festivals. And Toti Lamarque and Tita Legran do, harrowed and harrowing, with all that squandered brilliance and those scarves wound about their necks; they are advisors to the Green Cinema guy. Legion of False Honor, of lowly origins and dentist of choice to the intelligentsia; Automatic Answering Machine, who mistook the virtuoso pianist Excelso for the minister of the interior; Loreto the Magnificent, duplicator of preconceived ideas; the Bowwow Lady, who is completely unaffiliated and whose only claim to fame is embezzlement of several United States banks, extortion of retirement savings from countless elderly residents of Miami, and depleting the budgets of numerous museums (including Bellas Artes); she has been circulating incognito to this day, always accompanied by her lawyer and Janet Jackson look-alike Pelvic Thrust and by the president of Egremonía, the slow-witted Memerto Remando Betamax. (Egremonía is a recording label that spins out fast-food muffins, the stale kind that are layered with potato cheese and slapped straight on the grill.) In short, what we have here is a gathering of the swill. The flotsam and jetsam. Our legendary national dump, Cayo Cruz, in flesh and blood. Well, there might be the odd exception — maybe it's not as bad as I make it, there must also be many worthy people in attendance. To flesh out the guest list, I have relied on the erudite collaboration of the translator, author, and retired journalist Paul Culón, who is responsible for translating the works of Madonna Perón, Vil Ma Espónte, XXL, Gorby and Larissa, Maggie Thatch, Menem Talc, Polvo Escobar, and Volcano Fujimori into Esperanto. He has also collaborated on the song "Heroes for a Troubled World" and appeared as butter in *Last Tango in Paris* with Marlon Brando and Maria Schneider. He is personal friends with the picture of Che, the one that started reappearing on European T-shirts this summer. The place is crawling with ambassadors and cultural attachés from friendly and unfriendly nations, on the lookout for young flesh or dissidents to enliven their champagne-sodden evenings. The fan flares wide, as you can see, so wide-splayed there's no room for it to oscillate, hence to ventilate. The place is hotter than hell, hotter even than the deserted hall at Casa de las Americas, when they bestow their biannual Sahara Poetry Prize that always comes up barren.

Paloma Pantera finishes her recital and the room erupts in applause and flames; a length of tulle has caught on one of the candles lit for the saints and because of the blackout. It takes numerous jugs of water, but they finally manage to put out the fire. In the meantime, the lights come back on, and the whole neighborhood breathes a sigh of relief. Paloma Pantera, the Panther Dove, who has back-to-back performances all evening (she's expected at the Cercle Français and later at Eddy and Rey's Literary Paladar) rushes to take off the horrible makeup that has made her face into a Mexican mask. Then, I-and-me-and-me-and-I, choreographer of Germanic folk dances, anthropologist, and witch, plugs in his cassette/compact disc player and puts on a rap song to the delight of the hip local constructivists.

Cuca Martinez perches on the balcony and rocks back and forth in a lawn chair, an aluminum frame with a back and seat woven out of the plastic tubing used for hospital IVs. Her eyes are glued to the sky; she waits for an airplane to appear. If the Cuban sky is beautiful by day, then picture it at night — with the freshness and the perfect circle of the moon, so whorish and inaccessible and dangling her imaginary earrings like in the bolero by Vicentico Valdés, immortalizing her for the umpteenth time: *I have kept them for you, the moon's missing earrings, to make a necklace for you* . . . Tis not a night of pitch and dark. And yet, the sky is black as ebony, black yet sheathed in blue — thanks to Placid Phoebe and a bounty of stars. Cuca Martinez cannot believe her bleary eyes, up there on the moon, *moon, moon, blue moon,* the Sullen Skunk, disguised as a rabbit, looks over the galleys of the French translation of *The Color of Summer.* The vacant streets below, void of people and cars and light, resemble segments for a model of a labyrinth. The negligible movement on the street is not surprising, and not just because of the cemetery, but also there's no transportation to speak of and sudden blackouts predominate. Trees stand between us and the smaller labyrinth, the one formed by the cemetery and ensconced in the larger labyrinth of the living. The cupolas are mixed in with the tombs like small abandoned palaces or modern mausoleums for the heroic dead. The old lady views this place, which she avoids on principle, with a grimace. Her stomach is acting up again, she feels the knot in her gut and hunger feeding off her ulcer. She dreamily recalls a meal from the olden days; yes, a dish of meatballs à la Milanese would sure hit the spot, suit her to a *T,* and easy as pie, God bless us! All it takes is two pounds of ground beef, half a pound of ground pork, a quarter pound of minced ham, a quarter pound of Patagras cheese, two tablespoons of finely chopped onions, a clove of garlic, three-quarters of a cup of bread crumbs, a quarter cup of milk, two eggs, a quarter cup of flour, and a third of a cup of oil. First, you prepare the sauce, cooking the tomatoes with onions and bay leaf, a drop of white wine, a pinch of sugar, and salt and pepper. Then you shape the balls, dredge them in flour and fry them in hot oil until they're golden. Brown the finely chopped onion separately, then add it to the sauce. Mix everything in a pot and simmer covered for twenty-five minutes. Then, you can tell me about delicious! This dish will disorder your senses, leave your taste buds in disarray.

"Yoohoo, Grandma, wake up . . ." It's Bureau with Ringlets carrying a steamy mess on a platter. "Won't you try these meatballs I threw together?"

She looks around for a plate, doesn't see any, not even paper ones. He tells her to just hold out her hand, assuring her we're all family here. My God! What have we come to! Taste them, go on, they're not bad at all, a bit on the chewy side but hey, it's better than hunger and Polish lice. The coincidence of it was just too much! To fancy meatballs and have them appear out of the blue. La Mechu and La Puchu are rap dancing and chomping away, Fax is licking her fingers and putting the Bowwow Lady, who is stiff as a broomstick, through the third degree. Xerox Machine is wolfing the stuff down and keeping track of all the talk in the room, shoring up on gossip so that later she can deliver her scathing report to the neighborhood. The meatballs are gone in record time. And then, one of the VIPs has the sublime idea of asking Bureau with Ringlets, who is sipping a cocktail of rum and quicklime because powdered milk is a thing of the past (and to think that at the turn of the century, Nestlé had designated us for its first Latin American powdered milk factory), where he managed to find the ingredients for the dish.

"Oh, it was no big deal: first, I rounded up all my old shoes and boiled the soles in saltwater. As soon as they reached the melting point, I drained them and allowed them to cool; then I mixed them with quicklime and minced goose, the goo that's been flooding the market recently, and I rolled them like this (he shows them how) and I fastened them with rubber bands I stole at the office. Because they just refused to keep their shape, kept opening up like sunflowers, but the rubber bands worked like a charm. I did end up having to fry them in cod liver oil; I searched high and low for someone to loan me a few drops of oil, just until the next shipment comes in and then in six months I would return it. Where did you get the idea everyone I know is constipated? Anyway, most of them couldn't even recall the smell of oil. How'd I get the cheesiness, you ask? Oh, that's the taste of funky feet. Don't protest, darling, I wash my feet very thoroughly and go every Monday to Ánimas Street for a pedicure."

No one throws up; it's a luxury they can't afford. Cuca Martinez would like to puke, however. She gets a finger in as far as her epiglottis, but nothing doing; she thinks of her ulcer, always clamoring for a warm morsel, and takes mercy on her trusty partner in affliction. Nothing is coming up, anyway. Her state is so below par that her digestive system works at breakneck speed. All of a sudden, she doubles over in pain, her stomach in spasm. A long fretful line of guests, on or past the brink of shitting their pants, has already formed outside the bathroom door. Good thing she never leaves her house without tucking a precautionary paper bag inside her errand bag; you never know what can come your way — a croquette, a piece of pizza, an orange, a dose of the clap, you never know . . . There's no place for her to do her business discreetly. She looks for an out, and a path finally opens up in the crowded room; she walks out the front door, descends the stairs, crosses the street, and arrives in a sweat at the neoclassical gates of the cemetery.

"Halt! Who goes there?" asks the night watchman, soulless keeper of souls.

"It's me, Cuca." He gave her such a fright that her voice comes out shaky and strangely modulated, like a Mexican woman's when she's about to be flogged by her husband.

"If you're a tourist it'll cost you a fiver. You can't come here and just ogle our dead for free, like it don't mean nothin', come in here and mess with our dearly departed for free."

"Listen mister, I —"

"Don't you Mister me, it's Comrade to you. Don't you know they gave a newscaster the sack when he wished the ladies and gents a Merry Christmas and a Happy New Year! I'm fixed on keeping my job. So those imperialist Misters better not go getting the wrong idea about me. They don't scare me one bit. You were saying?"

"I was saying I'm Cuban, aiee! aiee! aiee!" and her spewing bowel overtook her.

"And what brings you at this hour to Bocarriba, home and neighborhood to those who repose faceup?" He sniffs around in disgust.

"I've come to pray for my departed mother."

"God! What a stink of shit. It must be Pea-eater! He must've broken out of his tomb again. I bet my right arm he's the one shitting the grounds again. He's one militant ghost, one of those cocky dime-a-dozen types, ate peas all his life and never got his hands on a bottle of milk of magnesia. His stomach so sick that even dead it gives him no peace. A very chronic situation." And with that, he forgets about the old woman and darts off to look for this Tropical Caspar and coax him back to his resting place.

With her thighs pressed together, she squishes off in search of a faucet, of water, it need not be baptismal, to wash herself from the waist down. Near the church, she comes across a spigot, so low it's level with the grass, and she squats to better wash her privates and her legs. She does the best she can with her panties and skirt and thinks of the awful cold she'll get from wearing these mucked-up clothes. She thinks she'll hang them on the branches awhile, give them a chance to air at least. She stretches herself on the wet ground and loses herself, with increasing absorption, in the beauty of a black sky thick with stars. When all of a sudden, she thinks she hears a voice, a hot and bothered, brazen voice from somewhere inside the meandering pathways. The heart-swelling voice of a woman, besotted by love and an expert in agony, is singing one of those boleros that drive folk to slip a noose round their necks and jump off high places, to go down in flames with their (not Latin America's) veins agape. Cuca feels not fear but dread, a terror so stupefying as to ripen instantly to a deep, spiritual calm. She tries to make out the whereabouts of the honeyed melody, but one meandering pathway seems as good a bet as any. That's when she notices the inky black sound is pouring from the vast above and beyond, not the leafy canopy exactly or any one tree in particular, but from that pacific stretch of magnanimity we like to pass off as the heavens above. It's the voice of a sky so black it's blue, a sky bristling with stars and beginning to look like a woman in the shape of a piano, a daunting black dazzler of a woman, smiling down from the poetic latitudes of false illusions. She, too, is plumped down on her back, or belly, sprawling into the utmost regions of what was just now the deep blue meadow of the sky, her waist and hips roll down in heavy folds to form a girdle of buoys, her ponderous cornstarch-dusted thighs like wondrous

The old woman rummages in the bag that never leaves her side and produces a Chinese lantern and shines it in her beloved's face. Her dismay, her shame, couldn't have been greater than when she murmured:

"But, Uan, my love, my life, you look brand-new, like you just came out of the box, like still wrapped in cellophane — you look young, younger than before."

"Well, I just had a face-lift."

She heard "face list," and thought he was talking about some new way of sorting out the bread line waiting for manioc or casaba loaves, but she didn't pay it much mind and took another step toward him.

"Give me that lantern. Now it's my turn to have a look." And he reached for the light, but suddenly she was less than willing.

"You stop right there. I've grown more wrinkled than a page from the international politics section of *Granma* when you crumple it to wipe your ass. Don't bother to look. I'll just tell you. I am none other than the love of your life."

Uan wonders how Naomi Campbell could have taken such a nosedive in a matter of hours. Just goes to show how disgusting science has become in this day and age. He had always said as much.

"I'm Cuquita Martinez, you miserable degenerate." And her voice, when she berates him, comes out like a purring, husky caress; she rolls the words as if the poetess Mercedes García Ferrer herself (who lived across from the Hotel Capri and could read the cards like nobody's business, and if she saw something, well, you had better grab your ass and step on the gas) were speaking. She speaks with such tenderness, all the years he went missing already forgiven, which as you can see does not mean forgotten, and she says: "Come to me . . . come closer, you fool."

They reach for each other, their bodies full of old and weighty memories more than love. They don't even dare touch lips, avoid showing their faces. Her head rests on his shoulder. He rests his chin on her colorless hair and sees blood, thick drops of it, landing on her gray head. A few minutes earlier, those grave robbers had split his nasal membrane. He caught them inside his mother's coffin with a sack of clothing and jewels into which they were just then stuffing the dead woman's gold teeth. She who had gone to naked but insipid dust. Caught by surprise, they tried to flee, but he somehow grabbed one of them by the shirtsleeve and they all had one hell of a rumble. When one of the thieves broke loose, he yelled for help or a policeman, but no one came. Well, not exactly, 'cause she was here, wasn't she?

"Uan, what have you done with our love?" asked Cuca Martinez, much like the poet, Bonifacio Byrne, with his *shredded banner*.

"And you, Cuquita, what have you done with the dough?"

And, because her ears were clasped in an embrace and because of the headstrong notions women get when it comes to putting their men on sky-high pedestals, she heard "woe" instead of "dough."

8

Lie to Me

> Lie to me for an eternity
> you make me happy with your falsity,
> What's another lie when life is a pack of lies,
> Lie to me some more
> You make me happy with your falsity.
>
> By Armando Chamaco Domínguez,
> as sung by Olga Guillot

OH, COME OFF IT, YOU SILLY BOY! Now's no time to bring up woe! Not when we're all cozied up like this! Woe, indeed! I'll be up at the crack of dawn, thank you, to fulfill my vow to Saint Lazarus. I will crawl all the way to the chapel in Rincón, on bended knee and balancing cinder blocks on my head, with my skull crushed if necessary, to offer up my thanks for the good fortune of seeing you — you, my bane and my joy — one last time before my fleas jump ship. From there, I'll go drop in on the little Virgin of Mercies and bring her a bouquet of white blossoms, if I find any; if I don't, any immaculate thing will do for my little Obatalá. Then, I'll go see my darling, my sassy little Virgin of Cobre, and do things up the way she likes them — with drums and violins and plenty of honey, sunflowers and plantains and pumpkins and custards. I don't know where in God's earth I'll get it all, but even if I have to sell my body to a tourist in

Malecón, I'll do it. Not that my body is worth much of anything, but maybe I could land myself some slow-witted Mexican who can't even tell the time of day because even the hands on his watch are limp. The deed done, I'll go to the beach at Cojimar to cleanse myself, and then, I'll slaughter a rooster for Yemaya, beloved little Virgin of Regla. Bless my soul! I completely forgot about her, Maria Regla — finally, she'll meet her father and he'll meet her. Am I right or am I right! Ain't life opera, a Brazilian soap opera! *Life is a dream and everything, everything ends* (not Calderon this time, but Arsenio Rodríguez, the Cuban composer):

> Live for the happy times
> And take what's for the taking
> 'Cause when it's all said and done
> Life is a dream
> And everything, everything ends.

Just because I'm living my minute of happiness does not mean I'm going to forget all about my daughter, neglect her future well-being, my sweet little mite, raised without a father, no wonder she's the way she is — so traumatized, so politicized . . . Hello, what's this warmish stuff trickling down my forehead and clouding my right eye? I can taste it now, it tastes vaguely sweet, sweat I bet, so much emotion he's broken into a sweat, poor darling. I can't tell you what warmth I'm feeling in my belly, even my belly button is tingling! My woe — he wanted to know about my woe, years and years of heartache, I haven't said anything yet. If I were to tell him about the yards and yards of gray stitched in black, I would bore him, spoil his evening. Well, I've put my pain on ice, anyway. In the same way you put someone in the deep freeze when you want to cut them cold. Stick 'em in the ice tray and you'll see how nippy things get. That's what I did, when I wanted my heart to cool down — I wrote my name next to Uan's on a strip of paper bag and stuck it in the freezer compartment. Had I not done this, then I would've most certainly ended up as dead as the Girl from Guatemala, *she, who died of love,* although some busybodies say that really it was a botched abortion.

I'll play it cool as a cucumber, I can't melt and give in so easily, just because he decided to turn up again after thirty-some years. I owe it to myself to cut a fine figure, fill my shoes so to speak. "Woe, darling, you were asking about woe? Oh, sweetheart, you can be so amusing sometimes, ha ha hee hee — I stuck it in the fridge."

For some incomprehensible reason, he pushes, almost shoves me, and holds me at arm's length by the shoulders. I believe he's looking at me in some amazement, but I couldn't say for certain because it is very dark, but his hands, clasping my shoulders like claws, give away what I imagine is the fierceness of his manly gaze. Because that's one thing about him, he was always very manly, none of that funny stuff, always skipping the niceties.

"Of course! Where no one would think to look! You went about it like a real pro!"

"Uan, my heart, you're bleeding!" And she cradles him like Scarlett O'Hara comforting a casualty of war in the brilliant panoramic shot of the wounded and dying littering the immense station in *Gone With the Wind*.

"It's nothing, really, just a splintered bone." He digs in his pocket and produces a bottle of magical nose drops that mend his nasal membrane in one amazing drop. "I take my hat off to you, Cuquita. Sticking it in the fridge was a truly professional move."

Professional? What kind of shit-eating poppycock is he going on about? Well, if that's the word I bring to mind — professional — if that's going to be his word for me, what're you gonna to do? Maybe that's how they talk in the USA. Suddenly the darkness lifts, frothing up in an instant like egg whites, as if this were midsummer in Saint Petersburg and these the white nights Dostoyevsky wrote about in that book. Hardly! It's more like the searchlights shining down on us from the treetops. Uan grabs me by the forearm, his large hand trembles. His face is now close to mine and he is staring at my mouth:

"Cuquita, you lost your teeth!"

"No, I had them pulled out, in protest, because it was taking you so long to come back."

must've been prettily paid to pay us such pretty respects; this sir and madam stuff is a topsy-turvy trick to make him seem more lowly and to fool us into thinking we're the grandees.

"For years now, she's been the reason for my visits to this country . . . among other things, of course, I'm also here on business . . ."

"We're aware of that. We're only here to make sure you're finding everything to your taste . . . if there's anything you need . . . if we can help in any way . . . we are at your beck and call."

"So, where were you earlier? When those lowlifes were profaning the place and robbing tombs, my mother's included? Hell, I was hollering my head off for a policeman."

"Make no mistake, sir, we aren't ordinary policemen. That is not our function. Furthermore, grave robbers have a special dispensation, they report to the sector's police chief. And now, sir, we invite you to leave these grounds."

Never had these eyes that one day will fill with earth, this very same earth that now stretches beneath my flat and strangled feet, seen such cold-blooded cynicism. Plenty of sirs this and madams that, but the truth of it is they're showing us the door, booting us out of here but quick. I stand by open-mouthed while Uan, in a complete departure from his usual cocky self, quietly thanks them, takes my hand, and pulls me toward the gate without even making a peep. There's more light out here, and I can see Omnivideo's balcony and the party inside still going full swing — paired-off couples fondling each another and mixed groupings dancing in the candlelight. Fax is hanging off the balcony railings with a phosphorescent stream spewing from her mouth. I cross the street holding his hand — hand in hand with MY BELOVED. I still can't believe he's here, right next to me, with me hanging on to his arm as though it were all the same to me, pretending to be hard as nails, playing at being the untouchable one, the heart of stone, the cheery bitch — what, me worry? To tell you the truth, I'm starting to feel sad about all this — his coming back just like that, like it was nothing, without so much as giving me a chance to get to the hairdresser's for a proper chignon. It's gray, okay, but at least I could've had a presentable hairdo. Can it be possible, did he really come for me? To see me, to find me? Now,

156

now, Cuquita, don't you go filling your head with false illusions; you heard the man say that you're one of the many, many, maybe thousands, of reasons for which he came to this country. After all these years of silence, of interdictions. Well, yes, because corresponding with family members in Miami was absolutely forbidden. I know plenty of families who stopped speaking, children who broke all ties to their parents so as to be able to keep their jobs and to keep their records clean. It was only at the end of the 1970s that they lifted the ban on travel to the island, and parents, children, and siblings came back bearing improbable gifts, loaded down like Christmas trees, with packets of coffee clipped to their hats and skirts, with dollar bills inserted into bars of soap and tubes of toothpaste and boxes of talcum powder and the hollowed-out high heels of their shoes. The *gusanos* (worms) had metamorphosed into butterflies and were more than welcome to come spend their money in the state-run shops and to keep the ravenous rabble in shoes and food and clothes. The reunions rekindled old loves and old woes, as well as new ills surrounding dollar bills. It took about a week for those on the inside to fleece those from the outside, and the initial enthusiasm went up in smoke and affection went out the window in family after family. But Uan's case seems to be a different matter. How can an official undesirable be here to establish a business? Well, what is it to me! I never cared for politics. He's here, next to me, clasping me by the waist, and that's what matters. Who knows, he may have plans to settle down, and we'll finally live together in our little apartment. Because his old place in the Somellán is off-limits, naturally; it's been confiscated and turned into offices for Sony. I know because I stopped by there the other day when a nostalgic urge drove me to seek out the terrace where I had surrendered my woman's virtue, my virginity; when the door suddenly opened, and a couple of guys came out carrying a three-in-one sound system with a Virgin label, can you believe it! They were followed by four men carrying a refrigerator, a beauty —one of those modern ones with double doors and a special compartment to dispense ice cubes — a dream come true. They allowed me to go in, and when I saw all the refrigerators, television sets, video players, eggbeaters, blow dryers — tens and dozens of every imaginable thing in the world in every size and shape — I all but forgot about the terrace where my modesty was defiled on a turbulent wind-blown night, when Uan was stiffer than a flagpole.

"You look dead to the world, Cuca, what's on your mind?"

"Refrigerators."

"Oh, the secret hiding place, of course, keeping track of the important things. Not that there aren't other important, more important, things, I know, but man can't live by love alone."

"Neither can woman, and in this hot climate, a refrigerator is of utmost importance — even if there's nothing to put in it. Do you know the difference between a Cuban fridge and a coconut?" I don't even give him a chance to throw his hands up in the air. "There is none, 'cause all they hold is water! Got you, didn't I?"

He stares at me in complete bewilderment, as if he were looking at a girl who'd gone off the deep end. I have to get a grip on myself. The interior of the car is just like a Fundora video. Never in my life could I have imagined such a contraption with its dashboard atwinkle with colorful lights and all sorts of clocks and even a radio-cassette player into which he's inserting a minuscule, silver record while asking me if I'm familiar with compact discs. "No, of course not" — I shake my head — "I'm so behind the times when it comes to these things." The only compact I'm familiar with is the stale Cerelac, denser than a brick, that they ration as a special supplement for the elderly. He's out of my orbit now, talking about lasers and precision beams and I don't know what else — the kind of technological advances, in short, that are as unbelievable as they are impenetrable. Anyway, that kind of stuff never interested me much, unless it applied to topmost necessities, like refrigerators. There goes my tit throbbing again, must be my nerves. A Valium and a small swig of home brew would do me a world of good right now, but I can't have him thinking I'm a down-and-out alcoholic and drug addict. I used to be, but now I'm crafty. If I'm going to come clean, I might as well tell you I've gnawed my fingers to the quick, there isn't a shred of cuticle left. My gums are completely blistered from chewing on too much nothingness. Bits of fingers must be embedded in my ulcer, it must be a festering mess of nail parings. He puts the car in motion with the elegance of a pitcher delivering a perfect curveball; the motor starts up like silk, noiseless as a magic carpet. I ask if he has enough gas, and he answers of course he has enough gas and what kind of question is that, Cuquita? I pinch myself to make sure I didn't die and go to heaven, I pinch myself again trying to sneak up on myself this time. No doubt about it, I'm alive all right — alive and drooling. But I'm not feeling much of anything; I wish I felt happy, happy enough to die of a heart attack, but it seems my heart is very healthy, a bastard of an oak. I'm dying to ask him questions about us, but I don't want to seem indiscreet or put my foot in my mouth or come out looking like a know-nothing or a fool. The car smells the way whores used to smell, of vanilla; he pushes another button —my God! it's air-conditioned, even! On the silver laser thingamajig, Elena and Malana Burque are singing about how *we so wished to be something, but it all came to nothing/our lives passed us like morning/passes into afternoon . . .*

Calle Veintitrés is blacker than the inside of a black cat; the sidewalks are deserted, and ours is the only car on the streets. The frosted glass facade of an old villa that once belonged to people who've left the country emerges from a shadowy tangle of trees; it has been converted into a Mitsubishi outlet for spare parts. Flags and murals camouflage last season's fluorescent Christmas greetings. Uan's expression is half consternation, half constipation. I explain that it's a special shop for diplomats, and he seems to understand. A fetid odor of pee and bad beer emanates from the Coppelia, that temple to ice cream from a bygone era. Someone told me some Spaniards purchased the first floor and now the Coppelia will be dubbed the War of New Dependency. And the new slogan will be: *Hurray for Spain and to hell with the freedom-fighting mambises!* Uan is wallowing in the past, wanting to know about places whose very shadows have vanished, about houses that have fallen to ruin and people who have died or left. We drive by the Moscou, the Montmartre, I mean, and for the first time there are tears in those eyes without crow's feet. They roll down those cheeks, smooth as cedar portals, and bounce off his chin onto a sopping silk tie that sports a reproduction of *Les Demoiselles d'Avignon* by Picasso. I know a thing or two, you see — thanks to my forays into magazines from abroad, supplied by the Greek, Xerox's number one boyfriend. I ask Uan to the wall of the Malecón for some fresh air, but he categorically refuses with ill concealed rage. Maybe later, there are too many emotions right now, he needs a long bath, a good rest. I pull a long face because I expect there'll be good-byes in the offing. But no, not at all, where did I ever get the idea, and he strokes my face, caresses my wrinkled forehead, and his fingers, eventually, work down to my neck and get lost in its sagging folds. He wants to see the apartment, meet his daughter. Maria Regla no longer lives at home, I tell him, and his face turns somber. At any rate, I need to talk to her first, prepare her for her father's return, that is if she lets me speak, because that Girl never lets you get a word in edgewise. It's the least I can do, to avoid terrible misunderstandings, psychological traumas. I notice him getting nervous, he's fixing his eyes on the rearview mirror and seems intensely preoccupied by something, and it's not Maria Regla.

"There's a car following us."

"You're just imagining things."

"They're parked half a block behind us, and the driver just made the foolish mistake of lighting a cigarette."

"You're scaring me."

"There's nothing to worry about; they must be checking up on me, it's completely normal. Until now, things have gone smoothly. Come on, Cuquita, take me to our little nest."

Little nest! He said little nest! I'm too old for this kind of excess. Menopause is well behind me, and anyway, they emptied me out when they removed the cyst. What people mean when they talk about feeling — well, I don't feel much of that anymore. But I could pretend, if he still wants me and won't run away again. Nest, indeed! Well, the apartment is a nest of sorts — chicken, not love. And not just because of the four chicks I got on my ration book and will one day, after they've been fed and fattened and survived it, have their necks wrung and end up in the soup pot; but because the place is a shambles, deteriorated beyond belief, in fact it's been declared unfit, and it's been buttressed with more staves and staffs than a forest. There's literally no room to sink another stick (a real one I mean, not a sexual one). But it's all I have to offer and he knows it, and I offer it with all my heart and soul. He starts up the car, and he's right, our pursuers immediately appear a short distance behind us. We take L Street to Línea (another black cat), we follow it to Calzada and turn right on M. Uan is nostalgically remembering the dwarf palms. I explain how consecutive hurricanes and the encroaching sea have swept away all vegetation. He parks the car in front of the building, and the second car follows suit half a block behind us. Before disappearing into the doorway, we say hello to Hernia, the lonely first-floor neighbor who camps out every night in a hammock because the storm of the century has destroyed all her belongings and most of her house. As I take the stairs, trying to think about other things, I notice the peeling walls that haven't seen a coat of paint since the building was built. The stairway couldn't have been nastier, gummy with filth; I used to clean it myself, but ever since I carved my mop up into little steaks and ate it, there's been no one to keep the place tidy. Someone stole the light bulb on the first landing; ditto the third. We finally reach our floor. As I open the door, I'm overcome by doubt, a hair away from agony. The TV is on and the test pattern fills the screen: that is to say, XXL is making a speech. The moment he's done, the set reverts to stripes, meaning it's off the air. Nadezhda Common Itch is snoozing in her cane rocker. Swifter than a wild beast and already flailing a shoe, Uan rushes in to squash my friend.

"Out of the way, Cuca! You're about to kiss your ass goodbye, baby!"

"You be careful what you do, Uan Perez!"

And on hearing his name, Nadezhda's husband, the Ethiop Rat, wanders in sleepy-eyed and buttoning up his pajamas. In one clean leap, a very terrified Nadezhda flattens herself against the wall. The Perfect Rat (the pet name with which Nadezhda and I like to tease him) immediately sees what's happening and dashes to the rescue of his ladywife.

"You be careful what you do! These are my dearest friends. Kids, I introduce you to the man of my life, the father of my child, Uan

must've destroyed his romantic detective thriller of a universe. I think I've just blown everything sky high.

"What do you mean I left you nothing?"

Birdsong intrudes upon his words, the flapping wings of hummingbirds and sparrows, the cooing of white doves. An early morning freshness floods the room. This first breeze soon swells into a squall; I go to each window and secure the shutters with hooks. I feel a thick strangeness pressing through my body. A dense, laden energy seems to be emanating from Uan as well. Pieces of paper blow in through the open windows, followed by leaves, branches, TV antennae, newsprint, towels and diapers still clasped by clothespins, flags, doors, glass, communal murals, ribbons, summer frocks, hair, dust, dentures — he grabs these in midair and waves them triumphantly. Objects of every kind come flying into the room, the metal ones stick to our magnetized bodies. This extremely peculiar event lasts forty-five minutes. Then, in a single whoosh, the wind snatches back everything it brought and a few more besides — my Selena radio, the vase with its plastic sunflowers, doilies and sundry odds and ends of no value. The altars do not budge. XXL's picture falls, shattering its glass — a bad omen. But the virgins stay put, each one at her station striking a pious pose, their pale faces feigning innocence. Suddenly Uan's body bobbles toward mine and mine toward his, drawn together like magnets, we lock but feel no wish to pet or neck or cuddle. Cold and insipid as side-by-side mineral deposits. The great wind suddenly lets up and a husky, smoky voice, backed by a sextet, surges from the Peanut Vendor's appartment and aeolian fury gives way to mellifluous song:

> Such salacity for a pocketful of peanuts,
> a pocketful of peanuts, a pocketful of peanuts . . .

And in every household, it's the bawdy, not the balmy, hour, because our hormones go hog-wild in hurricanes. The sexual tom-foolery of every tenant comes soaring up the shaft and past the four open windows and rings its symphony of moans and groans in our ears; because soundless fucking might be just the thing in Paris, where even flushing the toilet or switching on the lights is said to disturb the neighbors — I read it in *Elle* or was it in *Hola*? I think it was *Elle*, which is the more serious magazine of the two and does not go in for skewering celebrities and scandalmongery; still, if I had to pick, I'd go with *Hola* — it's juicier and how else would I get news about my favorite singers? Those magazines are my only balm; Xerox lends them to me as you know; she gets them from her number one boyfriend, the Greek whose boat is anchored in the bay as we speak, because someone absconded with the engine and nobody saw and nobody heard. Just then, Uan and I hear the Peanut Vendor shouting at his wife, who has a minor hearing impairment and fucks while listening to *Puente Familiar*, the Radio Enemy program on which families in Miami can broadcast messages to their loved ones. Her husband's booming voice drowns out the radio:

"Come here, precious thing, 'cause you're gonna get humped like you never been, you're gonna see the solar system in its entirety, you're gonna feel like you swallowed the moon — and Mars and Venus and the stars . . ."

And *precious thing*'s answer is to sing a bolero, made famous by Pedro Vargas:

> Let heaven above lose its stars
> and the wide sea its immensity . . .
> It's dark eyes and cinnamon skin
> that'll make me lose my mind.
> All I care about is you, you, you only you . . .

The Peanut Vendor goes into paroxysms of lust, unbuckles, and knuckles down to exact his due.

"Gimme your juicies, precious thing, gimme, gimme, gimme."

From a bed in another room in another apartment, a first-string working type beseeches her, too:

"Come on and let him have it, *precious thing*, so that maybe we can all catch some sleep, 'cause tomorrow is a working day and we're not made of stone!"

At long last, the Peanut Vendor lets out a hair-raising cry worthy of the Lezama Lima line that says *desirous is he who has traveled far from his mother.*

The folks in number twelve immediately take over where the others left off. The man's voice is heard saying:

"Open your legs, dear heart." Her response is a tired, sickly sigh — a sick and tired sigh.

"Mommy, do hearts have legs?" a small, sleepy child's voice wants to know. Silence reigns.

In the adjoining apartment, Fala and Fana, La Mechunga and La Puchunga, I mean, are gleefully cavorting with Memerto Remando Betamax. They've instructed him to perform a striptease, and they've curled up stark naked to make the most of a small diversion, the daintiness the president of Egremonia carries between his legs. With his underpants still tangled about his knees, Memerto flares his nostrils and sniffs around, intrigued:

"So, which one is the one who is supposed to smell of rotten papaya?"

"Aren't we the witty one! If I had just stunk up the place with a hot chickpea broth fart, I'd keep my mouth shut. Farts seem to follow us wherever we go!" La Mechu gives him her usual lip, while La Puchu introduces a finger into her vagina and discreetly sniffs it —just in case. I can tell because I hear La Mechu slapping her.

"Don't be stupid, girl, don't sniff yourself! You're going to believe this impotent fool!"

La Puchu puts a very scratched record by Olga Guillot on the old RCA Victor record player and blasts the volume to keep the neighbors from hearing what's going on in her dwelling:

> Know what I'd like?
> To go to bed on Friday
> Not wake up till Sunday.
> Know what I'd like?
> The sun in the night sky
> And ample love to flood
> Your senses . . .

"That's what I'd like, do not refuse me," Uan supplies the last lines of the song in a whisper.

My poor old flesh can resist no more; I feel like I'm on fire, like I could shatter thermometers if you were to take my temperature. But not down there; down there it's dry. My sex is cold and wrinkled and a disgrace. Plenty of tenderness, but desire is another matter. How can I say this to you, my darling, how can I tell you you came too late, all I am is an old woman now with a burning heart beating smooth and slow? An enlarged heart, overgrown from pent-up love and stifled passion. Naturally, I won't tell you about my escapades, my therapeutic, physiological sessions, because they don't count. Love is what counts. True love. But what if he's not my true love? What if I made a mistake and spent my life waiting for this fool and my real true love got away? Absence is a poor counselor and cajoles better than a pimp, but I haven't much time left. I'll just have to manage as best I can, I can't let this one get away, who knows when the next one will come along. What am I saying, what is this cold, callous talk, this is the father of my child we're speaking about. "A penny for your thoughts, Cuquita Martinez."

"I will deny you nothing, Uan Perez. Ask and it's yours, whatever your heart desires. Life, itself, if necessary."

"No, Cuca, that won't be necessary. I'm not asking for so much, all I really want . . . really need is the dollar."

I ask you ladies and gentlemen! Now, what's gotten into him! Does he think, now that I'm old and have suffered my life away, that I'm going around paying for it! Oh Christ of the Martyrs, how my heart aches, come on then, let the heart attack rip, because I cannot believe this man has come all the way from the native land of the dollar tree to take away my one and only dollar, the only one I've ever seen in my life, you understand, and that I just so happened to find by luck on the street. I'll just go Swiss on him; what else can I do, 'cause this is one guy who smoked himself a joint and didn't share it.

"What dollar do you mean, my love?" I ask in a dreamy way.

"Don't tell me that you, too, have forgotten . . ." And he dissolves into tears as if there were no tomorrow, like a penitent in

167

sackcloth lost in the open plain or the frozen steppe. "My life is worth nothing . . ."

"That's a song by Pablo Milanés. Mine is worth even less, doesn't even amount to a bean. And me, thinking you came for your daughter, for our love, for the good times to begin. Baby, don't be like that. Don't come telling me you don't have other dollars in your wallet. What difference could one more make when you have hundreds in the bank . . . don't you get started being stingy, 'cause you were always a very splendid man. Don't wimp on me now, I've never liked guys with a yellow streak, guys with cold feet. Don't be chicken-hearted!"

And again, his tantrum resumes; he's this close to banging his head against the wall, but our position impedes him from cracking his skull. Our bodies are still wedged together like a pair of terrific magnets. I put my hand to his head and stroke his hair, which amazingly is all there although he's taken to dyeing it mahogany. I counsel him to pick another shade, this one doesn't suit him at all, which makes him kick up an even greater fuss — he's practically baying by now. Between whimper and whimper, he tells me a story that sounds like the plot of a Humphrey Bogart movie. Unless he locates the bill, his wife and daughter face great peril, because the bill contains the secret serial number for a Swiss bank account that is of utmost consequence to his second family, the Mafia. And me thinking that by his second family, he meant us. His bosses there are in cahoots with the ones here and he has been sent to salvage the fortune. If he fails in his mission, he's already been told to not even bother showing his face — he might as well put a bullet in his brain, slit his wrists, dive off the Morro lighthouse and smash himself against the rocks. I like the last option best; it gives me goose bumps to think of the amounts of blood involved in the other two, how am I going to clean it up without a proper mop and no water. And now, I'll have the police to deal with on top of everything else. I come back to my senses. So, my love has come to this? Worth no more than a lollipop, a powder compact, a Coca-Cola? Not even, because Coca-Colas and cosmetics have gone up recently. I stroke him again, this time I touch his smooth tear-bathed face. I look into his eyes. Their emptiness terrifies me, they are lost in a dream, in the heaven of a crumpled piece of green paper. Taking his head in my hands, I make him look into my dull, weak eyes. Look at me, Uan, look at me. I have loved you so much . . . I am here, we are together. It's me, your old girl who loves you. I love you, I adore you, I'll buy you a cockatoo. I've never stopped loving you, not for a second of my life. Uan, do you understand what it means, a whole life? The one I thought I was going to spend with you. Look at me, please, look at me. Kiss me. I bring my dry and cracked lips to his silicone-injected ones, I force his mouth open with my rough and withered tongue. He smells like he always did, despite the store-bought smile with its porcelain teeth; he smells of tooth decay, scummy tonsils, Guerlain aftershave and mint. This is my man all right. The one who jeopardized me politically and sexually. And this is my kiss. My long-awaited kiss. He's poking around my mouth with his eyes wide open, his cold stare lost in mine. I close mine. His tongue is exploring my gums. I would give anything to have teeth right now. But such are the follies of youth, paid for a hundredfold at the end of this fucking life. His tongue is on fire now, he's running his hands all over my body, my skeletal frame I mean. I open my eyes. His are shut tight, inside my mouth he is speaking the words I've been watching for like a spider watches its web. I'm in a flutter down to my cuticles and I feel more than hear the magic words:

"I love you, Girl, I love you." And I fizz like a smitten mango shake.

Our bodies are released from their magnetic clasp, no longer swept together by a terrific gusting wind. His body travels through mine. Mine strolls through his. We are two, cautiously starting to feel as one. We lick each other's sweat and uncover old smells, the inborn smells of a given skin and its accidents. Unjoined, we study each other slowly, we leisurely consider new markings, the prints of time notched deeper than scars. We are overwhelmed by sadness, because we know how we've both lied, mercilessly, calamitously so as to go on living in our respective worlds — worlds filled with absurd, outrageous, shameless lies. The mood is so sentimental, I wobble toward the Virgin of Mercies and introduce my hand under the mantle embroidered with fine silver threads and extract my treasure from between her legs: my one dollar bill. Uan's pupils glisten with greed, even his mouth seems to water. He grabs it from me and holds it up against the light. From his jacket pocket, he produces an apparatus that can identify gold, precious metals, gems, and naturally, very special dollar bills. He collapses on the exhausted sofa and breaks all four legs. Good-bye sofa, I wonder where I'm going to find a carpenter and the wood to fix it. Might as well find a cure for love!

"This isn't the one," he moans.

"What do you mean, not that one?"

"This isn't the dollar I gave you when I left," he says, looking like the outlook is gloomy.

"What?" He gave me a dollar when he left! He must be either drunk or delirious. I don't remember any dollar. What I do remember is him saying he didn't even have a pot to shit in, a nickel to call his own. There's a knock at the door. Slowly but surely, I reach for the doorknob and turn it, not without difficulty, I really should see about oiling it. Two very circumspect men, dressed in guayaberas, stand there squinting at me. Their irregular features and pockmarked faces ring a bell, I have a feeling of having met them before, when it comes to faces, I can spot a delinquent right away, I'm an excellent physiognomist.

"Good evening, ma'am, we'd like to talk to your lover."

It just that takes that one word — *lover* — tossed about so brazenly for me instantly to recognize them. These are the same fellows who came looking for Uan on the day he went away forever, or almost. My instinct is to tell them he's not here, that I have no idea who they mean, and I stand squarely in the narrow space between the door and its frame. "Let them come in, Caruquita, they're acquaintances."

And I obey, stepping to the side like a true automaton and inviting them to take a seat. I even offer them my last teaspoonful of coffee. I brew them a weak but delicious cup. As soon as they are served, I of course disappear discreetly through the bedroom door. I am, nonetheless, strategically positioned to overhear their entire conversation:

"You know we haven't come to settle old scores but to pick up what's ours. You have until tomorrow, when you'll be attending a reception to honor Nitiza Villainterpol, who has been responsible for keeping the people well fed, energetic, and virile for more than thirty years."

"As long as we're talking about old scores, you have yet to tell me who killed Luis. That story has been more than buried, it's been engulfed by the quagmire of history. And as to this thing you say is yours, I have not found it yet, but when I do, I'm handing it straight to my boss. I have my orders and I intend to follow them."

"Don't play the damn fool, you know there's only one boss here. Don't forget you're on the island now. We'll be waiting for you." He runs his tongue over his teeth, licks them clean as he talks; can you believe such terrible manners!

"You can cool your jets waiting." Can you believe the anger! The balls!

The two fellows rush to their feet, they're snorting they're so furious, and walk out without saying so much as good-bye and leaving the door wide open. While they were talking, I suddenly remembered the other dollar, the folded-up 1935 one that Uan pressed into my left hand (the hand of the heart, the melody hand) before he walked out the door. Where could it have gone to? Dear God in Heaven, where did I put it? My head has become such a sieve. Ring, ring, ring, my ancient black Kellog is startled out of its silence. Who could it be, at this hour? Hello. Oh honey, it's you, what a joy to hear you. You couldn't have called at a better time. Today is the happiest day of my life.

"Mom, they didn't pick me for the TV newscast. I'm down, Mom. I'll be a frustrated journalist forever. I can't tell you how bad I feel. If only I could round up twenty pills, I'd swallow them all. I don't even have matches or alcohol or I'd set fire to myself."

"Stop being so melodramatic. Listen, I have good news for you. Well, I think it'll cheer you up a little . . . it's a bit difficult . . . I don't really know how to tell you this. It's important for the two of us to learn to communicate better. And you know that I have never, but never, lied to you."

"What is it, Mom? Just let it out. If it's the lump in your tit, I already know. Xerox already came by to blacken my week with her talk of *the malignant illness*. We're going to the hospital on Monday. This stuff is no joke."

"Well, Hail Columbia! People can't keep their mouths shut for a minute around here! No, no Reglita, forget about all the bad stuff, the sickness and the rest. No, honey, it has nothing to do with dime-a-dozen cataclysms. Now, sweetie, don't think I'm minimizing your rotten luck . . . but, I have a lovely surprise for you. I know you don't like surprises, but a good jolt can be a blessing sometimes. The car-diologist was just telling me that contrary to what people think, a good scare can do wonders for the heart, can make it strong and vig-orous, like Terminator. What you need right now is a major fright, the kind that lands you on your ass with a fractured tailbone, the kind that marks you for life, like cattle are branded with molten iron . . ."
I have such a lump in my throat I can say no more.

"Mom, are you there? Did you hang up?"

I can't make a sound. Uan snatches the phone from my hand. I snatch it back. He's not going to show up now, after a shitload of years, and steal the show from me. When I have been both mother and father to that creature, my daughter. Okay, our daughter. Either I give her the news or no one does. And with a boom and a bang, I blurt it out: "Reglita, my girl, your father wants to talk to you."

He takes the heavy handset, clears his throat, and greets her:

"Hey, kid, how's it going? Sure, I'm your dad. I came to see you, I was dying to meet you. Yeah, after so many years. You're not too angry at me, right? Too many terrible things have happened in our lives, but let's not think about hate now. I'll see you tomorrow? Right now? Where? You want me to pick you up? I'll be right there."

In one fell swoop, he sets down the phone and runs into the dawn, like a man possessed. I fall spent onto the sofa that is destined for therapy and bury my face in the pillow that smells of Perfect Rat because it's his favorite place to nap. I finally break into unconsolable tears, my soul like a rose apple, panting and swollen. I weep like I haven't wept in all these years, my tear ducts gushing like faucets without washers. I weep as if the world were about to end from so much undeserved happiness. Disaster is sure to follow, because who can trust such a bonanza all at once, everything happening so effortlessly, so much truth — diluted in a fair share of lies, naturally. How easily one forgets the hard times and grows accustomed to the good. I don't know how much time has elapsed since Uan left, just now I mean. I haven't stopped sobbing and sniffling. Downstairs, a horn beeps insistently. I look out the window and there is the most significant and moving sight I've ever seen: Maria Regla and her father leaving the car arm in arm to cross the street and reach the wall of the Malecón and turn around signaling me to join them. Before I step away from the window, I look and am hypnotized by what I see — a postcard Havana: the buildings border the bay like moored ships and the air shimmers with saline mists. In the dips between the rocks, the young splash in polluted pools, the beaches of the poor. Out of the city's scorched heart come its inhabitants, shadows of the dog days, trying to leave urban clamor behind and follow the brisk lead of the sea, its stench of rotting fish, its tars sharp enough to unclog nasal passages, its mosses collecting on the wall. An unexpected restlessness gives away the fearlessness of the young ones, their dreams of departure cut short by the beacon that watches the shore. Between here and there is an ocean of repellent waters that can ward off mosquitoes. The surf has swallowed up the Havana of my youth. Havana flinches like flesh, smarts like a sore or a scraped knee. But even like this, hurting and steeped in pus, she is beautiful. Beautiful as an adolescent slapped by her stepfather. Beautiful as a gash in the flesh with its rim of blood, a wound with lovely lips not unlike a cunt. I don't know why I'm thinking all this just now; if I had a pencil handy, I would write it all down as proof of a day on which I thought so prettily. There are so many beautiful words hiding inside one's thoughts, then they're gone, beyond our reach, never to come back. Out there, my daughter and my man and my city are waiting. What more could I ask for? I run downstairs, feeling jangly all over and vaguely feeling pee beading down my leg. They're already there, cuddled up on the wall, she rests her head on his shoulder. Overwhelmed with tenderness, he holds her by the waist. As I go to cross the avenue, a truck just barely misses making mashed old

173

lady out of me. At last, I'm with them, my two loves, they who denied me. The three of us disappear into an embrace, kissing without restraint. But alert, suspicious as cats. Expecting a claw to strike, separation, betrayal. We sit with our backs to the sea, facing the city; we watch her stretch her golden, humid limbs and rise as if out of a box, like a patient who, after a long coma, suddenly awakens and complains that the light is hurting her eyes. We watch the day rise up, like a meringue, and with it comes the old bitter taste; it, too, is rising and sticking in our throats.

9

A Thousand Disenchantments

A thousand disenchantments
could not atone for all my lost illusions.
A thousand torments
could not amount to all my sufferings.

By René Touzet,
as sung by La Lupe

*O*F THE MANY IMAGINARY PALACES and the handful of real ones
still standing in Havana as we speak, three cannot be overlooked:
the Salsa Palace, the Palace of the Revo—*lotion,* and the one of the
Capitanes Generales. Strategically ranked in that order of importance. At six o'clock in the morning, Uan is overcome by an urge to
visit palaces. His daughter informs him that the first and third will
pose no problem, but the middle one is out of the question. Uan gives
her a mischievous smile, to him nothing is out of the question.
Nothing and no one can stand between him and his pleasure. Reglita
cautions him that only those who heed advice will live to comb gray
hairs. He's lived all his life without the benefit of council or coun-
selors, never even tarrying long enough to listen to their breathing, he
haughtily informs her — and his health has never been better.

Havanarise. Whereas elsewhere on the planet it is the sun that
rises, here, we have Havanarises. At first light, the city ascends from

the sea or descends from the clouds to bare her dank and contrary self. And with the Havanarise, they set off for a stroll around the city. The previous night, need we say it, has taken a toll on many fronts: familial emotions, social hardships, and economic calamities — because of the missing dollar bill. Cuca Martinez, Maria Regla, and Uan didn't get a wink of sleep, didn't even doze off for a minute. And yet, they don't feel in the least tired; quite the opposite, in fact, they feel peppier than usual when they scale the wall of the Malecón to amble and circumambulate the streets of Havana, walking or driving around in the Mercy-Benz officially assigned to Uan for the duration of his delightful and rightful stay on the island. Everywhere they go, their pursuers or bodyguards are sure to follow in hot pursuit. For starters, Uan invites his ex-wife and daughter to breakfast at the Hotel Nacional. As they pass the Hotel Capri, home to the Salon Rojo Cabaret and to Uan's mafioso and macho universe, the memories are powerful as he stands there bemoaning how hostile his hotel beat has become. The training and playing field of his younger days is going to ruin right before his eyes, those very eyes that will fill with earth someday.

There was a time when Maria Regla would never have set foot in a tourist place or accepted to recognize this man as her father. But her political fanaticism has only resulted in too many moral blows over too many years, and she is increasingly reconciled to the idea that you only live once and to hearing the battle cry of *fatherland or death* as a deadly slogan for the efficient annihilation of an entire culture and its people, of an entire island. Also, it's been ages since she's even seen breakfast, the opportunity just had not presented itself, such a practice no longer figured in her life. No sooner are they inside the doors of the luxurious hotel than they find they're caught in a cross fire of aggressive stares — some are vigilant, others envious, all are uncomfortably perturbing. Cuca and Maria Regla immediately pat their amulets to activate them against the evil eye. All eyes are fastened on them and no one is looking away; they are being tallied up by hustlers, police pimps (I didn't leave out the comma between *police* and *pimps*), authentic foreigners with backpacks, fake foreigners packing a piece in their belts, buttons (not the kind you sew on but the kind who charge ten dollars to carry your bags from the front desk to the elevator door where they hastily drop them), receptionists and waiters with an exceptional command of English (we have an extraordinary gift for languages: just the other day the whole island could speak Russian, but when they gave the green light even the cat signed up for an English-language degree from the Lincoln Institute). After careful scrutiny the bored ones give up, now that they've ascertained there's not much to exploit, to capitalize on, as in *capitalism*. Because capitalism is the exploitation of man by man. And socialism? Is the opposite. To make a long story short, *fixity and inimical rumor* vanish from their macabre pupils when they are faced with the extreme incoherence of an old and gray lady in a shabby dress, the streaked, sweaty face of a young girl whose blue jeans are so discolored they're really white, and Uan, with his extravagant head of mahogany hair, thundering away with half of Manhattan on the diminutive cellular phone he's pulled out of his pocket. They are seated at one of the small patio tables so they can view (and be viewed), view the exquisite greenery hugging a blue, blue sea rimmed by clouds that seem to hover just above the canopy of trees. The special guest places their order so dismissively he's almost imperious — orange juice, ham and cheese sandwiches, and hot *café con leche* all around. The women's innards are off on a rapturous rendition of the *1812 Overture*, their hands and legs quake with ill-concealed anticipation. Cuquita's right eye twitches nervously, tics disastrously; Reglita's upper lip flutters in ominous agitation. A warmish sleep-inducing breeze soon has the women drifting off like babies — they even drool their shirts — while Uan is busy dialing numbers in Manhattan, wheeling and dealing across telephone lines. Finally, he interrupts his dispatch to the restless and brutal North, and wakes the women up by shaking their knees. The three exchange weak smiles and gaze at one another in puzzlement, timid again. Now that the *I love yous* and first caresses have been exhausted, they are bewildered to find themselves sitting together around a silly iron and glass table at one of the most beautiful and expensive establishments of its kind, the five-star Hotel Nacional. I'll have to hit up Havanatour for a commission; where would they be without me, I'm filling up airplanes for them. They're having a hard time initiating conversation, they don't feel especially inclined to talk about their pasts. No need to go stirring up shit. Leave well enough alone. Except that Cuca Martinez does have a need, a savage headlong need to speak of the passionate agony she has endured for thirty-some years of semifidelity and love.

(It seems to me . . . well, it's just a thought mind you . . . an opinion, you can take it or leave it . . . that she would do better to keep her mouth shut.)

I really don't think this is the right time for you to make an entrance, Lady Jane Cricket. Especially when the next chapter is almost 100 percent yours. You'll get your chance to spin and unravel, to reveal your genius and your extraordinary histrionic talents, but not now. So, see you later, alligator.

(You wash your mouth out before you talk to me, you stinky pig, and don't mess with my favorite characters, if you know what's best for you, or I'll blast you to kingdom come. You had better watch your step, sweetie, 'cause my crystal ball has you spending your next vacation in the tank, in Nuevo Amanecer or in Manto Negro. You'll be in a fine way then. Now, now, no need for you to get into a state — I'm going. But I'll be back, you're not going to get rid of me so easily.)

Can you believe that! She can be such a total pain in the ass! Good thing that up until now, she's more or less managed to stay out of things and give me a chance to build up my credibility as a transcriber. 'Cause don't forget, I'm only transcribing what the corpse dictates. Don't think it's easy to trudge around day and night carrying your revolutionary conscience in your backpack. To cut to the crux of the matter that occupies and preoccupies us, the breakfast is devoured in a flash by Cuca, her daughter, and her ex-husband. The women do not pass out from protein shock. Cuca mentions how bad she feels for the comrade pesterers who are shadowing or guarding them; not one bite has passed their lips, and they have them working ridiculously long shifts. She had even seen how their mouths watered when they had to watch them eat. At which her daughter jabs her so hard as to make the lump in her tit almost pop out of her mouth, thereby obviating any need for a surgical procedure. Regla clenches her teeth in a fake and sublime smile, and beseeches her mother to keep her mouth shut, to not even mention those fellows in passing if she wants to prolong the pleasure of keeping the love of her life by her side, if she doesn't want her dearly beloved to become her dearly departed. Uan is having the time of his life, charmed by the naïveté of his Havana family. Then, the faces of his American family abruptly steal into his mind, and Cuca's face is instantly transformed into a dollar bill, a missing dollar bill. At the same time that he is busily going at his perfect smile with a toothpick, he brings up the wretched dollar bill yet again. Does she still not remember where she hid it? Putting his hands to his chest, he implores her to try harder, to ransack her brains.

She has neither brains nor recollection, they've gone off to the afterworld without her. She sits in a pleasant daze, delighting in how her beloved gesticulates. It's always the same thing with him, he's always worried himself sick over the most insignificant things. Well, maybe not altogether insignificant, because if the dollar doesn't turn up he'll probably come home to find his other wife and daughter drawn and quartered and packed into plastic bags inside the freezer. A horror worthy of the Sunday afternoon feature or of *The Fifth Dimension*. She pokes around and around in her lost memory, in her birdbrain. And finds nothing, not even a speck of evidence, the trail as cold as can be.

"All I can remember, Uan my love, is my suffering and disenchantment, my tireless love for you. *Now, as I look back/I'm so weary/far from hating you. Believe me,/I've forgiven you/all I feel now is the pain/of my mistreated love.*"

Holy Saint Lazarus! What a relief to heave up one's heart and soul and feelings in one convulsive churn. I tell you she outdid herself, those words really drove the nail home. Good thing La Lupe came to her rescue with those lines from one of the most exquisite boleros, because Cuca's mind at moments like this, critical moments, turns into an aquarium where neurons float about on eternal holiday. Inert as split peas in a barrel.

"How about we walk a while?" the Girl suggests, to diffuse the situation, and because out of the corner of her left eye she just caught sight of some booted guys in blue wielding clubs and carrying guns in their holsters; in other words, most certainly cops, checking for passports and IDs, the kind of guys who would ID their mothers if they were to come across them. Those whose papers aren't in order will have to slip them cartons of Marlboros under the table, if they want to leave the premises unharmed and sleep in their own beds and not in one of the cells of Unit One, where people say they send you off to sleep with kicks and blows and wake you up in the same way. Our three subjects find themselves in the area targeted by the agents and try to eclipse themselves quietly. One of the cops is alerted by their serene slow motion toward the exit and moves to block their way. He is immediately spotted by the bodyguards/shadows and with one swift kick they leave him splayed on the pink marble floor. Uan is thinking that at least they were of some use, spared us from the hassle and wasted time of presenting documents that are so real they're sure to raise suspicions and therefore be deemed fake.

Outside the sun glares like hellfire. Even Uan's Ray Ban sunglasses are powerless against the piercing splendor and whiteness of this day, worthy of a knife blade resting in a puddle of milk. He reaches for the car door and burns himself on its scorching handle. The interior feels like a pressure cooker inside which red beans bubble, hot enough to boil humans. The leather seats are so piping hot that as soon as Maria Regla seems to have settled down, her ovaries dilate, she ovulates and menstruates in record time. Now, there isn't a single pharmacy throughout the land that carries sanitary napkins; they are rationed at a rate of ten per year and no one is ever sure in which month they'll be available and they only distribute them to women of menstruating age, naturally. So the only solution is to go to a diplo-shop, they'll be sure to have them even though they'll cost you an arm and a leg, a package of ten sells for nine dollars and fifty cents. Maria Regla is very excited at the idea of visiting a diplo-shop, because Communist women love to shop. Cuca is agitated, her blood pressure shoots up and she needs one of those pills you place under your tongue, but she doesn't have one. But she is not about to set foot in a diplo-shop. She could die of shame at the idea of Uan squandering his money on sanitary napkins and blood pressure pills. Not to mention she still owes him a dollar, which try as she might she can't remember where she put. Her ears are flushed and her eyes so dilated they could jump their sockets, she froths at the mouth. They have no choice but to rush her to a hospital. At Calixo García, they've run out of the darned little pills that go under your tongue. The doctors in attendance are as nice as can be, and offer them first aid. On realizing Uan is half foreign and hails from a country that can open the heart and mind of almost any Cuban, when they peg him as someone from Overlandia, they direct him to Camilo Cienfuegos, a dollars-only hospital specializing in retinitis pigmentosa. Many an eye has come flying out those windows in the split second it takes to switch on the backup generator when there's a blackout.

There they can kill two birds with one stone: they can buy the lifesaving pill and a package of ultra-plus pads. So much time has elapsed that the Girl Regla has bled through her filthy jeans onto the leather seats of the Mercy-Benz. Furious and half regretting having returned to Cuba the Beautiful, Uan scrubs alcohol into the seat and manages to leave it damp but unbloodied. Regla will need to change into some clean clothes. But Uan has already set his mind on going to one of the diplo-shops to outfit Cuca Martinez and the Girl with appropriate clothing and shoes if they are to accompany him to his evening function at the Palace of the Revo, where they will be holding a ceremony followed by a reception in honor of Nitiza Villainterpol, the grande dame of revolting Cuban cuisine, who has just been officially made a card-bearing member of the Cuban Communist Party. A thousand six hundred milifools turned in their cards when hers was issued; now they are milizanies. Uan knows he'll be attending tonight, because an invitation found its way into his pocket earlier in the day. He discreetly parted his pocket's linen flap and zeroed in with a disapproving eye on the contents of the white card printed in gold relief.

They take the car. Maria Regla slips a flattened egg carton under her so as to not mess up the seat again. At breakneck speed, they race in the excruciating heat toward La Maison on Fourteenth and Seventh Streets in Miramar. Just getting into the place is like obtaining a valid passport to enter eternity. They even have a man, a very proper sort starched from head to toe, opening and closing the front door. He has a humble smile for Uan and he vaguely grimaces in the direction of Cuca Martinez, but when Maria Regla walks in with an entourage of flies buzzing about her thighs he does a double take and asks for ID. The father solicitously intervenes — that won't be necessary, she need not bother show anything because she's his daughter. The majordomo assents but is not entirely convinced, these foreigners have such hippie-ish and filthy children that if it were up to him he'd ship them all off to the fields to cut sugarcane. Who knows, anyway, if she's really his daughter, maybe she's his lover. And he remains absorbed by such ruminations that are of utmost importance if the country is ever to emerge from underdevelopment.

Maria Regla eyes a rack of dresses so splendid they are almost tediously extravagant, made out of tulle and other stupendous fabrics, next to these is a stand overflowing with golden and silver leather bags, then there are the evening shoes. She lunges toward the goodies, but only after she's played at being the doormat, the dead duck obedient daughter looking at her father with calf-to-slaughter eyes. He grants her wish with a wink and even goes so far as to suggest she take her time to pick out what she needs. Cuca Martinez is numb with shame, she constricts her body until it's puckered as a prune; hiding behind Uan's back, she cautions her daughter in pantomime to not spend one additional cent, to pick out only one thing so she can change out of her bloodstained and fly-blown pants. With a small tap, Uan shoves Cuca inside the boutique and dragging her behind him makes a beeline for a black lamé dress festooned with blue spangles. He holds it up against her body and asks her to try it on. Even if she were to lose all her marbles, she would never put on such a ridiculous getup, and what she says is:

"Even for gold and riches, I would never masquerade in such a scandalous costume."

"Your tastes have clearly changed, because when I met you, you were wearing an almost identical dress."

Cuca searches her mind. It's true. A very nice little number, a tad roomy around the tits and ass, it had belonged to her friends, La Mechu and La Pechu. It's touching of him to remember, so she accepts the gift but won't hear of trying it on now, she'll put it on tonight, it'll be a surprise. Her love and her bane erupts in garish, knowing laughter. She does too, so heartily you can see the fine veinage on her purplish gums and her uvula. He suddenly strikes his forehead with his left palm as if he just remembered something and gropes around with his right hand inside his pant pocket. Triumphantly, he produces a set of teeth, the same dentures he had snatched out of the air in midflight when they flew in through the window that dawn.

"Here, Cuquita, these are for you. Put them on. You see, not only did you get me but you got your teeth back too."

"Not on your life, even if you were to offer me filet of beef too tough to chew. How do you know they didn't belong to a dead man!"

"They didn't belong to no dead man, Cuquita. They probably belonged to some person who was fast asleep with the window wide open and the hurricane just lifted them out of the water glass on the night table."

"Even worse. I'll just be guilty that someone is walking around toothless because of me."

"Because of the hurricane, you mean. Why don't you just put them on in the meantime, and if someone turns up to claim them, you'll give them back and end of story."

She hems and haws, turns them this way and that, they're good-quality dentures, not bad at all. He's right, she'll just borrow them, and if someone turns up looking for a pair of dentures fitting this and that description, she'll give them back right away. She finds a mirror and pops in her new smile; she looks like a different person; twenty years younger, a thousand sufferings lighter. Submerged in another mirror, like Alice knee-deep in wonders and ringed by a Hula Hoop of flies, Maria Regla tries on dress number thirty-one. Uan loads up perfume bottles, faux earrings, an assortment of hand-bags, a pair of patent leather shoes for Cuquita, three more pairs in a variety of styles and colors for his daughter, a dressy as well as an everyday garment for the old woman, and fifteen outfits that include ensembles, mini- and maxi-skirts, blue jeans, and every glad rag the Girl fancies. Cuca Martinez is mortified. Her own Reglita, so simple and modest when she was a girl, growing into such a vain and greedy hussy. Uan prepares to pay with a gold credit card, the women stand by nervously biting their lips and expecting something to go wrong at any minute.

"Here, Reglita, put everything back where it came from. Take my things as well. We don't need anything, Uan dear. If I had known you were so short on money that you had to pay with coupons, I would never have allowed you to even set foot in this place." Cuca Martinez is now very upset and motioning to Reglita to take it all back.

"What's wrong with you? Don't be stupid, this is a bank card, I have the right to use it, it's backed by money." He restrains his dejected daughter, who is already walking away with the stuff.

The salesgirl, who is busy with other customers, does not notice the card at first. The minute she sees it, she gets a *yeyo*, which is something like a groovy breakdown.

"Hey, girlfriends, come and see how this fellow has come to complicate my life," she yells, turning her back to call the other girls. "You're going to have to wait a long while, honey. There are only three credit card machines on this island, and I'm going to have to track one down by phone and send someone to pick it up. Tourists! When it comes to stinginess they beat the whole world hands down, why can't they have real cash like everybody else and pay up front!"

Our three shoppers listen to all this without saying as much as boo, stiff as pokers, their body temperature plummeting to zero.

"Do you speak Spanish?" The salesgirl shouts this, because like any good Cuban she tends to confuse nonspeakers with the hard of hearing.

"Yes, of course, but I wasn't expecting this," he mumbles.

"Well, expect it and more too. And where are you from, if one may ask?" She's getting flirty.

"From here," and his voice is a mere filament, like polyester thread for sewing raincoats.

"From here and you weren't expecting this?" she challenges in disbelief.

"He left when it all began, and hasn't been back in thirty-six years, that's why . . ." Cuquita rushes in, trying to straighten things out, but the woman cuts her off.

"Lucky you! You did the right thing, old man! Chuchín, get me the main operator and see if they can locate a card-swallowing machine that works. Oh, because that's another tragedy, every single time I stick a card inside that wretched machine it snaps it up, and I have to cut it up with a scissor to get it out."

Beads of sweat settle like pretty, fragile bubbles all over Uan's ashen face. Looking like he'd like nothing better than to tear the salesgirl limb from limb and making a great effort to remain clam, he politely inquires as to the whereabouts of the rest rooms. Once she's tossed him an *ask around out there, love, that's not my job,* Uan leaves in search of a safe haven where he can operate discreetly. In the privacy of the john, he unbuttons his linen shirt and feels for the clasp of a wide body belt that is taped to his skin and catches on his chest hairs. A number of bulging bags hang from the belt. He opens one and pulls out two thousand dollars, greenbacks. He returns to the counter.

"Forget the card, I'll pay cash."

"Listen, honey, make up your mind, shit or get off the pot. 'Cause the order already went out. There's nothing I can do if the card-swallower is already on its way. No, no, keep your money, we'll all just have to wait now. Anyway, no way I'm going to take hundred-dollar bills. Like what planet did you come from? Do you realize the amount of work — I have to copy each serial number with your passport number and home address next to it! I mean what's to tell me they're not fake?"

Uan turns to his female companions and asks them to please step outside and wait in the car. Very slowly, very calmly, he places the packages on the counter, and ascertains that the other customers are gone or distracted, and that the other salesgirls have stepped into the storage area for some reason or other. He looks her full in the face, his eyes like daggers pinning her panicky ones, she looks away, busying herself with a stack of bills. She opens drawers nervously and looks for what she claims is an eraser that tastes like strawberries. Uan raises a delicate hand and lands it with a tremendous dry snap on her cheek. A second later, he pushes a hundred-dollar bill into her hand, which he then kisses like an English lord:

"This is for you. A souvenir. Now, you're going to take my money right away, or I'm going to report you to your boss for gypping me out of a hundred dollars. It's absolutely traceable, because every bill is printed with my name. It's nothing, just a silliness of mine, you see. I suggest you ring this stuff up as fast as you can or I'm going to split your skull in half. And don't go copying the serial numbers, and you're not going to see my passport, and you'll never get your hands on my address. What do you say?"

"Yes, sir. Understood, sir. Right away." She is white to the roots of her hair.

Five minutes of terror got her a head of white hair and more wrinkles than Robert Redford.

"Ask for my forgiveness, you rude thing," the mafioso commands her in his mildest voice.

"A thousand apologies, sir," she murmurs.

"Why so many? One will do. And louder, I want to hear."

"I apologize, sir," she shouts, damaging her vocal chords forever.

"You see how easy it is. I'll be seeing you, you tasty bitch," and he reaches a hand to her cheek and squeezes a ripe pimple, splattering pus on the glass counter.

Uan emerges through the mansion's white-washed door with his arms full of Cubalse shopping bags. Cuca Martinez breathes a sigh of relief, at least nothing involving security guards, prisons, or the red devil had occurred. Maria Regla grabs the bag with her blue jeans and goes back into the store to find a bathroom, where she washes herself by squatting on a sink and dries herself with a page of the *Tribune* and puts on new pants. She doesn't throw out the old ones because she thinks she can get a pair of fringed cutoffs out of them.

They head straight for Old Havana. Seated in the Mercy-Benz, Cuca misses Ivo's Chevrolet. She remembers him fondly, feels she might be betraying him with Uan. Ivo, tired of waiting for her to make up her mind to marry him, went ahead and shacked up with a tart from Cerro, now he didn't even drop by for months on end. Who cares, when the man who drives her wild is sitting right there driving this monster of advanced technology. Again she blesses all the saints who watch over her and thanks them for the miracle. Could she even have imagined it, just a few days ago, that she would be reunited with the love of her life or driving around like this, like a queen in a limousine, and clutching a slew of Cubalse shopping bags filled with nice presents. Although food would have been bet- ter to tell you the truth, but she wasn't about to behave like a spoiled girl wanting this and that and that one too. This car can really fly, it hasn't been ten minutes and they're already in Malecón. The sun glit- ters in the surf. A golden sea rocks back and forth, and the waves crashing against the wall bathe the city in their ardent, radiant foam. In the blinding light, the silhouettes of skeletal and half-naked chil- dren can be seen running along the wall, young girls with deep rings under their eyes and much too much makeup for this hour of the day lean their fluorescent-clad bodies into car windows and haggle with the tourists. Fancy boys hunt or fish for women, men, or whatever the cat dragged in. At the intersection of Prado and Malecón, they stop at the light and Cuca overhears the outrageous exchange between a fancy boy and a tourist from Argentina. The boy, who must be sixteen at the most, is hassling the woman, who must be at least fifty:

"Come on, pretty lady, for twenty buckaroos you'll get a night you'll never forget."

"Listen, kid, when something costs me twenty dollars I never forget it," says the *gaucha,* and gauchely evades him.

"Come on, pretty mama, I'll suck your cunt if you buy me a meal," the boy insists.

"Aren't you ashamed of yourself, you, the child of such a great revolution defiling the memory of Che?" the ideological tourist asks opportunistically.

"I have to eat, damn you; die, you old red bitch!" he shouts as he darts into the middle of the street and almost gets run over by a car. Cuca quietly wipes away her tears. She could never have imagined that such things would happen in this country. Maria Regla has turned her face away and looks out the other side, there where the sea still offers up one of the most beautiful sights ever to befall human eyes. At another time, she may have spoken up in defense of the revolution, but those days are already far, very far, behind her. She no longer wants to change the world, just herself. And not only her wardrobe but her mentality as well. Uan parks the Mercy-Benz in front of a shop that sells armies of miniature soldiers, and they set out on the tourist circuit, the usual folkloric route: Plaza de Armas, Palacio del Segundo Cabo, where they are denied entrance on the pretext that it is now occupied by a publishing house, even if it hasn't put out a book in more than a thousand years. They visit the Palace of the Capitanes Generales from top to bottom, and Uan takes a picture of Maria Regla leaning against the phallic scepter of Ferdinand the Seventh. They take Oficios to the Fountain of Lions, which is right next to the convent of San Francisco de Paula, where the true horrors of Old Havana begin: vacated rooming houses, ruined mansions, gaping cavities at the beginning or in the middle of city blocks, neither hide nor hair of the buildings that were once homes, offices, shops, cafés, restaurants, professional establishments. The hardest part is thinking what happened to all the people. Cuca Martinez has the sensation of swallowing something sharp, she has a bad feeling which she cannot place, and she suddenly feels very sad at seeing her city reduced to dust and stones, emptied of its people. Unhavened Havana. Havana Deserta.

"It would take more than five hundred million dollars to rebuild this place." Uan is in shock.

A smell of mildew and dust and grease emanates from inside one of the rooming houses. Finally, they find survivors of this catastrophe, this simulated self-bombardment. The Americans did not have to invade us, we invaded ourselves. There is a swarm of stakes supporting the structures, the extensions and lofts threaten imminent collapse, each one houses ten to fifteen people, it is said they sleep in shifts. It's not right. Maria Regla gets off of her cloud and comes down here where the reality is thick and dense.

"I was thinking it might be a good idea to do a story on the inhuman conditions in which these people are living," she breathlessly says and again, she's off soaring on her cloud. In a minute, she begins looking all around her.

"Go on, you! I don't think they'll allow it or publish it," her mother miserably sighs.

"I would do it for myself," the Girl protests.

Deep silence. A troop of barefoot children comes surging out of a crumbling colonial mansion that has paving stones for the passage of old-style chaises and gigs still intact; they're running behind a mustachioed man with a young face and gray, almost white, hair.

"Writer, writer, take my picture, write about me! What are you looking for? Your family? Maybe I'm your cousin or your brother or whatever you'd like me to be!"

The visitor dispenses ballpoint pens and candy, pats the children on their heads, strokes their cheeks, then crestfallen, he turns into the first street, wiping away a tear. The children euphorically proclaim:

"He said he was French! He writes books! He said his family used to live in this house!"

The image of Edith Piaf comes to Cuquita's mind, such a beautiful woman despite her arthritic hands and physique, such talent, that voice like eternal adventure, like endless and unfathomable excess. She wants to run after the Frenchman and ask him what happened to the Parisian sparrow, how did things turn out for her in the end, but she doesn't dare. A woman steps from between the ferns and vines that overrun the patio and proudly shows them a book the author had signed with his own hand — *De ton cousin, Erik Orsenna.*

They sadly cross the Plaza Vieja and walk down San Ignacio to the Church of the Espiritu Santo. Uan takes pictures of the small square and of Acosta Street, where his grandmother's friend Mercedes, a *santera* with clear eyes, used to live. They walk on past the parish of La Merced until they reach the port. They come back up Calle Cuba; when they reach the square of the Convent of Santa

Clara, their steps slow down — if they only knew the number of baseball games he and his school buddies played in this square. On reaching Muralla, they take a deep breath, but don't get your hopes up — the street no longer smells of anise. Maria Regla has caught her parents' nostalgia, she is discovering her city. Her father points out a defunct bank from bygone times on Amargura, they reach Obispo, and when they enter the Sarrá Pharmacy, they are dismayed to find that the old-fashioned flasks and medical instruments, true relics they were, are gone — well, when even medication has disappeared how can you expect to find all the rest? They end up in the part of Havana that's been restored, the area they show tourists and know-nothings. The Plaza de la Catedral is teeming with Mexicans wearing Lacoste, and Italians who refuse and refute the truth of a socialism gone to pot, and Canadians reeking of Coppertone but still pale as the Nela cream cheeses that have been banned from our tables, and French people following in the footsteps of Sartre and Simone and Gérard Philipe. A handful of Hungarians and Bulgarians loiter in this living museum to their past, but in the tropical version.

The family decides to have lunch at La Bodeguita. But it's out of the question, they don't have a reservation and priority is given to visitors from Overlandia. They try El Patio, but tables aren't available there either. Defeated, they go back to the car. Finally, they end up at Paladar 1830, not the secret service hangout, but the eatery that seems to have been tacked on to the main restaurant because everything from the chef to the food is the same. It's a home-style smorgasbord taxed to the heavens. Cuca feels a little apologetic about going for seconds so many times, but as everyone else seems to be doing it, she timidly keeps coming back in search of a good bowl of soup, any kind of soup — fish, chicken, tomato — as long as it's not *solianka*. Uan waits at a table that's tucked behind a corner. While the women are busy helping themselves, one of the pursuers or bodyguards jumps on the opportunity to pull up a chair and sit down facing Uan:

"Looks to me like you're getting much too sentimental. Do you have the dollar?"

While keeping an eye out for Cuca and Maria Regla, Uan shakes his head; then, speaking firmly, he expands:

"I don't, but when I do, as you already know, it's going straight to my boss in New York. So, let's avoid pointless discussions. No more comments."

"We'll see about that. By the way, the Official Residence is off-limits to your family. They can come to the reception, naturally; they will provide a good cover. As far as everyone is concerned, you've come back to donate funds for the launching of a new rum distillery and reestablish family ties. You don't live in the USA but in Santo Domingo. Got it? Now don't behave like an ass, because asses don't make history. You must've been informed by your boss that we agreed to let you into the country to find the dollar bill on one condition — you turn it in to us. We'll settle up with him later. We've had our eye on the old lady for years, we must've searched her house more than a thousand times, we took it apart tile by tile. And nothing. You better find out if she has it or it's goin' to cost you heavy."

"She forgot where she hid it. What if she doesn't remember? What if it's lost?"

"That's your problem, Uan. Aren't you the famous Uan? So prove it. If you ask me, I'd say granny knows plenty more than she's letting on. Either you bring it in tonight or you're headed for Villamarista, straight for the room with the small animals. Think of the suffering you'll bring on your families — 'cause you have two families, right? Maybe you want to take granny and the girl along to be your ladies-in-waiting? It's too rich!"

Pleased with himself, the spy says good-bye and disappears between the columns and tall windows that open onto the swimming pool. Lunch proceeds silently, except for the odd banal comment on how exquisite the avocado and tomato salad drenched in olive oil is and how the coconut custard is out of this world and how the owner must steal with his left hand when he wants to relieve his right, and why not? When the state is the biggest thief of all! Ain't that so! And then they have the gall to point the finger at hard-working people, to put placards around their necks accusing them of being money grubbers. Bullshit! They're the only ones who've been grubbing money around here for the last thirty years or more! And then changing the subject, they bask in the pleasure of having been asked to such a super place and express their gratitude for the fabulous food, and how life, after all, can be beautiful, benevolent, bringing them back together like this. Uan barely touches his food. Cuca gives him a questioning, worried look.

"Oh, nothing really, well yes, something important, in fact . . . about the dollar, I think you should try a little harder. I have to find it by eight o'clock tonight. If not, I'm a lost man."

She thinks this is peanuts compared to the hell she's been through and very confidently takes his hand in both of hers and assures him it will turn up, he shouldn't let this poison his existence, and everything has a solution except death. And because of the unfortunate choice of words, she immediately bites her lip, she can really do it, now that she has a mouthful of teeth, she sees how she's really bungled it this time, because that's precisely the point isn't it — either the dollar or death.

"You don't worry, just go to the Official Residence and let me take care of things. Come pick us up whenever you're ready. We'll be waiting for you, more beautiful and brave than ever and loving you as never before. And I'll be holding it in my hand."

He drops them off in front of their building. As soon as he starts up the car again, Cuca is flooded by a premonition — what if she never sees him again? — and maniacally pulls on the handle and climbs back into the car.

"Is it true? Did you love me?" and her dentures almost fall into the ashtray.

"As I loved no one else." Their dry lips meet. The bitterness that fills Uan's mouth befits his shameful behavior, his dirty conscience.

The old woman feasts on bad breath and tooth decay, on scummy tonsils and chewing gum, and is swimming in bliss. Maria Regla comes between them, she, too, wants her share of tenderness. Uan finally drives off down Calzada toward the Malecón and in the direction of Laguito. Mother and daughter make a mad dash for the stairs, on the first landing they bump into Xerox, who despite her hurry to find out the winning illegal *bolita* lottery numbers, looks

192

them over from head to toe taking note of the three immense shopping bags, or rather sacks, from a diplo-shop they are carrying, but she doesn't even stop to say hello. She's very taken up with the clandestine lottery business, but she is especially keen to get an invitation to tonight's event for herself along with Fax, La Mechu, and La Puchu. Nothing in the world is going to keep her from the reception for Nitiza Villainterpol, she deserves being inducted into the party, the horrible bitch has a cooking show on TV on which she gives people recipes for fried kitchen sponge. Xerox has already been informed that Cuca and her daughter will be escorted by the Girl's father, people say he's a millionaire who has come to get new businesses off the ground. Later tonight, she'll have plenty of time to fill in the particulars. On the second landing, Yocandra and her Chinese bicycle are stuck. They free her wheel with a shove, and she proceeds to the next floor where the Nihilist and the Traitor are waiting and wailing for her. On the third landing, Fax is trying to contact Jackie O in a last-ditch effort to find a solution to Hernia's problems; she has read about an upcoming Jackie O auction in a romance magazine, and she thought maybe Jackie could set a few things aside before the event, at least spare a mattress for poor Hernia who has lost everything and doesn't even have a bed to call her own. In the apartment, Nadezhda, La Mechu, and La Puchu are waiting; they are giddy with joy and jealousy, they hug and kiss their friends and rave about the return of the Jedi, the Uan I mean. Cuca, who is this close to a heart attack, drops the clutch of bags on the floor, and asking her friends to help her, she puts her shoulder to the wheel and launches Operation Seagull: the search for the missing dollar. Maria Regla, who is droopy with sleep and utterly indifferent, collapses on the swoon sofa. They turn the apartment inside out, the armoire upside down, the vanity table likewise; they shake out clothing, split seams, tear out linings, review the trinkets that grace the altar one by one, peel back walls, and break through the dropped ceiling. Finally, Cuca ties a red bow around the leg of a chair and implores San Dullo to return what is not his to keep, she raises burning eyes to the sky, falls to her knees with her hands clasped in a pious gesture, and intones a prayer (it comes out sounding powerfully like a spiritual

193

sung by Ella Fitzgerald) to San Antonio. She suddenly breaks off midprayer and squints up at the ceiling, studies its leafy upper reaches where the buttressing posts disappear into the foliage tumbling from the flowerpot where her malanga flourishes.

"Nadezhda, get up there! How could I have forgotten! I planted it. Stuck it in the flowerpot on the same day he gave it to me, the day he left."

Nadezhda and Perfect Rat, who just now came in, depressed because of a summons by the territorial militia troops, scurry up lightly and scratch around in the soil. The Ethiop Rat tunnels down to the bottom of the flowerpot. And there they spot it, wedged inside the roots, humid and almost rotted. They descend in triumph, the rodent delicately balances the dollar bill between his teeth and solemnly delivers it to Cuca. The moment it reaches her hand, she feels a divine balm coursing through her from head to toe. Another vow to fulfill. Another round of suffering. She knows she is holding the only thing that could drive her beloved away from her forever, and again. In tears, she throws herself on the bed like Greta Garbo, clenching her fists and savoring her misery. Succumbing to frenzy and exhaustion, she soon falls asleep and dreams she and Uan are clapped together, dancing at the Montmartre to the tune of a slow, heart-wrenching bolero sung by La Yiyiyi, that is La Lupe, the rascally queen herself:

> Did I ask for anything but loyal understanding?
> Did I not give you everything your hands could hold?
> I wish I could've made you a gift of light,
> but it was not to be.
> Now, you want the stars and the sun from me,
> but a god I'm not, so
> ask of me things I can give you,
> like myself unconditionally,
> ay, ay, ay.
> Tell me, what did I ask of you?
> Go tell the whole wide world
> there's never been a love like mine.

That evening, in their carnival queen finery, the girls step into their respective carriages: Cuca Martinez and Maria Regla Perez Martinez (they decided to go with the father's surname as well) with Uan in the Mercy-Benz; Xerox, Fax, Hernia, La Mechu and La Puchu, and Yocandra and her two husbands, with Ivo, as usual, in the old Chevrolet (these cars, as everyone knows, can fit between ten to fourteen people, if they squeeze). The journey is very eventful because of numerous blackouts and roadblocks. It's a good thing all the invitations are genuine, and every single one of them seems to be found in good standing, without grave criminal, read political, antecedents, hence not dangerous.

In the car, Cuca Martinez tactfully relinquishes her most prized possession, not her virginity or her love as she had many years ago, but the dollar bill. Overwhelmed by gratitude, Uan squeezes her hand, brings it to his lips, and kisses its veined and spotty surface. He gently releases the dollar from Cuca's wrinkled grasp. Feigning calm, when in fact he's about to self-destruct, he uses his sophisticated treasure-detecting machine to ensure that he has at last found the thing he was searching for. His face is joyful as he looks ahead, smiling into the black monotony of the night broken only by the luminous cones of the headlights.

The Palace of the Revo couldn't have been uglier if it tried, with its immense front parking lot and staircases worthy of Caesar. Render unto Caesar what is Caesar's. And columns so high and mighty they trigger vertigo. After crossing the vestibule, they have to check their bags as well as all strange and superfluous objects —anything from cameras to Pilot brand pencil cases. Cuca hides Nadezhda Common Itch and Perez the Perfect Rat in the osseous vale that used to be her cleavage. She insisted on bringing her little friends; she wouldn't hear of excluding them from such a happy occasion; what's friendship for, if you're not going to stick together in good times as well as bad. Most of the guests are already here like the Martians in that chachacha by the Aragón Orchestra: *the Martians are already here/and they came dancing the chachacha/rico cha, rico cha, rico cha* . . . It's more or less the same crowd as at the Hoi

Polloi (only Panther Dove is missing, miffed because she wasn't asked to sing, and His Ex-Superfluous, who has been sent away on a mission) with a few new faces like Jabuco Cochino, for example, a designer of Asian haute couture who is waiting for authorization to launch her fashions on a catwalk simulating the Great Wall of China, the event to be held at La Maison. And the great cucalambent poet Johnny Pursued, the vice minister of agricultural and agro-ideological foreign planning; Candelona Serving High Seas; main opponent of small aircraft operations in semiterritorial waters, the Minister of Acupuncture and Apiculture, Baba Dar Javalos, better known to the boys in his neighborhood as Bend over Babar; Roba Y N'á, Alardón Fumé, the veteran pilot Paul Enroque 007, and Official Dissident, whose presence serves to discredit and dispel all that stuff about human rights violations. The Red Witch confesses to Bureau with Ringlets that she could die for the low-cut tulle dress Maria Regla is wearing. His wife-husband Leonarda da Vinci sticks a pin in a ragdoll in the shape of the great poet Johnny Pursued. Argolla, Laca, and Arete gossip about the remote possibility of winning an exit visa in the lottery — the thought that homosexual roundups could be reinstituted and land them all in jail has them scared shitless. The handicapped queens, Optical Neuropathy and Peripheral Neuropathy, usually so numb and oblivious, are also very excited at the news of twenty thousand entry visas to Úrsula Sánchez Abreu. Loreto the Magnificent colloques — the gallicism is intended — with the Three French Graces and their respective Nursemaids One, Two, and Three; he is very displeased to see the Bowwow Lady leave arm in arm with Fax. Desequilibrium Crespo is grandly describing the film he'll be directing, with Maria de Medeiros in the leading, role to Excelso Pianista, Abad Tamaño, and Legion of False Honor. Upside Down Bunions (who has had only one orgasm in her life and that back in the 1960s with a bearded opportunist who had never been in the vicinity of the Sierra in his life but couldn't shave because he suffered from facial mycosis and got half the world into bed by boasting he was one of the bearded ones in the mountains), who is a television producer and gets paid *for having ideas,* is visiting us for the millionth time to see if she'll finally land an interview with XXL.

She'd be better off scratching lotto tickets — she'd probably have better luck if she tried for the millionaire draw on TF1. Toti Lamarque and Tita Legrando, along with Rumana Engaña, are compiling a list of participants for the New Year's Eve Suitcase Draw —what you get isn't exactly a trip, more like a walk around the block, but hey, maybe you can welcome in the New Year in someone else's neighborhood, like Guanabacoa. In short, we are gathered here today with the cream, the skim, and plenty of scum. They are kept waiting at least two hours in a large hall with granite floors. They've brought in so many gigantic ferns, you'd think you were in the foothills of the Sierra Maestra. I'm beginning to understand why so many journalists love coming here; it's like going to the mountain, since it's not going to come to them. While on their outing, they interview XXL and write books with obvious mountain motifs, with titles like *Hoary Cuba,* and they move around in a world of revolutionary heroes. When the two hours have elapsed, the dividing screens are rolled back and they cross a long hallway, and off in the distance a line begins to form. It seems Cuca Martinez is destined to find long lines wherever she goes, even here, if you can believe it. And she, feeling under the weather poor thing, is jumpy and crampy and this close to a heart attack.

A silver-plated iron wall that tries to capture the flimsiness of aluminum opens automatically; it's really a sliding door made of an exceptionally light material much like a shower curtain. Its dimensions are in the spaceship range. And who to our wondering eyes should appear, not the trekkies from *Star Trek* but XXL in flesh and bone, suited and beaming and powdered like a French Louis (the kings not the coins) and advancing to the head of the line in giant steps. A few steps behind him, believing himself to be as elegant as ever but really looking as absurd, in his linen suit and panama hat, elated and so full of himself you couldn't even fit a bird seed up his ass, comes the Old Man. The very same guy, down to his shoe size, as the New York Mafia fellow. Uan is overcome by dizziness, but he handles himself very professionally, his recovery is quick and nonchalant. Well, let him have his fun while it lasts, 'cause a great ordeal, a major *yeyo,* is about to strike him in the next chapter. Even though the sylvan thicket makes movement difficult, XXL manages to greet and welcome everyone personally, complimenting them on a dress, a wig, a pearl necklace, a pendant, a turd whilst proffering his hand. Flashing cameras capture every handshake as unrefutable proof, future evidence to send people to the gallows, to find them guilty beyond a doubt at trials that have yet to come. The point is — smear away, implicate everyone, there's enough shit to go around. Anyway, even those who aren't splattered by the camera's flash will end up crapping their own pants when all is said and done. The bedpan can fall out of the sky when you least expect it.

10

Forgive Me, Conscience

Forgive me, conscience,
my sweet, dear friend,
your verdict was tough
but well-deserved,
after what I did that night.

By Piloto y Vera,
as sung by Moraima Secada

WHEN EVERY COMPROMISED and compromising greeting and prostration has been carried out, the throng of colorful celebrities spills into an even bigger hall, lit by immense fluorescent tubes. A two-kilometer-long table laden with exquisite food and drink stretches down the middle of the chamber. Cuca Martinez thinks she's in a movie and asks herself, not without trepidation, if this is not indeed the last supper.

(Don't play with fire, you'll get burned. If I've told you once I've told you a thousand times — drop the irony and the silly jokes. This is one place you're going to have to behave yourself, so take it easy. Touch nothing, and let no one touch you. And if you have to use the bathroom make it snappy, don't go hanging and poking around 'cause the cameras are everywhere. The one I'm starting to feel real sorry for is Uan; of course, he asked for it. Well, ain't life a barrel of laughs.)

Well, I don't feel a bit sorry for him. There's only one victim here and her name is Cuca Martinez. As far as I'm concerned, he can take his problems and piss off. Let him deal with his karma. Look, they're already coming for him. Cuca Martinez has to let go of his arm because two men in shiny gray suits, cut from the same cloth they used to ration out so people could outfit themselves for work in the fields and which they still use in a khaki shade for prisoners' shirts (dubbed the XXL style by certain European fashion designers), are asking Uan to accompany them. Forsaken, the old woman seeks out the company of her friends. Arm in arm with La Mechu and La Puchu, she sidles up to the real table that she still thinks must be science fiction. Maria Regla puts an arm around Xerox, and together they scan the room for Fax, who, plate in hand, is already at the head of the line and lunging over the tamale casserole. Uan has been escorted to a special chamber where XXL has gathered the foreign press and is disclosing the forecast of a spectacular citrus harvest. The circumference of this new breed of orange will be equal to that of the earth and each fruit will produce more juice than all the oceans of the planet put together. You will see. You will see.

(We will see indeed! Here we go fucking up the flora and fauna again. At least we won't have colds; instead, we'll have ulcers galore. Things will be just dandy with all that acidity sloshing about in our stomachs, but we'll have tons of vitamin C stockpiled in our bodies [the human not the labor ones]. I try to be specific, because you can never be too careful with language around here — what with the official lingo and the sanctioned jargon and the street talk, the confusion can be something awful, you practically need an interpreter to move between neighborhoods. But every cloud has a silver lining, because at least there is metalinguistic vigor and rigor [mortis]).

Uan finds the Old Man waiting for him; he is his usual cocky self, but the hand he offers in greeting is cold as ice. Because of the air-conditioning, he explains. He seems much too friendly and wants to know if his minion finds the place to his liking, is he comfortable enough, was he able to see his old family, is there anything he can do to help him. No, nothing, Uan is shaking his head and sweating, in spite of the mammoth air-conditioning unit that takes up an entire wall. He is overcome by an urge to break the old guy's nose; it's hairy and teeming with blackheads. With all that money, you'd think he could get himself to a beauty salon for a waxing and facial.

(Have you gone off the deep end, sonny! Don't you get it! The guy thrives on his own nastiness!)

Lady Jane Cricket, I forbid you to use me to address the characters directly.

(And now, they're censoring me, on top of everything! Didn't she say this was going to be my chapter?)

Well, it is, isn't it? Do you think I'm telling everything I know? It's not like you don't rap my fingers with a ruler every time they get carried away on the keyboard! Well, don't you? And even worse, like when you smashed them with the butt end of a machete for cutting sugarcane? Behaving like the good revolutionary conscience you are. If you weren't always standing over my shoulder, I would already have spurted up my hemorrhoids and all. This chapter belongs to you because you, Miss Self-censorship, have played your part to a T.

The Old Man is quiet. The other one hasn't said anything either. The silence is so thick you could cut it with scissors. Uan, who hasn't taken his eyes off his boss, looks completely stumped and arches an eyebrow, as if to ask what the hell are you doing here, his nostrils are flaring as though he's been trapped, his ears flush intermittently as though he's been duped, his mouth contorts in fear, and he looks like a man with few friends.

"I understand your confusion. I decided to come personally and pick up the dollar. Do you have it?" the Old Man asks, feigning indifference.

Uan reluctantly admits he does and pulls out a pack of Vogues, extralong and semiaffected cigarettes, and lights one up. It's been fifteen years since he's smoked the last one, but he still carries his favorite brand around in his pocket for superstitious reasons and as a show of toughness, to prove he gave up the habit without resorting to extreme measures or going stir-crazy. The Old Man puts out his hand and doesn't even say please. Uan places a small white envelope on the outstretched hand, and an aide-de-camp immediately whisks it off to ascertain the authenticity of its contents. In three minutes, he's back. He nods and causes the most beatific and hypocritical smile of an entire lifetime to cross the Old Man's face.

"Well done, young man. Mission accomplished. You'll get your cut, of course. I admire your bravery. I know how tricky things can get. I, myself, am caught up in the most incredible mess right now — last night, at five past eight, I appeared simultaneously on NTV and on CNN and both programs claimed to be live and direct. Imagine! The local chain said I was at the Assembly for Popular Power and CNN had me in Washington meeting with congressmen at the exact same time! I hope it passes unnoticed or unseen or however you say it?"

"Unnoticed." His mouth fills with saliva, he'd like to spit but swallows a good mouthful of bitterness instead.

They are seated on an olive green leather sofa. Uan's ears begin to buzz, strained by his interlocutor's chafing voice. His eyes survey the room like a video camera. In the distance, a hand sets down a glass of Bloody Mary on a small corner table placed near a woven mahogany armchair. His eyes zoom in on a photograph in a gilt rococo frame. In it he sees XXL and the Old Man and Luis standing between them, they're holding one another by the shoulder and are full of life and good cheer somewhere in the Sierra Maestra. Uan turns white as a sheet, he feels his eyes go hollow, as if his eyeballs had jumped their sockets and left them rattling like diving boards.

"What is that picture?" he asks, making a tremendous effort to stay cool, when he is way beyond cool, way way beyond, already feeling the stinging stab in the back that will turn him into a political prisoner or have him extradited to Sing Sing, the jail José Feliciano sings about, for life.

"That snapshot? Yes, it's Luis." And completely unfazed, he continues to rub Uan's shoulder affectionately. "He didn't have faith in us, you know. But let's leave the past behind, we have nothing to gain from it. Let's think of the present or even better, the future. The only way to achieve immortality is by sticking with XXL. I've fought him for years, our ideologies, to the degree we have any, are different, but we have come to see that we must make our peace, we have interests in common. The most recent being the Fountain of Eternal Youth, it's taken him years but he finally found it. He went through Isabel de Bobadilla in his negotiations with Hernando de Soto. He's very proud of it, I think he'll break the news to the press tonight. He also gave me a small bottle of FLP, For Large Penises, a remedy developed by the Institute of Biotechnology to take care of the erection problem. They're currently working on FLC, a similar product for women."

Uan buries himself in the sofa; he is biting his knuckles, there is blood where his teeth broke the skin, tears of helplessness stream down his face; blood and tears run down his arms. He feels absurdly alone, stupidly snared, hopelessly trapped among three families — his New York family, the Old Man, and the one here. He only came for the dollar bill to protect his American wife and daughter, but now that he's here, he feels a deeper attachment to Cuca and Maria Regla, maybe because he feels more indebted to them, they were the first ones after all, for having caused them so much harm.

(I am not going to leave him alone. Even if it's my downfall. It's not right to make firewood from a fallen tree. I told you, some things are just too terrifying to think about and shouldn't be written. But now that you've written them down, you can't back out. You can't take responsibility for some things and not for others. Gray areas are for traitors. You would've done better to keep quiet instead of bungling things and betraying people. But now that you've opened your big mouth, all you can do is let her rip, and I'm behind you. Of course, all you'll get in the end is the destruction of a human being, his total annihilation, and his troubles exposed for all to see. What's the point, I ask you? Why do you need to break the poor guy's balls when he's already up to his neck in hooliganism? Why do you have to pop that picture on him out of the blue, his poor dead friend in the company of his good pals or assassins? And that cynical old bastard mouthing off all those stupidities, killing the poor fellow all over again. Politics are a bad counselor. How many times have I told you not to get mixed up? Aren't you ashamed to face those other two, whose pictures you have hung in front of your desk? Doesn't it break your heart to let them see the stuff you're up to, the stuff you write? Aren't you afraid your beloved, exemplary writers will abandon you and stop protecting you, get bored with all your busybody meddling?)

One, taken in Havana in the 1960s, is a black and white photo signed by Chantal Triana. In it, José Lezama Lima is sitting in what looks like a sunlit doorway; his right hand rests on a Formica table; his guayabera is superwellpressed, the front pocket holds a bottle of asthma medication; his left hand strokes a pack of cigarettes. The second one is a beautiful portrait of Marguerite Yourcenar, taken by Christian Lvowski, a friend of Jean Mattern, who so kindly made me a gift of this limpid image of the Belgian writer, her half-smile lined with intelligent wrinkles, her eyes sunken, the childish gape of her mouth, stray gray hairs obscuring the ear from which a pearl dangles. In a curious way, it is the pearl that is the focal point of the picture — as if to suggest the purity of the pearl is in that face, in that soul, like a treasure brought back from the ocean depths. There is also a photograph of my mother. I'm surprised you forgot to include her in your list of sublime photographic subjects. My mother, faraway, my mother beyond reach. She, too, is smiling and stands surrounded by other mothers who don't seem any less happy. Happy to live without their children? Happy in the expectation of bad news? Anyway, she's always happy in the pictures she sends me, so I won't worry I suppose. She is sitting so close to the edge of the sofa she looks like she's about to fall off, I always want to grab her when I look at that picture. She wears the green sweater I bought her at the Ronda Universitat in Barcelona, and a pair of tawny latex slacks that zip up the front, apparently it's quite chilly in this picture of my mother sitting in my apartment in my Havana. Behind her, I can see my books and my knickknacks, I see irreversible loss, perhaps. My mother, the wellspring of all my fears. My nightly dream. Thorn in my flesh. My fount of courage. My mother who taught me how to be a mother. When it is not our children, it is our mothers we leave behind as hostages. No, I do not feel shame, I am not upset. Yes, I do, I am. I feel everything at once. In front of these faces, I feel rage, pain, valor.

They look on in approval, and in disapproval, why must everything be positive all the time. They have lived their lives, done what fell to them to do. And I have to take on what's mine to take on, take care of my things. The dead one implores me at the top of her lungs, breathing down my neck. I cannot keep quiet. To hell with those who stifle their destinies. Let's get back to Uan, I have no intention of leaving him stranded. Mystery whispers a song in his ear:

> I had so wished it and dreamed it,
> anticipated it so,
> and when I saw you by my side,
> I left the past and its chains behind.

And with these lines, he finds himself back in the here and now; he takes out a Guerlain-perfumed towelette and cleans his hands one finger at a time; with halting steps (and breath), he makes his way to the great hall where he will meet up with Cuquita and Reglita. The room is a buzz of refried beans and frivolity. The honorific and horrific induction ceremony is over; Nitiza Villainterpol is officially part of the party that's falling apart at the seams; she is being rewarded for her culinary genius — her three million inedible recipes for the ingredient-free kitchen. After the usual speech and show of false modesty, the famished beasts attack the groaning board. As you can imagine, not even one of her three million concoctions is on the menu. Cuquita had not seen such feasting in centuries, it looked like a telethon for starvelings and no matter how they ate and drank, the trays and drinks kept coming. If it had been a glutton competition, they would have been awarded a collective medal. The world has never seen such pushing and shoving and reaching for fried pork rinds, or a handful of plantain chips or plantain fritters, or a taste of tiny fried bananas, or a helping of fried or roast pork, or a heaping of Havana-style minced meat (the good kind, made with real beef), or lobster tails or shrimp in garlic, or a spoonful of dozing black beans — in other words, it was an eat-your-head-off event. The tamale casserole is a house speciality, so are the French cheeses, which aren't really French but imitation, but even XXL says the copy is better than the original. We are world champions, even when it comes to French cheese. The guests need only sniff the corks to get drunk out of their heads and wits. The bread is fresh from the oven. Cristal and Hatuey are the beers of choice. For dessert, there is Coppelia ice cream — a Cuban agent stole the recipe from an American firm — strawberry and chocolate, what else.

Cuca has eaten like a ghoul, her stomach so bloated she looks like a thread with a knot for a midriff. La Mechu has not stopped saying, wow these people sure know their chow, and La Puchu has not stopped slapping her for the idiot she is and asking her who else did she think would know about chow? Fax is still trying to sell her autobiography to the Bowwow Lady, who tells her she's only in the market for street art she can buy for a song. And an immense confusion ensues, because Xerox has just unearthed a network of art thieves in the modern gossip notebook she borrowed from Automatic Answering Machine (who in turn got it from one of the Three French Graces); curiously, all the injured or embezzled parties are on shaky sexual ground, as well as being intellectuals and avid collectors; of course, they've also wreaked havoc in a number of museums and art institutes; they're definitely a deft and nimble crew with the luck of the lucky. Automatic Answering Machine dismisses Xerox as incorrigible and wanders off, smitten by Paul Culón's buck teeth. Yocandra embarks on yet another philosophical debate with her two irreconcilable husbands. Adobo Mayomber, the Maceo sympathizer, is keeping an eye on her and bolting down pork rinds; he is an intriguer by profession and has recently become obsessed with the promising new trio of Cuban cinematography: Thirst and Surf, Ear of Bread, and Auspicious Insomnia, who are having their first concrete encounter with a protein croquette, they've never tasted meat in their lives. Maria Regla is flirting with Licensed Programmer. As his name indicates, he is in charge of programming for National Terrorvision, TVUUUHHH; he explains they're so happy with how the abbreviation turned out, because it gives terror-spectators an accurate idea of the horrors in store. Licensed Programmer is the brains behind *Distribution of Foodstuffs*, the most informative show on TV. In truth, Licensed Programmer is newly back on the scene, after many long years of compulsory retirement, his reward for being too bright for his own good and trying to do more with less. In the early days of the social experiment, Licensed Programmer was picked for the difficult task of traveling abroad as a buyer; they say he singlehandedly saved Alfa Romeo from total bankruptcy in the 1970s, when he bought their entire stock of discontinued cars; they became our taxicabs. But his true troubles began when he was given loads of money and dispatched on another buying mission; right off the bat, he was shown a fleet of very pretty machines and told how the fate of yet another factory hung in the balance if someone didn't turn up soon to take these babies off their hands. Licensed Programmer felt so sorry for the manufacturer, he bought the whole lot, never even bothering to ask what they were for. He finally got around to reading the instruction manual when he went to pick up his cargo from the Havana Customs Bureau. And that's when it dawned on him he had purchased a squad of snowplows, and that's how he ended up as the director of a cultural program in Pinar del Río. Things didn't go so well there either; one morning, he received the following telegram: PLEASE COMMA HOST CHAMBER GROUP TOAST OF THE PARTY. To which he promptly responded, being neither a lazy nor a trusting man, certain the telegraph operator had made an error: TOO OVERWHELMED BY WORK TO HOST IN CHAMBER STOP HAVE NEITHER MATERIALS NOR MEANS TO GIVE TOAST OR PARTIES. Well, that was the end of him for many long years. Until now, when he's resurfaced blithe as air, rising like the phoenix from its ashes, still convinced that he's never made a mistake in his life, his only faults being excessive diligence and partisan goodwill. Leveling with Maria Regla, he asks her if she's interested in swapping sex for a spot on TV. She says yes without missing a beat; disappointments and missed opportunities have worn her down. Look at her father, after all — he used to be the enemy and here he is, an honored guest.

Cuquita's first mistake was to pull out her trusty bag and start filling it up with food, laying in reserves for tomorrow. Two guards appear at her side the minute they see her stuffing the bag with goodies. Cuca Martinez is completely unfazed and keeps going about her business, she is securing her future. The future for her consists of tomorrow's breakfast, lunch, and dinner. Pretty soon, she's distracted by a wriggly feeling in her skinny, saggy breasts. She thinks it's the lump, but no, the lump is fast asleep, tired from a full day's thumping. Oh little Virgin of Cobre, it's them, Nadezhda and Perfect Rat! And now she makes her second mistake. She pulls out the roach and the rat and without a second thought sets them down to eat on a tray of fried plantains. The producer Upside Down Bunions is the one who raises the hue and cry as she makes a flying jump for the curtains. And the place goes haywire. Cuquita has only one thing on her mind: she must get her friends to safety, and holding the bag in one hand and picking them up with the other, she makes a dash for the exit doors. Uan grabs his daughter by the arm and they run off after her. As always, there's a phalanx of guards outside the doors. But old slyboots signals behind her and yells:

"Run, run! We've been invaded by rats and roaches!"

"Invaded!" The word is enough, the guards need not hear the rest.

The pathetic gorillas swallow her every word, old ladies don't tell lies, and dash down the hallways and past the doors and jump into the fray, the out-and-out mayhem that's taken over the main room, the Red Room, nothing to do with the Capri of course. Uan and Maria Regla catch up with her in the parking lot. They rush to find the Mercy-Benz; when they're safely inside, Uan takes his time to start up the car, they gently roll away so as not to arouse suspicion. Ivo's Chevrolet soon appears behind them with La Mechu and La Puchu, Fax, Xerox, Hernia, and Yocandra and her two husbands. Uan scrabbles around in the glove compartment and comes up with one of those compact cereal discs, he removes it from its wrapper and plastic sleeve and delicately prods it with one finger and it slips into the laser record player. Moraima Secada's voice fills the charged atmosphere:

> I filled my head with dreams
> and drank to glory
> knowing all the time
> I was no longer my own man.

Cuca Martinez sighs loudly, as if to interrupt the song. Which would be tantamount to interrupting her own life. And Uan, who is sad and feels responsible for everything that went wrong and guilty to the marrow of his bones for injuring this woman's love over and over again, switches it off. Again, you could cut the silence with scissors, it's denser than corduroy in that car. Maria Regla breaks the ice:

"How about we go dancing, ladies and gentlemen? At the Salsa Palace. Come on, don't make such long faces! This isn't a funeral procession, after all. Don't let all this get you down! Hey, you only live once."

Cuca's lace hankie cannot take any more nose blowing; Reglita's consoling words have given rise to tears of joy. Nadezhda and Perfect Rat, peeping over the black lamé balcony of her décolleté, are visibly moved as well. Uan puffs out his chest in fatherly pride and looks like a weight lifter who just made Olympic gold. Without pause, the tires of the Mercy-Benz zip round to reenter the mysteries of the Havana night and they blast off toward salsa heaven.

(Now, you're talking! I thought you'd never get me out of that sniff-my-ass, kiss-my-feet affair. But the Salsa Palace is a completely different story, it's for folks who are not all there or anywhere. And frankly, that's more my style, wiggling my ass and letting the bilirubin skyrocket while I'm somewhere else. Letting the good times roll and the juices flow — things don't get better than that, my sweet. Have you ever been to a porn flick? What am I saying, you're too young! But how about when you were abroad, did you ever go inside one of those little shops of horrors where they sell immense dongs with thorns? Aah! forget it! You were cut out to be a nun! Anyway, I think it's high time you went to the New Continental, one of those Chinese theaters on Calle Zanha. True, you'll have to sit through an incredibly dated Chinese movie without subtitles and then the newsreel and then a film from the backward school of Latin American Cinema, but what do you care, you're not there for the features or to write a review. You're there for the free-for-all, the higgledy-piggledy going on all around you. Now that the motels have been closed down, the New Continental is the place to bonk, it's cheap and you get to suck in Chinese, what more could you ask for? That's why they call it the Milky Palace. Wonderful stuff, sweetie! Ah, *voilà!* It is here already — aren't I just too French! The Salsa Palace, where we will make a mad dash for the dance floor, hurling ourselves into the arena to be eaten by lions, stepping into the ring to be pulped by Stevenson — oh how I would love for someone to smack me round the face and spank my ass, to leave me jingling with pleasure and wallowing in sweat, but no blood, never blood. Sugarcane sap is the only thing flowing through my veins, ain't it so, gentlemen! So, come on over big boy, give us a rub with your tool, go on ahead and make yourself at home, come on install yourself, don't stall. And you, don't be such a prude, come, let's dance! I'm warning you, you're on your own if you're not coming. What's wrong with you? Aren't you supposed to be my soul sister? My accomplice and all that, like in the poem by Benedetti! Go on, let your hair down, what are you — shellfish! Look at her, putting on airs! Little Miss Anonymous! Doesn't eat, doesn't dance, doesn't sing — nothing, not even fruit. Well, the fruit part is understandable 'cause they've dropped off the face of the earth. Look, doesn't it break your heart, even your characters are hot for the here and now: Cuca Martinez and Uan flailing about with the Charanga Habanera and melancholic with Isaac, he's been looking terribly skinny lately. Maria Regla doing the limbo with a pretty boy from Los Sitios. La Mechu and La Puchu carrying on together as usual. Thank goodness their breakdowns are behind them, 'cause, honey, those women suffered big-time in the summer of '94. How come you skipped that part? You see, you censor yourself all by your lonesome. Don't you roll your eyes at me! How dare you shush me! I'm the boss here, after the dead one, I know. Okay, where were we? But don't think I'm going to forget about La Mechu and La Puchu so easily . . . Hernia dislocating her limbs and letting off steam, doing the salsa-rap. Fax hooking up with a Canadian investor, and if she keeps offering him her tits as a desk, he will most certainly be publishing her memoirs. Xerox jumping up and down and sniffing out evil, keeping track of everything in the notebook she stole from Automatic Answering Machine in all the confusion. Yocandra and her two Rodin thinkers sit like three scholars in a row. Intellectuals are the one thing I can't stand! They grow up in a slum, hungry as mice, with someone banging a rhumba on a trash can just outside their window, they read four or five books, they move from Cayo Hueso to Miramar, and suddenly, they think they're Chateaubriand or Lord Byron or Mme de Staël. But I'm sure that's nowadays, because I would bet my jugular that Gabriel de la Concepción Valdés, Placido to his pals, was not so full of shit and he was plenty smart too, and look how they shot him full of holes when that Escalera conspiracy stuff was going down round 1884. Well, you gonna join or what? Join Up! Oh goodness me, I sound just like that pushy slogan for the Union of Communist Youth. She sings along with La Charanga:

> Find yourself a sugar daddy
> over thirty but not quite fifty . . .
> and you'll get everything your little heart desires,
> Juaniquiqui!)

I had no idea Lady Janes could disgrace themselves like that, such indecent behavior and nothing I could do to stop it. But she's right about one thing: between a computer and a drum, I'll take the drum. Cuca Martinez and Uan are elated, reliving their finest hour, and they couldn't be in finer form — now that's what I call dancing. Plenty of cruiser dudes from Vedado would kill to master those old-time steps. The crowd falls back, making a circle around them and clapping to the beat, tourist cameras flash with Japanese abandon. Cuca's radiant happiness is the envy of more than one visitor from those pale and well-fed European lands. Not to be demagogic about it, don't think I'm making allowances for the propaganda of hunger that would have you believing we're all happy here even though we have nothing to call our own. Make no mistake, Cuca is happy because she loves. Because she, sirree, as you see, is again in the arms of the man who drives her wild! In any event, just now, they both feel like they're about to drop, they're out of breath and their hearts are beating a mile a minute and they tell Reglita they're ready to leave.

Mercy-Benz — a vehicle that's getting to be more human by the hour — trundles along one of those Old Havana streets, down there, where Reglita lives. Uan, anxious to see how his daughter lives, used the pretext that he didn't want her going home alone at this hour of the night. In its ray of moonlight, the patio fountain looks like something that could have come from Florence. The girl leads the way, her parents come after, chagrined by the dark and dank, by the spiral staircase insubstantial as onion skin. They enter a cavelike hovel of a room, superkitschy posters of variety singers like the exiled Annia Linares adorn the walls, there is a small Spanish Mortification table (I apologize for the sameness of the decor, but that particular style took Cuban living rooms by storm), a clay pot filled with papier-mâché flowers sits on a plastic doily, the cot where she sleeps has weathered every position in the Kama-sutra and it shows. A loud bedspread, stitched from chenille remnants, covers the cot; Maria Regla, who is allergic to chenille, spends her nights sneezing under that cover. A hole in the wall serves as a closet, across it hangs a curtain of discarded film strips, given to her by Donatién, her friend who works at ICAIC. Yellowing, moth-eaten, well-thumbed books are piled up in a corner. Uan sighs in dismay, so this is how his daughter, the journalist, lives. Not that there aren't journalists all over the world who live in similar or worse conditions, but that's not the point, is it? Are we talking about making things worse or making them better? It's not a matter of choosing the lesser evil, is it? Of nullifying, impoverishing, degrading the conditions in which human beings live? Is it development or underdevelopment we're after? Is human advancement measured in degrees of poverty or of development? Is poverty a synonym for dignity? Come on, Lady Jane, set me straight on this:

(That's a tough one. No matter what I say I'm bound to have one of the two camps jumping all over me. *Better I should keep quiet, not say a thing . . .*)

You piece of opportunistic shit! You really disappoint me! I don't know how I could've trusted you, you folkloric scum!

(Don't insult me or there'll be hell to pay! When will you learn that life is a long, long train of disappointments. And the ride is free. I cannot answer that question. Sorry, I can't help you there, can't toss you a lifeline on that one. How do you expect me to have an answer,

212

when even the developed world doesn't have one? Go on, write it down, say we'll just have to wait. And add, with faith, hope, and charity, like in that Mexican movie.)

Seeing her parents in such low spirits, Maria Regla hugs and covers them with warm, slobbery-as-okra kisses. She is sad but feigns indifference, and sees them off with a simple:

"Mom, Dad, sleep well. I'll see you tomorrow."

And now the time has come, I believe, for me, Lady Jane Cricket, to tell you about the events La Mechu and La Puchu lived through in the summer of '94. At this very moment, Cuca Martinez is on her way home, riding down the Malecón and pensively staring at the ocean engulfed by the thick, black night and remembering that other summer night, just a year ago, when La Mechunga and La Puchunga mysteriously asked her to get Reglita and come meet them in the Rincón de Guanabo. When she and her daughter arrived at the appointed place, the twilight had not properly set in, a dark blue quality filled the air, and a marine breeze incited one to adventure, to bold crossings worthy of Captain Cousteau. Which is precisely what La Mechu and La Puchu had in mind, a bold crossing to the turbulent and brutal North. They got tired of waiting around for the gas to be turned back on, of marathonic blackouts, of eating poorly fumigated beans, and the pair of them had fallen in love with Wacky Squirt, an orphan who swore he was not about to waste his life on this satanic island and who was twenty years their junior. They decided to throw care to the winds and their bodies to the high seas and go with him on his homemade raft. Cuca Martinez knelt on the shore and sobbed, begging them to reconsider, to stop and think a little, just this much, and she showed them the tip of a fingernail, of the great danger they were putting themselves in. Meanwhile, Wacky Squirt secured bundles, rolled up lengths of rope, and double-checked everything down to the last detail. Maria Regla did not utter a word, she stood there with her arms crossed, her eyes on the horizon, tears of rage rolling down her freezing cheeks, the wind blowing her hair about and making her face look sharp.

"Shut up, Mom!" she finally exploded. "Let them go, if they

want to risk it all and end their days as shark feed. And me thinking the two of you had changed! Saw you as my family! You tricked me. You never loved me."

With tears in her eyes and a lump in her throat, La Puchunga moved toward her:

"Don't say that, sweetheart. Of course we love you, but we can't go on like this, my angel! We don't fit in this society. Do you know that I've spent the last week looking high and low for any kind of anti-spasmodic medication, those badly fumigated beans did me a lot of harm, you know. I thought I'd go across the puddle and see if I could find that wretched medicine and get my stomach some relief. Sure, we've fallen head over heels for Squirt, but that's not the main thing . . . You've seen with your own eyes how much we've suffered. Reglita, our lives were snapped, clipped in the bud. They never really accepted us —"

"Stop explaining," La Mechu angrily cuts in. "Did she stop to think of us when she went off on her militant duties?"

That made no difference to La Puchu, who still wanted to kiss the Girl good-bye. Maria Regla turned away and shoved La Puchunga from her, the older woman lay embedded in the sand in a ring of tiny seashells. Cuca, who was swimming in grief by now, put her arms around her friend and helped her up. She walked alongside them until the water reached her neck, and even when the raft disappeared into the night, Cuca still stood there saying good-bye and half-drowned by the sea. A few feet away, Maria Regla was burying her face and her rage in the sand.

La Mechu, La Puchu, and Wacky Squirt rowed and rowed like zombies. At long last, they were picked up by an American boat and delivered to the Guantánamo Naval Base. They lasted four months in those tents. Desperate, missing Cuquita and Reglita like crazy and incited yet again by Wacky Squirt, who was so disheartened by how his plan had backfired and missing his girlfriend, they decided to escape back to where they came from, except this time they would go by land and cross the minefield that separates the Cuban territory from what until now has been the American, but who knows who it will belong to in the next century. The women miraculously made it, but Wacky Squirt got caught, his leg blown to pieces. They went back to help, to salvage what was left of him. The trio got a hero's welcome. Back again to normal or paranormal life. Wacky Squirt, minus a leg, sought comfort in the arms of his young lady. The women took over the young man's care, they were no longer interested in being his lovers, just his aunts. The truth is, all three silently suffered through the trauma of mutilation. But clearly, the young man was the most affected, and he didn't hold out much hope for another chance.

Cuca would prefer to forget the incident. Neither she nor Reglita knew if they should've been happy or sad when they saw their two friends coming back. After all, they had gotten used to thinking of them as free. Cuca closed her eyes and stuck her head outside the car window; the sea breeze mussed up her hair and ruffled her eyelashes and ordered her thoughts. Dear God! She could've lost her dearest friends forever! How could she have allowed them to go off like that, to endanger their lives like that!

They cruise down the Avenue of the Malecón for the last time. Coated with salt and wind and dreams, they finally pull up in front of Cuca's building. At the door, she invites him inside. He smiles, and it is this last image of him smiling that she will remember. This is the night, it is understood, when everything that happens to them will end up in the *last time* file.

Just as they're entering the building, a couple of very flustered-looking comrades intercept Uan. They pin their distress on what they describe as a minor blunder on Uan's part. He should've known better. How could he have been discourteous to the Old Man? Now, the guy had suffered a heart attack and was in a critical state. It all happened immediately after his conversation with Uan; first, he turned pea green, then, he spat up a black clot. In the ambulance he was choking, gasping for air, his chest completely blocked. You really stuck your head in the lion's mouth this time, and then you spat. There are limits to indecency. In short:

"You are detained," which always sounds nicer than "under

arrest" or "in custody." "We invite you for questioning at Villa-marista, and then in the morning, you'll be deported, Esteemed Persona Non Grata."

Cuca Martinez claps a hand to her mouth and stifles a scream. She doesn't faint. She takes a deep breath and carefully sets down Nadezhda and Perfect Rat on the doorstep. Immediately, they begin digging a tunnel. I have no idea why everyone thinks of tunnels as symbols of freedom. Nothing could be easier than plugging up the entrance and drowning the runaways. She firmly takes her man by the hand. If they're taking him, they'll have to take her too — that's the message. A member from the rival gang is now sitting at the wheel of the Mercy-Benz, and just like in a Walt Disney cartoon, the car's bumper grimaces in disgust. She'd like to come along? No problem. And they herd the pair of them into the backseat. The journey is long and dreary, somber, like a trip to nihility should be, to Cayo Cruz, to the cemetery of garbage. He is not afraid. Neither is she. They sit close together, holding hands in the backseat. Bride and groom. Married at last. Cuffed at the wrists and bound with chains of iron. You can't be too picky, a wedding is a wedding.

(They're not afraid, you say? They're shitting bricks, you mean! They can just hide it better than others. The last thing you want to do is show these ruffians you're yellow with fear. Sign here please, sir, and the little lady, and drive on in. The problem is going to be when they get there, not that there is a there, and they separate them. That's when the shit will hit the fan and the real willies will get going. When they throw her in the cold room and him in the hot one. When she's about to turn into an iceberg and he's turning into onion soup in the pitch black dark. Even though they'll sometimes shine a light about two millimeters from his pupils for hours on end. Then they'll turn off all the lights again, and that's when the small animals come in. The pets, as they say. A female caiman for her, a male one for him; the national reptile, looks just like the map of Cuba. They're there for a night, a week, they can't say for sure. And at the end of that time, which is the end of all time, they'll let them go. But not just like that. Are you crazy! He'll be driven straight to an airplane and catapulted into the stratosphere as Persona Non

Grata. She'll be dropped off on a street in a small town she'll instantly recognize. Her hometown, Santa Clara in the old province of Villas. She is grateful, in her mind she bids her friends La Mechu and La Puchu a sweet good-bye. Good-bye sweet ladies, sweet scramble-brained ladies, woozier than oozing batteries. Good-bye Nadezhda Common Itch and Perez, the Perfect Rat. Bye, bye Fax, bye Xerox, and Hernia and Yocandra. She's thick with dreams now, kisses the forehead of a newborn. Maria Regla, don't kill your mother, child. Your Cuca Martinez loves you all. On a radio in a neighboring shack, a very old recording of Moraima Secada, the mulatta who died of love, is playing:

> I have forgotten all those things
> in the world that
> make pleasure short
> and sorrow long.

Cuca Martinez moves her sad mouth and mouths the words to the rest of the song:

> Forgive me, conscience
> I know you were right
> but at the time
> only feeling mattered,
> reason did not count.

Reason did not count. Reason did not count. Reason did not count. Reason did not count. Reason did not count. Reason did not count. Reason did not count. Reason did not count. Reason did not count. Reason did not count. Reason ... Crash! Piiiiiiiiiiiiiiiiiiiiiiiiiiiiiiiiiiiiiiiiiiiiiiiiiiiiiiiii. Ischemia Arteriosclerosis. Brain death. Vegetable. One way to salvation.)

11 and Finale

Havana Nostalgia

Nostalgic, I yearn for you
but destiny forbids it,
when, Havana, beloved land,
when will I see you again?

By B. Collazo,
as sung by Celia Cruz

IT'S VERY EARLY MORNING. Our daybreak here, in the tropics is red, warm, much too perfumed, garish. As he ascends the stairs of the aircraft, Uan takes in the landscape of Rancho Boyeros, funny name for an airport. He takes a last deep breath of Havana air. Nothing, not the palm trees, not the riotous vegetation, not the people hanging over the banisters of the airport terrace — every last one of them consumed by the anxiety of a loved one's imminent arrival or departure — not the pathetic enforcers of that modicum of power conferred by walkie-talkies, not the electrified fences in the far distance, not the sadness of this ugly airport, gray as an egg carton, not the blue sky, nor the immense sun, nor the clouds like cotton candy, none of that will ever equal his yearning for this smell, the smell of Havana — difficult to describe, impossible to shake off. A smell that is both fluid and overpowering, a smell he could use to describe the aromatic flesh of Cuca Martinez or his daughter's fragrant cheeks.

He turns and disappears into the airplane, he's so wobbly you'd think it was his first time.

Maria Regla dashes down the dank stairway of the edifice she calls home — 305 Empedrado, between Villegas and Aguacate. She is euphorically happy, life is meaningful again now that she's been reunited with her father, she sees the error of her rigid ways, the wrongness of her political correctness. Also, thanks to Licensed Programmer, she's finally landed herself a story. She'll pay her pound of flesh, of course. But she feels so fortunate right now, she can even look at this flophouse where she lives and see it as a palace. In fact, the place must have been palatial in its day. The inner patio boasts a nineteenth-century fountain, an old waterless Triton, weathering rainy seasons and ignorance. Only Maria Regla knows the old, beached marble is a deity from Greek mythology, the other residents mistake him for Saint Lazarus and every December seventeenth, they used to burn candles in his honor. Now, they don't even have candles for blackouts, so forgive them Old Babalú Ayé, they still pray to you every day, with even greater fervor now they're out of candles. Maria Regla is glad she lives on the edge of Centro Havana and not in the filthy heart of Old Havana, though she wouldn't mind a little place in Vedado or in Miramar, or really, in her heart of hearts, in Miami, hush your mouth shameful heart! Still, she is very proud she bought this room for twenty thousand Cuban pesos, at a time when twenty thousand Cuban pesos was a respectable sum of money and people were selling their properties like hotcakes and the local currency still meant something. She had purchased it with the sweat of her brow, with savings that dated back to her first position as a salaried journalist (they get paid a pittance). And, why delude oneself, with additional clandestine savings from selling all kinds of junk on the black market, everything from tinned deodorant to blurry photocopies of books by Alain Kardec, very sought after works, critical materials in the training of many progressive *santeras*. Maria Regla is still tearing down the spiral staircase at breakneck speed, the old, rotting wood creaks beneath her feet, in those places where the steps have completely disappeared she jumps and the entire structure resounds with her every landing. A fine dust falls from the building's quaking dome, whitening her hair, her eyelashes, her shoulders. She's rushing off to her next assignment, so happy she's trembling; finally, after an eternity of waiting, she has landed herself a story on the only remaining newscast on TV. Licensed Programmer decided in her favor because he trusts in her intellectual abilities and because she's one of the remaining few; journalists are no longer returning from foreign assignments. She's been asked to report on a very topical issue: the rural free market. No way she's going to miss this opportunity; no one is going to stop her this time. This is her third chance to prove her stuff as a journalist. Twelve years out of school and she's only had three jobs. Maria Regla's feet are coming down hard, her heart, too, is beating hard, bursting with song and hope. When she's almost reached street level, she realizes that five more steps have collapsed in the night. It's a long way to jump, she'll have to leap and hope for the best. She pushes off, the old-fashioned legal folder she inherited from the grandfather of one of her friends is wedged under her arm. Suddenly she's airborne, for a full five seconds she hovers in stop-motion, like in a kung fu movie, she considers the dangers of landing, of reaching ground, but she has no choice in the matter. How could she? She's only an inexperienced professional, holding two degrees — thanks to XXL and the revo and all that other stuff we already know by heart — whose only choices have been either to jump on the bandwagon of bullshitters she is condemned to live with or to retire to her room and lock the doors. She touches down like the negligible hundred-pound thing she is, her feet lightly regaining the building's front-door step. But her fall is the drop that overflows the cup, it's the last snippet of a burning wick, the haphazard unpinning of a hand grenade. One hundred fifty years of cement and stone and wood and sand come instantly crashing behind her. One hundred fifty years of history. One hundred fifty years of life. The boardinghouse caves in and they're all sleeping. Every last one of them dies. The building succumbs to dust. Nothing, not even an ouch, only the huge thwack of a boot, and then silence, transcendental, beautiful. Somewhere inside the rubble, a cassette player mysteriously turns itself on, and a forbidden voice floats in the cloud of dust:

221

Havana, will those days ever come back I ask,
Havana, to walk the Malecón in search of your moon
Havana, to see the brightness of your beaches again
Havana, to find your smiling streets again,
Havana, I may be far but did not forget,
Havana, nostalgic, I yearn for you.

The cameraman waits outside, smoking a Popular and leaning against the hubcap. He barely makes it to the opposite sidewalk. From across the street he can see a young woman's hand emerging from the rubble. He runs to her side, calls for help, firemen come, ambulances too. The first body they carry out is the journalist's; she was closest to the surface.

(Is that how things happened! You are breaking my heart with this story. Dear God in Heaven, Yemayá on High! Couldn't you have done a little something for her. That poor mother is going to die of cardiac arrest. The leading national cause of mortality and morbidity. It's too much, too many blows. But then again, she's half gone, disconnected from reality. Anyway, I would have wished for things to turn out differently. But if that's the way it's gonna be, well that's the way it's gonna be and end of story. No use messing around with destiny! I say onward with electricity and progress! But still, I really wished her the best.)

And for the dead one, too. She's no different from anybody else, she doesn't want to die, especially now with so many opportunities coming her way. Now, she's just been reunited with her father. But that's life for you, a romance novel, a Venezuelan soap opera. Speaking of Venezuelan soap operas, why don't we bring her back to life? I mean, in those stories, where there's a will there's a way. So why don't we brush her off and set her back on her feet. She wants it so badly.

(Yeah! Do it. Resuscitate her. She didn't deserve that death, buried in the rubble of a collapsed rooming house, so unpoetic, so vulgar. Do it for your mother's sake, come on, I'm begging you, go on, give her mouth-to-mouth. Don't be mean-spirited. Artificial resuscitation, come on!)

I wouldn't ask for anything better, but don't forget, she has to give her permission. She's the one dictating the book, remember. Yeah! Didn't you get it? She's the corpse, Maria Regla, and she's been dictating the whole thing from chapter 1 — word by word and comma by comma.

(You're kidding! Well, all the more reason then. Come on, show a little gratitude. So she's the one who has been busting like a mule, not you. Ask for her permission. I'm sure she'll say yes. She must be dying to live again.)

Fine, I'll ask. But I want to make one thing clear, we've both worked equally hard.

Give leave father, give leave mother, give leave echu Alagbana, give leave house echu akuokoyeri, give leave corner 3 and ficus tree, salutations godmother, you of the second chair, salutations to the one who watches over Orula, salutations to my head, salutations to all the orisha, and salutations to the ancestors. Salutations to the privileged head, orisha of ocean depths, thy son be king, be alert on the roadway, the deer belongs to Obatalá, give word Obatalá with the right.

Rewind footage. Take two. Exterior. Day. Scene without death of Maria Regla. Roll cameras. I mean, hand write! The cameraman smokes a Popular and waits, leaning against the hubcap. He catches the falling bundle in the nick of time. Luckily, it drops straight into his arms. It's the languid body of a young woman. Cradling her in his arms, he runs toward a waiting Lada. Once they're inside, the driver, who is dumbfounded and cannot say for certain if he has witnessed a fire or a quake, puts the car in motion. The crowd of curious onlookers vanishes into dust and smoke, a billowing fog that reeks of sewage rises up to the defiled and polluted sky. Firemen's sirens and hooting policemen's whistles put the whole city on alert. When Maria Regla regains consciousness, they're already on Calle Línea and going past Vedado. Soon they'll be in Miramar and then in the outer suburbs and the small towns and on and on until they reach the appointed place, where they plan to interview the bumpkins.

"Holy Virgin of Regla! What the fuck happened back there? All I did was jump. I knew it, I could feel it in my bones, when I was up in the air, I knew something was going to go terribly wrong! Someone's always whispering these things in my ear before they happen. Sweet Mother of God, they all died, the children — Angelito, Patricita, Rebequita, Elenita, Carlitos — oh my God! And what the hell am I doing here? Where are we going anyway?"

The driver gapes at her in the rearview mirror, the cameraman turns around in the front seat and he doesn't look any less stunned. Neither one can emit a sound, the cataclysm has devoured their voices. She understands. She stops crying. She smooths her hair, sticky with dust and sweat. She rests her elbow on the window and grips her skull with her hand, her fingers disappear inside her hair. She realizes she's lost everything. The story is all she has left. And do it she will. Then, we'll see.

A vaporous somnolence comes over her, she is lulled by sea air and despair. Everything itches, her pupils, her gums, her brain. Still, she has no wish to close her eyes; she forces herself to look at the landscape, the faces, the streets. The filthy streets, shorn of trees, mangy dogs frantically rubbing their raging flesh against the pavement, recently decapitated cats still wriggling in pools of blood or flapping on clotheslines. Barefoot, hungry children in rags; the smallest ones run naked. Embittered, diseased, muttering women. Younger ones languishing in bakery doorways. Men thinking up new ways of killing one another; the women would do it for them, if it were not for the children. The elderly burn in funeral pyres on every corner. They have no houses or money or water or electricity. Only taxes. They call these people the *indigent,* and they are the majority. They drive on and things change; houses with bars on their doors and windows, new, shiny, recently painted dollar shops with plastic curtains and frosted glass to deter curious eyes; neon signs — RÁPIDOS, CUPETS, FOOD AND GASOLINE FOR SALE, DOLLARS ONLY. The shoppers who leave these places, no one notices them when they're entering, are a completely new breed. They carry nylon bags loaded with red meat and Coca-Cola in cans, they wear blue jeans and Florida palm trees on their shirts, there are polka dots on their tennis shoes, and their cheeks are pink. Even though they're always carrying on like dissatisfied *gusanos,* they still seem to expect something from this regime, they are the hypocrites, their hatred of the ration booklet is profound. At one point or another they must have worked in the secret police — a group that is largely exempted from shortages — or maybe they're the fortunate ones who have not been forgotten by their relatives in the United States, or they are whores and pimps who've struck pay dirt, or blackmarketholics who deal in cigarettes and rum and marijuana and cocaine, they are the *tourists of the world, unite* etc. — They call the people who emerge from such places, their number growing by the day, *diplopeople.* Behind grimy curtains, in closely watched neighborhoods, locked up with their terror, chewing their nails to the quick, cloistered in their mess, yelling at the toilet bowl, hugging the telephone for dear life, black and blue from beatings, placing all their hopes on journalists from abroad, or from beyond abroad, these are the minority they call the *dissidents.*

Paranoid and deeply depressed, yet pretending to be lively and euphoric and very sure of themselves, vain and proud of ideas they claim are unprecedented since the beginning of time, certain to make loads of money, strong, healthy, invincible, indestructible, they are the living bastion of mediocrity; exemplary, spectacular, arrogant, and of course corruptible — excuse me incorruptible — irreplaceable, powerful, immortal sons of bitches, and these are the *leaders.* I think I've summed them up nicely. Maria Regla lists them according to the current social order: the leaders, the diplopeople, the dissidents, the indigents. Shit! What's gotten into me? How could I skip the *survivors!* Read — artists, philosophers, writers — if they don't foul things up and end up belonging to one of the preceding groups.

This is the city that Maria Regla sees. Deserted avenues, except for the occasional diplocar running over the occasional diplodog. A diploLada with white diplomatic plates pulls into the diplogarage of a diplorestaurant. A diplowhore swaggers by, her diplobelly stuffed with diplo pork and beans. A recent college graduate looks on in envy and wonders if it would not have been better to pursue a diplocareer on the Malecón. She suddenly remembers the diplospeech diploXXL made on the day she received her ration booklet and she is swept by a fervent urge to pursue a religious vocation: *We have the best educated and healthiest whores in the world.*

A song by Pablo Milanés is playing on the car radio:

> Life is worth nothing,
> if I have to delay
> every minute of being,
> and die in a bed . . .

They say the lyrics are inspired by the last letter written by the Rosenbergs to their sons. Maria Regla cannot help herself, she's sobbing like a fool and doesn't even care to justify her tears. Yet she also cannot help but smile when she hears the silly variant sung by the driver, who is beyond good and evil and has no clue she's feeling so blue:

> Life isn't worth a Lada
> if what I really need
> is a Nissan to sell,
> if you don't like it
> go to hell . . .

He makes the most of a red light and sticks his head out the window to flirt with a hefty woman, an American horsey type, stuffed into a pair of Levi's.

"Hey, lady! You a capitalist?" The woman turns to see what's up, but he's already answering himself, "I think so, 'cause I see you still keeping the masses oppressed."

The rural landscape is gaining ground. The greenery looks like it used to in old movies, the palm trees wait like brides, and all that other foolish stuff that is so essential to the Cuban soul is also there in all its eternal redundancy: the blue sky, the fetid smell of tar mixed in with rotting grass, clouds like clumps of talcum powder, the purity of colors . . . everything looks as it always has, every segment of road, every single kilometer rolling past her eyes. Except for the billboards with their militant message of SOCIALISM OR DEATH;

COMMANDER IN CHIEF, YOUR WISH IS OUR COMMAND; HERE, NO ONE IS GIVING UP; WE ARE ONE HUNDRED PERCENT CUBAN; IMPERIALIST MISTERS, YOU DON'T SCARE US ONE BIT . . . These are slowly giving way to billboards bearing strange messages from the 1950s: plump and smiling infants urge us to GROW FASTER WITH NESTLÉ; Manolo Ortega, the old declaimer of official speeches, turns up on another advertisement, he is young and thin and unstarched, couldn't be more casual as he cheerfully invites us to a HATUEY BEER, THERE'S NO OTHER LIKE IT. A budding film-maker promotes Pepsi, an actress Guerlain perfume. WE WANT PAN(CAKES) AND AMERICANS instead of WE WANT THE PAN-AMERICANS, in reference to the games, and so on and so forth for mile after mile. There's not a soul or a bumpkin in sight. Just the countryside and billboard after billboard from the 1950s. The girl doesn't entirely understand it. Maybe it's a dream inflicted by aliens. Without coherent transition. The driver is whistling "Only You," the hit song by the Platters; he's dressed in a suit and tie, so is the cameraman. Her hair is short and permed, she is wearing a sleeve-less yellow number, cinched at the waist, then comes the flaring, roomy skirt; her feet are in comfortable flats, the kind for dancing rock and roll. Her exhaustion does not lessen her bafflement; she strokes the formidable and comforting vinyl seats of the '58 Chevrolet. They pull up into a small country town, the cameraman opens her door and offers her a helping hand.

She takes it and hops out of the car. The town is in the midst of some kind of celebration. TV cameras are rolling. Maria Regla looks worried, she's already getting pissed off — another coup d'état, someone has beaten her to it. Suddenly, she notices that the cameras are beautiful unwieldy machines, the cameramen are all wearing suits and ties. She senses that she's in another era. There's no rural free market here; these people are participants in a game show, a dowry draw, a raffle for newlyweds to win houses and eggbeaters and General Electric refrigerators (they've dropped the trips to Miami, later they will resume, but the raffle will have another name . . .).

The participants are dressed in their Sunday best, they're curious and merry and clap and hope for a winner . . . A group of pregnant village women steps up for a turn. They'll try for the layette. Among them, Maria Regla notices a woman who looks remarkably like her: ever so slanted eyes, button nose, bold lippy mouth, a chin like a mango. She could have been her double, a darker double. The woman, who looks to be in her eighth month, pulls a slip of paper from her bag and hands it over to Germán Pinelli (didn't he live to be a hundred?). She's won! The layette is hers for the taking as well as the made-in-the-USA mosquito netting for the baby's crib, probably the last of its kind because the Pestana store that carried it was nationalized shortly thereafter. The master of ceremonies puts in a good word for this glorious year, 1959, in a bit of jovial propaganda, then he asks the woman what color mosquito netting she'll pick for the baby. She answers, shaking like a leaf, "white with pink ribbons." Then Pinelli, persistent in his stupidity, wants to know why that color?

"Because children should be dressed in white" is all she has to say.

"But you live in Havana, what brings you here to Santa Clara?"

"Before giving birth, I wanted to come and see the place where I was born." This is greeted with loud and mighty applause.

The skinny Germán Pinelli decides it's time to move on to the detergent competition, and being the hypocrite he is, he uses a sly elbow to push the young woman out of the frame. Maria Regla, who is afraid to lose her in the crowd, follows her and gently takes her by the arm. The woman is too tired to even question the gesture, she doesn't take her eyes off the slip of paper that says she's the winner of a baby layette.

"Excuse me, I would like to interview you . . ." Maria Regla senses a mystery here. "How old are you?"

The woman does not answer, she loses her footing and almost falls flat on her face. Maria Regla steadies her and wipes the sweat off her brow with the hem of her skirt.

"Tell me your name, where do you live in Havana?"

The woman looks like she's going to faint, she vomits.

"I'm sorry. Maybe you can come back tomorrow. I don't feel too well . . . My name is Caridad, and I work at the Cafetera Nacional, in Havana . . . But now, I'm here, visiting. Strange . . . you look like me. I live over there in the little blue house . . ."

"I'll come back. Your life interests me, maybe we could do something together for television . . ."

Maria Regla blushes, ashamed of her words. This forlorn pregnant girl gives her such a strange feeling. She promises she'll come back not tomorrow but the next day. It's a long trip and she has to go back. Go back where? she wonders. To a nonexistent house or to a nonexistent era? Both ideas terrify her. Still, she promises to return in two days. Distraught, she kisses Caridad on the forehead and gets into the Chevrolet. The car starts up. Again, the countryside, the advertising billboards. Beautiful young men and women, luminous skies, haughty, seductive palm trees, wild green vegetation, malicious clouds, a whiff of toasted, grated coconut, but also miasma, much miasma . . . Then, the city with its pros and cons. With its hills and its sinkholes. The city, like a rancid cheese. Its insides gashed by senseless tunnels. Havana like my mother, still young, still the only universe I know, still my future. Havenme, you, my prison city. Havenme, you, my freedom, with your virtues and your vices; sad, faded city, you, scandalous, mortifying city of joy.

Maria Regla looks at her dusty hands, her frayed jeans, at the holes in doors where the handles used to be. The seats of the Lada are torn, coming apart at the seams. The cameraman sleeps, the driver hums a song by Los Van Van:

"The butcher is the ace man, the butcher is my main man."

She quizzes the cameraman:

"What happened? Where did we go?"

"We went for the assignment. It didn't work. How can you not remember? No one would speak on camera . . . People are scared stiff, they have plenty to say to one another, but the minute they see a camera, they freak . . . Come, you can stay at my place tonight."

She's plunged back into reality, into this superficial reality where she's not bound by time or home. Her family probably heard the news on the radio or maybe they read it in the papers. The cameraman tells her to not delude herself, that kind of stuff no longer makes the news, collapsing buildings are an everyday thing these days. Her mother must have given her up for dead, buried in the debris. And what about her father! Oh dear God! And again she cries, she's upset, afraid. Yes, she'll go stay with the cameraman; she's so disheartened and tired, she can barely walk.

The cameraman lives in Vedado, in a small apartment he shares with his mother, his father, two aunts, and an assortment of siblings and cousins. His wife lives with her parents. That's why they don't have kids. He sets up a folding cot on the balcony, there is no other place for him to lie down. In the living room, Maria Regla flops down on the sofa-bed where he ordinarily sleeps. She stares up at the shadow play on the ceiling and can't stopping thinking about that young woman from 1959.

She keeps coming back to the strange events of that afternoon so often the cameraman finally concedes there may be some truth to her story, or her nightmare, but he, for one, didn't witness any of it. He turns to face the other way and swiftly lapses into methodical snoring. At the crack of dawn, Maria Regla is already up and harping on the same old tune; the fact that she lost her house and all of her possessions seems to have slipped her mind. Or at least when the cameraman brings it up, she shrugs it off, insisting it's of little or no consequence. What she needs right now is a car, she wants to go back to the village. The water jug will return to the well as often as it will take for it to break . . . or mend itself. The cameraman, who is beginning to feel sorry for her and who is as good as they don't come anymore, convinces his older brother to lend him his Lada. They immediately set out for the countryside.

The back country looks the same, except this time the billboards do not change. Even though their message is essentially the same. Soon, they come upon a sign with neon or fluorescent lettering: COME AND EXPERIENCE THE TEMPTATION, it reads, and in the foreground there's a huge black ass wearing dental floss. SMOKE HOLLYWOODS, GO TO HOLLYWOOD. FLY CUBANA AIRLINES. And so on and so forth . . . all the way to Santa Clara in the old province of Villa Clara.

The town is a total shambles, a deserted wreck of a place, if it were not for a handful of barefooted adolescents playing jump rope with an old strap for tying down horses. Maria Regla walks up to them. She's very nervous, bewildered by the scene she sees before her and the capricious vagaries of time. The girls, who are skittish at first, stop playing and wait for her to speak:

"Do you know a pregnant woman named Caridad? She was here yesterday, she told me she lived in the blue wooden house . . ."

"Caridad, Caridad . . ." The sunburnt and disheveled girl is hard on the scent.

"The only little house I know that used to be blue is that one . . . ," and she points to a rooftop somewhere behind the thicket. "And the only person who lives there, far as I know, is the crazy old lady who just moved in, they call her Cuca."

"My grandmother told me," another girl chimes in, "that Cuca used to live there when she was a girl, and she's come here 'cause she wants to forget all about her life. And her brains are completely fried, and she spends the whole frigging day talking about how she made a date with a journalist many years ago and how she's waiting for her to come, 'cause they're going to tell the story of her life on TV, they're going to make it into a soap opera!"

"So, what year are we in now?" the journalist wants to know.

"Well! Nineteen ninety-five, of course!"

Maria Regla's heart makes a somersault. She walks toward the thicket. The girls go back to their jump rope. The cameraman snores inside the car. Their clothes didn't change this time, nor did the car. Did it really happen, can time switch around like that? And why take the past as a model? Why not the future? Why not dream, imagine the future?

(You hold it right there! It's been very moving up until now. Notice, I didn't interrupt you one single time, but what's all this philosophical talk about the future? Drop it, it doesn't suit you. You're not Maria Regla, you know. You are her subordinate. Did she ask you to resuscitate her? Well, did she? No. 'Cause if she did, I'll keep my mouth shut, but as I remember it, I was the one who had the brilliant idea of bringing her back to life. You asked for her permission, and she was happy to grant it, but don't tell me you brought her back from death to make her talk shit. You have no right to mistreat the poor woman like that. What's all this crap about the future this or the future that? Can't you see there's blight on the sugarcane and people have it plenty tough around here for you to start asking them to contemplate the future! First we need to deal with the present. And you, little sistah, can take your concern about the future and go tell it to the marines! I know your little speech inside out so let's not get going with that again. If I've said it once, I've said it a thousand times, but this girl must be hard of hearing — go live your life, my love! You're never going to solve it. This situation is fucked up but good, it cannot be solved, it's a chronic malady, honey. The body is dead as can be but no one has the energy to bury it and call it quits. Why make all this worry for yourself — about the city, and the country, and the buildings falling like flies, and the countryside going to pot! What were you expecting? That we would build Tokyo in the Caribbean? Must be the steady diet of split peas that has played havoc with our intelligence. That's probably why they keep them coming. It's our national poison. When what we need is a magical potion, like Asteríx, something to makes us grow strong without food. We don't have a single red blood cell left in our bodies, but hey, we're going to make mincemeat of the most powerful empire in the world! Everything was going very well until you started in on the future. So be a good girl and skip all the stuff about the future. Okay? Are we clear? Fine, you may proceed.)

Have you ever heard such brazen impudence in your life! Your wings are getting too long for your own good, Jane Cricket. If you ever interrupt again without a justifiable cause, I'm going to slap your face. You let me get on with my philosophical musings, 'cause I happen to know what I'm doing. Plus, you know it's my one weakness, my only fantasy, to make philosophy out of a recipe for split pea. Split peas *à l'anglaise*: soak the peas overnight. Sautée chopped onions, shredded ham, and the peas in butter over high heat. Add a nice broth and allow the mixture to boil until the peas have softened. Season the dish with salt, pepper, and grated nutmeg, add a pinch of turmeric or a strand of saffron for color. Thicken the sauce with mashed hard-boiled eggs. Cover with sausages and serve.

(Tell me, besides the split peas, where the hell do you expect me to find the other ingredients? Never mind, maybe you'd be better off writing letters and banal poetry. Go on. Another generation down the drain. When I stop and look around me, all I see is things going from bad to worse. So, go on, go on about your business.)

An old woman sits by the doorway and rocks in a battered chair. It squeaks, but who has oil to grease it? When she senses Maria Regla standing there, she turns away from the rosebushes. There can be no doubt about it. It's her mother, Cuca Martinez in person. The smile is the same as before, timid and tired.

"I have waited so long to tell you everything. Now, I think I can . . ."

But Cuca Martinez is talking as though this were 1959. She's numb to reality, arteriosclerotic, she doesn't recognize her daughter. She even notes the girl's familiarity in passing. But, and she moans, her daughter died, buried in the rubble of a Havana boardinghouse. Still, she cannot bring herself to believe it. She knows, because of a very unusual pang in her heart, that her girl is still alive, waiting for her somewhere. She begs the journalist to write down her life as a soap opera for TV, but she'd like it to be like one of those they make in Brazil, because Brazilians are geniuses when it comes to that, they're soap opera monsters, they're number *uan*. An unexpected tear rolls down her face. She pauses in meaningful silence, then picks up where she left off — it's got to be the best thing of the summer season, with plenty of suspense, intrigue, and very long, at least three hundred chapters long. A perfect little scandal of a show!

Maria Regla refuses to accept she's talking to a spirit. Even though spirits are far superior to the living when it comes to telling stories, because of their nostalgia and their pain and their helplessness. Maria Regla wants to make her mother understand that she's here, it's her, the Girl, her mother was right, she's alive. Very much alive, here in her heart. Cuca Martinez gets going like a house on fire, her story begins way back in the 1930s. Maria Regla can only listen, that's all there is to it, she'll tape it and later she'll find someone who is truly alive to write it up for her. Of course, she'll do it. Then, we will see. And from somewhere inside the palm trees and greenery, the compassionate voices of Clara and Mario filter in to corroborate the ending:

> If in the end, I have to write
> the story of my life,
> If in the end I have to speak
> of the deepest hours,
> then, it stands to reason
> that I'll talk mostly of you
> who else but you, coming
> first in my heart as you do.

(That's a very appropriate and dignified ending. It's very pretty and quite effective. You've outdone yourself. Congratulations. Not exactly out of this world, but it's not bad at all. Do you think Cuca Martinez will like it? And what about Maria Regla, what does she think, what does she say? Tell me. Did she like it?)

She can't read, and neither can anyone read it to her. She's dead. Remember? And the dead feel no pain. And now, I'm left high and dry, empty, alone in spite of . . . I look at the pictures again. My photo album; my only link. My daughter plays with her father in a park in Madrid. I sit on a bench and watch them. I would give anything and everything for my mother to be there, here. I think we at least did one thing well; this happy little girl in her red dress with the white polka dots playing on the swings. *Elle nous raconte une naïve histoire de monstres en français.* In French, she tells us a naive story about monsters. Her monsters are nothing like mine, or like those of Cuca Martinez or Maria Regla. But they are her monsters. In order to face my monsters and help her defend herself against hers, I turn to my only weapon. I look in a book of Cuban history, by Manuel Moreno Fraginals, and I read these lines written by Beatriz de Jústiz y Zayas, Marquise of Jústiz de Santa Ana, in 1762:

> You Havana, capitulated?
> You in lament? and ruination?
> You under foreign dominion?
> The pain of it, beloved homeland, the pain!

Translator's Note

The following entries may help clarify some of the particularities of the historical, political, and cultural context of this work. I also take this opportunity to express my gratitude to Eyda M. Merediz for the many patient hours she spent helping me decode the obscenities of language and power. Thank you, my friend.

Page 1. Guillermo Cabrera Infante (born 1929), Cuban novelist, author of *Three Trapped Tigers*, *Infante's Inferno*, and *Mea Cuba*, currently lives in London.

Page 15. José Martí (1853–1895), patriot, poet, essayist, national hero, and father of Cuban national consciousness, died in battle at Dos Rios.

Page 35. José Lezama Lima (1910–1976), poet, essayist, novelist, and lawyer, was Cuba's most highly regarded writer, author of *Paradiso* (1966).

Page 43. Eusebio Leal, prominent Cuban historian, currently heads the rebuilding and restoration of Old Havana.

Page 44. Virgen de la Caridad is the patron saint of Cuba. Her sanctuary is in El Cobre, and her counterpart in Santería is Oshún. Christian saints and Yoruba deities (Yemayá, Eleguá, Obatalá, Changó, Babalú) are interchangeable in the pantheon of Santería, a syncretic faith that combines Roman Catholicism and the Nigerian Yoruba religion. Santeros are the clergy, mediators between the world of the living and the world of the spirits, or the *orisha*.

Page 49. Máximo Gómez (1836–1905), general and hero of the Cuban War of Independence.

Page 56. Red and black armbands were the insignia of the twenty-sixth of July Movement, named in commemoration of the 1953 attack led by Fidel Castro on the Moncada military barracks in Santiago. Although the attack failed, it rallied public support for Castro's rebel army.

Page 62. *Período especial* (Special Period) is how Castro dubbed the post–Cold War years of economic hardship and material scarcity.

Page 63. *Granma* was the fifty-eight-foot-yacht on which Castro, together with eighty-two men, launched his invasion against Batista on December 2, 1956. This action also failed, and Castro went into hiding in the Sierra Maestra mountains to prepare his guerrilla campaign. *Granma* is also the name of the official daily paper of the Cuban Communist Party.

Page 63. *Gusano* (worm) is a term used to refer to anti-Castro Cubans.

Page 64. "Havana Belt Agricultural Project" refers to long-standing reforms (instituted by the Agrarian Reform Law of 1959) that have put 80 percent of the Cuban territory to agricultural use under state jurisdiction.

Page 69. Playa Girón is known to Americans as the Bay of Pigs. The trade of prisoners for baby food refers to the exchange of the 1,180 captured men for medical supplies and foodstuffs.

Page 71. The Committees for the Defense of the Revolution (CDR) are the neighborhood policing committees that were first organized in 1960.

Page 82. "Country school as opposed to schooling in the country-side" is a reference to two distinctly separate institutions. In the first, junior high and high school kids volunteer for forty-five days to help meet agricultural quotas. In the second, children are assigned to boarding schools outside the urban centers and come home only on weekends.

Page 91. Popular belief has it that Matías Perez took off in a hot air balloon and never returned.

Page 96. Martha Sánchez Abreu (1864–1909), patriot and philanthropist, donated a beautiful theater to the town of Santa Clara.

Page 98. Commandant Marcos was the leader of the Zapatista Liberation Army in the province of Chiapas, Mexico.

Page 98. Régis Debray, French Marxist and author of *The Revolution within the Revolution*, formed close ties to Fidel Castro and Che Guevara. He was arrested in Bolivia in the mid 1960s while trying to track down Che for an interview. He served as an advisor on Latin America to François Mitterrand.

Page 116. "Enemy Broadcast" refers to Radio Martí, the Miami-based radio (and later television) station critical of the Castro regime.

Page 139. Alicia Alonso is prima ballerina and current director of the Cuban National Ballet.

Page 142. "The Sullen Skunk" is a reference to Reinaldo Arenas (1943–1990), prominent Cuban novelist and author of *The Palace of the Very White Skunks* (1991). He left Cuba in the 1980 Mariel boatlift.

Page 149. Bonifacio Byrne (1861–1936) was a patriot, poet, and journalist.

Page 159. Mambí (plural Mambises) is the name given to the Cuban rebels who fought in the Ten Years War (1868–1878) and in the Cuban War of Independence (1895).

Page 171. "Nitiza Villainterpol" is a play on Nitza Villapol, famous television cooking show host. Other Cuban public figures and members of the Politburo, who may have attended the functions at the Hoi Polloi and at the Palace of the Revo, include Vilma Espín, José Ramirez Cruz, and Armando Acosta, to mention a few.

Page 194. Militias of Territorial Troops (MTTs) were organized to fight sabotage from exile groups.

Page 203. Hernando de Soto (1498–1542), Spanish conquistador of Peru and governor of Cuba and Florida, married Isabel de Bobadilla, who led the interim government of Cuba while her husband set off on a trek from Tampa Bay to Arkansas. De Soto drowned in the Mississippi River.

Page 206. "Maceo sympathizer" refers to Antonio Maceo (1845–1896), the "Titan of Bronze," second-in-command of Cuba's army in the War of Independence.